Portrait of
LIES

OTHER BOOKS AND AUDIO BOOKS

BY CLAIR M. POULSON

I'll Find You

Relentless

Lost and Found

Conflict of Interest

Runaway

Cover Up

Mirror Image

Blind Side

Evidence

Don't Cry Wolf

Dead Wrong

Deadline

Vengeance

Hunted

Switchback

Accidental Private Eye

Framed

Checking Out

In Plain Sight

Falling

Murder at TopHouse

a novel of suspense

Portrait of LIES

CLAIR M. POULSON

Covenant Communications, Inc.

Cover image: *Bow of Cruise Ship* © Zennie, courtesy of iStockphoto.com

Cover design copyright © 2015 by Covenant Communications, Inc.

Published by Covenant Communications, Inc.
American Fork, Utah

Printed in the United States of America
First Printing: August 2015

21 20 19 18 17 16 15   10 9 8 7 6 5 4 3 2 1

ISBN 978-1-68047-244-8

To Alma and Loyle Rasmussen

PROLOGUE

"What are you going to be when you grow up? An artist like your mom and dad?"

Trey Shotwell had been asked that so many times as a little boy that he had learned the only answer he could give to satisfy his mother was some variation in the positive. Usually, he would say, "Yes. I'm going to paint pictures." Never did he dare say, "I'm going to be a policeman." And yet, in truth, that was all he ever wanted to be.

His parents, Rita and Simon Shotwell, were internationally known artists. Rita specialized in portraits and did very well. Simon painted mostly landscapes, nature scenes, and wildlife. He was more than well *thought of* throughout the world. He was considered *world class*. His works were some of the most sought-after paintings.

Young Trey had begun doodling even before he could write, and the abundant natural talent he'd inherited from his famous parents was apparent in those doodles. Later on, he did do some serious painting. His oils needed some work but showed powerful potential. His pencil sketches were outstanding. He even did some watercolor. Amazing work, overall.

Trey was fifteen before he let the cat out of the bag. It was at the graveside following his mother's funeral. She'd been murdered, gunned down during a robbery of their London home. Three of Simon's paintings and two of Rita's had been stolen, along with most of her jewelry. The jewelry was worth a lot, but the paintings were worth a small fortune. The officers of New Scotland Yard were working hard, they assured Simon, to find whoever was responsible for his wife's death. Since there were no witnesses, it wasn't even clear how many people had invaded the home, though the police were certain there were multiple burglars. As of the day of the funeral, the police had only one lead. A neighbor had seen a black panel van on the street about the time of Rita's death.

Standing beside his father near his mother's flower-draped casket, Trey shocked everyone within earshot. "I will find who did it, Father. When I am old enough, I will join the police, and I will search until I find Mother's killers. They will not go unpunished."

"Son, the police will do their work," Simon said as he put an arm around his teenage son's shoulders. "I know you are angry and hurt— we all are—but you must not let this terrible crime be a roadblock to the great work you have ahead of you. You are an artist, Trey, and not just any artist: you are a genius. Your mother would want you to put all your energy into becoming one of the best artists in the world."

A neighbor, a good friend of Simon's, affirmed his words.

Rita's brother, Lukas Nichols—who had surprised Simon and Trey when he showed up at the funeral—said, "Let him alone, Simon. He's just a kid. He'll make his own way in life without you prodding him along."

Simon scowled.

"Whatever he does, he'll succeed. He's not a slacker like you," Lukas added.

"And you're out there making a living?" Simon asked.

Lukas, a slightly chubby man, who, at five eight, was a couple inches taller than Simon, replied with a sneer. "I do fine, dear brother-in-law."

"Never asked anyone for a penny? Is that what you would have all these people believe?" Simon waved an arm toward the crowd that was standing nearby. "I couldn't count the thousands you begged from Rita, and because she was such a caring person, she always gave you what you wanted."

"You could afford it. So could she. But I didn't just take it; I borrowed it for investment purposes. Then she cut me off with no good reason a few months ago," Lukas complained. "But I'm a resourceful man and willing to work as hard as anyone. I'll do okay, and you'll get repaid. You just watch."

Simon shook his head. "You can be assured that Rita's decision to quit giving in to you was final. There will be no help from me if you ever come begging again."

"I don't need your help, Simon," Lukas said haughtily. Then he turned to the boy. "Trey, don't listen to your good ole dad. You do whatever you want. If you need me, I'll help you. I hate to see you become a cop, although that would be better than wasting your life playing with paints and canvas. Make a life for yourself, like I am."

"That's enough, Lukas. You may leave now. You've done enough damage," Simon barked angrily.

Lukas laughed. "Gladly. It embarrasses me to be seen with you." He turned and strutted away.

An uncomfortable silence surrounded the grave. Everyone watched Lukas. He stopped at a car about fifty meters away, where he was met by a woman no one recognized. She was short, had closely cropped brown hair, and was dressed in expensive clothes. She and Lukas got in the sleek black car with the woman at the wheel and drove away.

After the pair was gone, other mourners added words of encouragement, telling Trey not to pay any attention to Rita's feckless brother. Trey listened politely, but he was not persuaded. He knew what he wanted to do, and the horrendous crime that had deprived him of his mother only cemented his determination.

As the mourners dispersed one by one, Simon said, "Son, painting is all you've ever wanted to do. Don't let this terrible tragedy distract you from your goals."

Trey stiffened and said softly but firmly, "No, Father, painting is all you and Mother ever wanted me to do. I've always wanted to be a police officer. I enjoy painting, but for me it will never be anything but a hobby. You may not believe me, Father, but I will hunt down the people who did this." He looked to where his uncle and the dressy lady had just disappeared. The man was a sponge, his father had told him before. He soaked up what others worked hard to make but did little to contribute to society. Trey guessed that the attractive woman was probably just the latest person who was being taken advantage of. Lukas was the kind of man Trey wanted to protect society from. On that account, he was in complete accord with his father. He despised Lukas.

Trey could tell Simon Shotwell was gravely disappointed at his son's words, and he was even more disappointed as the days and weeks and months passed. Trey dabbled with his art but read every book he could find about the world's great detectives, both real and fictional.

Trey's betrayal of his father's dreams was painful, but it was not the only pain Trey would inflict upon his father. When Trey began to attend the meetings of the Mormon Church with a couple of friends, his father, a faithful member of the Church of England, was cut to the core. He tried to persuade Trey to abandon his study of "that cult."

Trey did not. His father forbade him from joining the Mormons, but Trey continued to attend meetings and soon had a large circle of Mormon friends. He also spent time with a number of different police officers from New Scotland Yard. Those men, his *older* friends, encouraged him to not give up his goal to become one of them.

Though Simon was upset, he loved his son and didn't want to lose him. But he felt like that was exactly what was happening—his son's Mormon and police officer friends were dragging him away from his father.

Since the death of his beloved wife, Simon had felt like a stranger in his own home. It was empty and filled with painful memories. He was often heard saying he wanted to leave London. When asked where he would go, he named a place he had visited several times. He felt a strong pull from a faraway country: Australia.

Shortly after Trey's seventeenth birthday, Simon announced to his son that they would be moving to Australia. Simon had already begun applying for citizenship there and was excited about it. In the back of his mind, he thought the move would help his son forget his desires to join a church Simon didn't approve of and remove him from the police friends who constantly encouraged him to hold fast to his goal to become a police officer.

Trey argued about the move, not wanting to leave his friends, his school, and his neighborhood, but one thing his new religious beliefs had instilled within him was to honor his father. And honor him he did. He abandoned his resistance and told his father he would go. A month later, they packed their belongings, auctioned off what they couldn't take, sold their London mansion, and prepared to immigrate to Australia.

Before leaving for Sydney, Trey spent as much time with his friends as he could. His Mormon friends told him how to locate the Church in Australia. They told him that when he turned eighteen, he could be baptized without parental permission. He promised them that he would and that he'd let them know all about it.

His police friends told him that if he ever chose to return to England, they would help him get the training he needed to join New Scotland Yard. And they promised him that they would help him in his quest to find his mother's killers, who had never been found. The paintings had never resurfaced either, and he hoped to someday find them too. Those friends cautioned him, however, that the likelihood of success was very small. But Trey Shotwell was not deterred.

One man always came to mind when Trey thought about his mother's death: his Uncle Lukas. Since the day of his mother's funeral, neither he nor his father had seen or heard from Lukas Nichols. For that matter, not a single pound of the money he'd *borrowed* from Rita had been repaid. They doubted he even knew of their move to Australia and frankly hoped he didn't. They certainly didn't want the man to follow them there.

ONE

THE MASSIVE CRUISE SHIP GENTLY rocked from side to side on its way from Australia to New Zealand. The last port for the passengers, who had embarked on the cruise in Sydney, was to be Auckland, New Zealand. They had left Melbourne, the last of the Australian ports the ship had visited, that morning. Now, on a beautiful moonlit night, they were churning their way to New Zealand, where they would make several more stops. Detective Inspector Trey Shotwell had his head down and was running hard, circling the entire ship on the outdoor walkway, part of the promenade deck, oblivious to the rocking motion. Trey was in top physical condition, and even though he was taking a lengthy, well-deserved vacation from his job with the New South Wales Police Force, he was determined to keep his body in top condition.

He slowed slightly as he rounded the back of the ship and glanced at the frothy, churning water. Then he picked up speed again and moved forward at his normal pace. It was late, and the walkway was mostly deserted. He'd tried running during the daylight but had found he couldn't keep up the punishing pace he preferred because there were so many passengers walking in both directions. He was constantly having to adjust his pace to pass them or work his way through them if they were going in the opposite direction. Thus the late-night runs. At other times he worked out with the excellent weight-lifting equipment in the ship's large exercise room.

The first day on the ship, Trey had met another passenger who also worked out, but Hans Olander lifted weights that Trey knew he'd never be able to lift in his entire life. Hans was a Swedish wrestler. At six ten, Hans was not only fourteen inches taller than Trey, but he was also nearly double Trey's weight at around three hundred pounds. But the difference in size didn't hamper the two men from becoming fast friends. They laughed and talked about their divergent pasts and hopes for the future. Trey came to think of his new friend as a gentle giant.

Trey shared an ocean view stateroom with his father, world-famous artist Simon Shotwell. Even though Simon hadn't been happy about the fact that his son had joined the Mormon Church and become a police officer, he didn't hold those things against Trey. He'd been able to find some comfort in the fact that the young man had given up his dream to return to London and join the New Scotland Yard force and had instead chosen to stay near his father in Australia, a land they had both adopted without reservations.

Trey loved his department and the work he was doing in New South Wales. Despite his misgivings, Simon made sure Trey knew how proud he was. His son had joined the police at the age of nineteen, just two years after they had immigrated to Australia. Through hard work, a lot of study, natural intelligence, and an aptitude for crime detection, he had been made a detective shortly after achieving the rank of senior constable. And to Simon's delight, Trey spent a lot of his free time painting, eager for pointers from his father. In Simon's expert opinion, Trey's painting was outstanding.

As Trey ran, engrossed in his thoughts, he couldn't help but notice an attractive girl sitting on a lounge chair on the deck. Each time he circled the ship, she was still sitting there. She'd been there the previous night too—a book in her hands and her eyes glued to it—but she had disappeared after he'd only circled three or four times. As far as he knew, she hadn't looked up from her reading once, but now, as he approached her location on his fifth or sixth time around, she looked up, caught his eye, and smiled shyly, displaying perfect white teeth and two small dimples. He gave a nod, and she nodded back. Her hair was golden, long, and shiny, and it moved rhythmically as a gentle ocean breeze caught it. It was chilly this late at night, and she wore a pink jacket that matched her long pants. The jacket was zipped clear to her chin.

He swept by without slowing down or breaking his stride. The next time around, the book was lying beside her on a cloth bag that looked like it might contain one or two more books. She was staring out over the dark sea, her face somber, her knees pulled tightly beneath her chin.

She glanced at him briefly as he passed. Her eyes again met his for a fleeting moment. It was hard to be sure, but her eyes looked dark blue in that short glance.

Once again she smiled shyly. And once again, he swept past her. When he looked over his shoulder a moment later, she was again staring out to sea, sitting motionless, seeming deep in thought.

When he came around the next time, she was still sitting in the exact same position as before, still staring into the darkness, the breeze blowing her golden hair across her face. There was no smile, no eye contact this time. It was as if he wasn't even there. But he glanced over his shoulder again and was surprised to see that she was watching him now. She lifted one of her hands and wiggled her fingers. The gesture, small though it was, made his spine tingle.

Round after round, he passed by her. She eventually went back to reading. On about his twentieth lap, she had a different book out and was reading intently. He slowed down a little, looking closer at the book. He knew that book. He loved that book. She was reading the Book of Mormon. She looked up from her reading and smiled at him again.

"That's a great book," he called out.

Her eyes—definitely dark blue, he saw—widened in surprise. But then he was again past her. Once more, he looked over his shoulder, and once more, she was watching him through the veil of golden hair blowing gently in front of her face. He was ready to quit for the night. He slowed to walk the final round to cool down. The girl was still there, but she was putting the Book of Mormon in her bag. She stood up just before he reached her. She was several inches shorter than he was. Her slightly wavy golden hair cascaded halfway down her back.

She had her bag in one hand and looked toward Trey as he approached. When he reached her, she smiled again. "You must like to run." She had a pretty American accent.

"I do," he said, stopping beside her. "I'm Trey Shotwell."

Her eyes widened. "Are you the same Trey Shotwell that has the portrait of a young boy displayed in the gallery?"

"Yes, but it's not very good," he said modestly.

She held out a dainty hand, which he took in his own. "My name is Aariah Stanton," she said. "And I think the portrait is amazing. You must be a professional."

"No. Much to my father's chagrin, I just dabble," he said.

"Wait. Is your father Simon Shotwell?" she asked excitedly.

"Yes, and *he* is a great artist," Trey said.

"You can say that again," she agreed. "Was your mother Rita Shotwell?"

"Yes, she was killed ten years ago," Trey said, surprised at the girl's knowledge. "She was also very good."

"I've seen a couple of her paintings. She did mostly portraits, according to what I read," Aariah said. "Like that one of yours. You have her talent."

"I wouldn't say that. I don't do just portraits, although I like them. I don't have time to do much painting though," he told her.

"Well, I think your painting in the gallery is great," she said.

"Thank you. Are you going inside?" he asked.

"Yes, and you?"

"I am. I'll walk with you if you don't mind," he offered.

"That would be nice," she agreed, lowering her eyes demurely, and the two of them fell into step and moved toward the nearest entrance to the interior of the ship. "Are you a Mormon?" she asked, patting her book bag. "You saw me reading the Book of Mormon and said it was a great book."

"I am a Mormon, also much to my father's chagrin," he said. "He wouldn't let me join when I first wanted to. That was when we lived in London. I think he thought I would change my mind when the two of us moved to Australia, but I didn't. As soon as I turned eighteen, I was baptized. He's come to accept my decision. My father's a great man."

"Do you ever regret joining the Church?" she asked.

"Oh, no, Aariah," he said. "I love the Church. Why do you ask?"

"I've gone to your church and even thought about being baptized, but I don't know if I should. I still have some questions."

Trey opened the door they had just reached and signaled for her to precede him inside.

She hesitated. "Could we walk around the ship one time?" she asked with a hopeful look. "Maybe you could answer a few of my questions."

"If I can," he said as he let the door swing shut and turned back to the promenade deck.

She grinned at him. "If you can walk that far? I've been watching you. You're in great condition."

He grinned back. "No, I meant if I can answer your questions."

"I'm sure you can," she told him, still grinning.

"I'll sure try, Aariah," he said, liking the feel of her name as it rolled off his tongue.

"If you aren't a professional artist, what do you do?" Aariah asked as she swept her long hair from her face.

"Disappoint my father," he said with a chuckle. "I told him I was going to be a police officer the day my mother was buried. Even though he dragged me all the way down to Australia, my desire didn't change. He says it's not why we left London, but I think he thought getting me away from my police friends in London would change my mind."

"So you're a policeman?" she asked.

"Yes, I work for the New South Wales Police Force," he said.

"That's awesome. I have an uncle who's a cop in New York."

"Is that where you're from?" Trey asked.

She nodded. "Yeah. My mother is Australian, but she met Dad when she was in college in New York. They married and settled down there."

"Then you must have family in Australia."

"My grandmother lives there. And I have other family there too, but they don't live very close to my grandmother. She gets lonely since my grandfather passed away a few months ago. I came here to spend some time with her and try to help her get on with her life without him." She was silent for a moment, and they walked along, the light breeze continuing to blow her long hair around her face—a pretty face, Trey noted, one that would be fun to paint. But she looked somber again. "My grandmother saw me reading the Book of Mormon, and it upset her."

"I'm sorry," Trey said. "I know how that feels. But don't let it stop you, Aariah. She'll still love you. My father still loves me."

For the next few minutes, she expressed some of her concerns about the Church and its doctrine, and Trey answered them the best he knew how.

As they approached the door again, she said, "Thanks, Trey. You've been a great help. But I still have more questions. Maybe we could talk another time?"

"I'd like that." They went inside. "What deck are you on?" he asked.

"Eleven, and you?"

"Ten," he told her.

They headed for the elevator. "I wish I had a different stateroom," she said. He looked at her and was surprised to see her looking troubled.

"Do you have one that doesn't have an ocean view?" he asked.

"No, it does. I love the view; that's not the problem. It's the two guys next door."

He took her by the arm and stopped. She faced him. "Why?" he asked anxiously.

"They aren't good guys. I hate how they . . . look at me. They leer at me. They scare me."

"Would you like me to walk you to your door?" Trey offered.

"Oh no, you don't need to do that. They just, you know, look scary. It makes me wonder why they're on the ship. I think they mostly just get drunk." They reached the elevator, and Trey pushed the up button. As they waited, she asked, "Are you going to be at the art auction tomorrow?"

"Yes, I am. Are you?" he asked in surprise.

"I don't paint very well, but I love art," she said. "I'm planning to go. I wish I could buy that one of yours."

Trey chuckled. "That's a kind thing to say, Aariah."

"I mean it, Trey. It's a wonderful painting."

After a moment he asked, "Are you alone on the ship?"

"No, my grandmother and I are traveling together. She's never been to New Zealand, and she is so lonesome that I talked her into going on this cruise, hoping to get her mind off her troubles," she said. She frowned as the elevator door opened. "She hasn't had much fun, I'm afraid. I think all she wants to get out of this trip is to persuade me to have nothing more to do with the Mormon Church."

Trey offered her a sympathetic smile and then pushed the appropriate numbers. "Will she be at the auction? I'd like to meet her."

Aariah chuckled just as the elevator stopped at Trey's deck and the door opened. "I don't think so," she said. "She's not into art like I am. And she's a bit of a grouch at times."

"I'll watch for you," he said. "You can sit with my father and me."

"Really? I'd like that," she responded, her eyes bright. "If it's okay with him. I really admire his art."

"I won't tell him you're reading the Book of Mormon, only that you like his paintings," Trey said with a grin. "Actually, he'd be fine with it anyway. See you in the morning." He stepped away from the elevator and watched her face as the door closed. She looked worried. Trey didn't consider himself a knight in shining armor, but he made a dash for the stairs and bounded up them two steps at a time. By the time the elevator door opened, he was standing in front of it.

Aariah looked shocked. "How did you do that?" she asked. "You aren't even breathing hard."

"I'll walk you to your door," he said with a grin.

Relief washed over her pretty face. "Thank you, Trey."

Her room was a short walk down the hallway. When they stopped in front of it, he said, "I think your stateroom is directly above mine. I guess it would be. Other than the first numbers, they match. Mine's 1088." Hers was 1188. "If you tapped on the floor in Morse code, I could probably hear you."

She gave him a puzzled look. "I don't know Morse code."

"Neither do I." Trey shrugged. "But it sounded good."

She began to chuckle, but it caught in her throat as the door beyond hers opened. Two men stepped out. One looked about forty years old; the other was probably three or four years younger. They weren't evil looking—unless you looked into their eyes. Which Trey did. The older one had brown eyes, the other, green, but it wasn't the color that interested him. Evil lurked in those eyes. Both men had dark-brown hair that fell below their collars but was clean and neatly brushed. Neither of them had a lot of fat on their bodies. They looked quite fit. The older one seemed to be about the same height as Trey but maybe just a little heavier. The other one was taller by an inch or so and even a little heavier than the older guy. Both reeked of alcohol.

Aariah was struggling with her key card. Her hands were shaking. The two men started to slip past them, but the older one stopped and said, "Kind of early to be turning in for the night, gorgeous. Why don't you leave the English bloke and come with us. We'll buy you a couple drinks in the lounge."

"No thanks," Aariah said without looking up.

She finally found the card and unlocked the door, but she didn't push it open. She stood frozen in place. Trey placed a hand on her shoulder and watched as the two men continued down the hallway. When they turned toward the elevators and were out of sight, he said, "They're gone now."

She looked up at him. Fear filled those dark blue eyes. She brushed a long lock of golden hair from her face. "Thank you, Trey. Do you see why they frighten me?"

"They're full of hot air," he said, trying to calm her fears. In truth he wasn't at all sure it was just hot air. There was something menacing about them, especially the older of the two. "Aariah, you know my room number. You don't need to tap on the floor with Morse code. Buzz me on the room phone when you're ready to go to breakfast, and I'll come meet you here."

"Grandmother and I will probably eat in the room," she said with only the slightest touch of smile at his attempt at humor. "But if it's okay, I would like to call you before the auction."

"It's at eleven," he said. "How about if I just meet you right here at ten thirty?"

She nodded, relief in her eyes. "Thank you, Trey. I'd like that a lot. I'll see you in the morning then. And, uh, it's really been nice meeting you."

"Yeah, same here," he said.

He walked slowly back to the stairs and down the flight he had come up so quickly, his thoughts centered on seeing Aariah again. There was just something about her . . .

He went to his room. Aariah's neighbors knew he was British, yet he had not said a word, so it couldn't have been his accent that gave him away. If anything, after ten years in Australia, he probably had more of an Aussie accent than an English one. Trey could tell that the older one was most certainly British; *his* accent did give him away. The other one . . . Trey had no idea, as he hadn't said a word.

He opened the door to his stateroom and saw that his father was where he'd been when Trey had left, seated in front of a relatively small canvas and busy painting. That was where he'd spent most of his time on the cruise so far. He put his brush down and stood up, stretching. Smiling at Trey, he asked, "Did you have a good run?"

"I did. It looks like you're making good progress," Trey said. "I love the colors of the sky. It gives the painting a dark but beautiful mood." He leaned closer and studied the canvas for a moment. It was a seascape, one with a dark and threatening sky with streaks of bright lightning. There were fierce whitecaps on the ocean. He straightened up. "I love it, Father," he said.

Simon nodded in appreciation. "You could do better than me—if you wanted to," he added with a smile.

"I'll never be as good as you are. Anyway, I love what I'm doing," Trey said. "And you know I do a fair amount of painting. I appreciate your help, but it's not my first interest. But who knows, maybe the painting I have in the auction will bring in a few dollars, and that would be fun for me."

"I know you love your work, Trey, and you're very good at it. Don't think that I'm not proud of you, because I am. But I think you'll be surprised at how well your painting does tomorrow. Even though it's only a hobby to you, you are still very, very good. I'm sorry. I don't mean to harp at you. I am grateful you paint as much as you do."

Trey smiled at his father. "I'm looking forward to tomorrow's auction. There are some very wealthy art lovers on this cruise. I've seen several of them admiring your work, commenting about how neat it is that you're on the ship. A couple of men said they hoped they could meet you, that it would be an honor."

"I do enjoy meeting people who appreciate what I do," Simon said softly.

"It will be fun to see what your paintings bring, Father. Now, I better get showered so we can both get some sleep."

"Yes, and I suppose I should study some of the other artists' paintings. But you know how I am. I don't like to examine other painters' work too closely. I worry that mine aren't as good as some of those others."

"That's not what I heard people saying when I was down there. I spent an hour studying the paintings this afternoon," Trey said, as he felt the uncomfortable stirring in his gut that he'd felt earlier in the gallery. "One of yours is on display. It's the best one there. And I'm not the only one that thinks so. They brought several paintings out to display that have not been shown previously. I heard someone say that more will be displayed tomorrow."

His stomach continued to churn. He thought about mentioning the concerns he'd had when he was looking at a portrait of a Scottish farmer that had reminded him of one of the ones his mother had painted, one of the two that had been stolen the night she was murdered. She had called it *The Scottish Farmer*. The other stolen one was a companion painting she called *The Scottish Farmer's Wife*. But he kept his thoughts to himself. He would rather see if his father noticed what he did. The painting was not exactly like his mother's, as he had remembered it, but it was very, very close.

"I'll go down to the gallery in the morning after breakfast if you'll go with me, Trey," Simon said.

"Great! I would enjoy that, Father. They'll have a few more paintings displayed then. I think another one of yours will be brought out." Trey gave his dad an affectionate pat on the shoulder. "Now, I really do need to shower."

TWO

SIMON, WHO LOOKED A LITTLE pale to his son, ate an unusually light breakfast.

"Are you okay, Father?" Trey asked. "You don't look very well this morning. Is it the rough sea?"

The ocean was quite turbulent that day, the first turbulent water they had experienced on the trip, and Simon nodded. "Yes. I need to take something for it. You know I get motion sickness."

"I'll go up to the stateroom and get you a couple of pills while you look at some of the art in the gallery," Trey suggested.

Together they went to the gallery, and Simon was soon absorbed in studying the paintings displayed there. Trey slipped away and ran up the stairs to the tenth deck. When he got back with the pills and a bottle of water, his father was looking worse than before, but it was more than just seasickness. He was staring at a painting with a look of rage on his gray face. Trey followed his father's eyes and felt a jolt. The painting that he had wondered and worried about the previous evening had been moved when additional paintings had been added. This one wasn't where Trey had remembered, and he hadn't expected his father to see it yet.

"Father," Trey said slowly, "what are you thinking?"

Simon raised one arm and pointed at the portrait. The old farmer was leaning on a pitchfork, gazing toward a building storm. "Rita painted him with green eyes," Simon said, his voice trembling. "Now they're blue."

"What are you saying, Father?" Trey asked, even as he knew he'd been right when he saw the painting the day before.

"Look at it," Simon said, pointing again. "Doesn't that look familiar to you?"

"Yes, it does. It looks like the one Mother called *The Scottish Farmer*," he said. "But that doesn't mean it isn't one someone else painted that is very similar."

"It's not just similar," Simon said in a growing fury.

"If it is Mother's, and I don't know how you can be sure, but if it is, then someone has painted over it and added a signature."

"That's right. Your mother had not yet painted her signature on, Son. But it is Rita's painting. She died when it was stolen, Trey. And now it has been . . . been . . . desecrated!" Simon was shaking.

"Let's go up to the room, Father," Trey said, putting an arm around his father's waist. Simon was trembling and stubbornly planted in front of the painting.

"Dad, I'm a police officer. I'll look into doing something about this," Trey said with determination; his goal of the past ten years may no longer be at a dead end. This altered painting, if it was Rita's, as they both thought, could be a clue to the murder of his mother. But that was all it would be—a clue. He'd stayed in touch with officers in England, and even after he decided to work in Australia instead of London, he hadn't lost his determination to search for his mother's killers. He'd always thought that finding one of the stolen paintings would be at least a beginning to solving the case. He had good friends in New Scotland Yard who would love to hear what he and his father had found. One particular officer came to mind: Detective Inspector Willie Denning. Trey decided right then that he would call his old friend later, when the time in London was such that he wouldn't risk getting Willie out of bed.

Trey moved his arm from his father's waist to pull his iPhone from his pocket. He took several pictures of the painting while Simon continued to stare. Trey looked closer at his father's face. He realized with a jolt that Simon wasn't really staring. His eyes were moving very slowly, taking in every detail of the altered painting.

Kneeling down, Trey snapped a close-up of the artist's signature. Ainslee Cline. Whoever had worked on altering this painting had been very good. "Rita was going to sign it here," Simon said, pointing. "The area has been very skillfully painted over."

Trey stood up and slipped the phone back into his pocket. "I'll come back with my camera and take some better pictures," Trey told his father. "But are you *sure?*"

Simon's eyes finally left the painting; he looked directly at Trey's face and nodded. "I'm sure. When you bring your camera, be sure and take a close-up of this," Simon said as he stepped closer to the painting and held his finger over a spot in the lower center of the painting.

"What is it?" Trey asked as he peered closely at the spot his father was pointing to.

"Rita and I always make marks to identify our paintings, unofficial signatures of a sort. This is one of hers, this little piece of loose thread in the old man's pants. She always did that. I do the same thing."

"Father, that's great!" Trey pulled his cell phone out again and snapped a picture of the spot on the old man's pants. "But how do we prove she intentionally painted that loose thread to identify the painting, and why haven't you ever told me this before?"

The frown on Simon's face relaxed, and he raised a finger. "I'll take those pills now," he said. After he swallowed them, Simon said, "Rita and I always kept journals as we worked on a painting. In the journal, we would record where we put the official signature, but we would also record the unofficial signature and its location on the painting. In fact, we usually did more than one on each painting. I don't remember what else Rita did on this one, but her journal will tell me. I have the one of *The Scottish Farmer* in the safe at home. Is that the kind of proof that would help?"

"That's absolutely brilliant. Yes, that will help a great deal," Trey said.

"Give the credit to your mother. It was her idea, not mine."

"It's brilliant, that's for sure. Did you tell the officers in London about this when Mother was killed and the paintings were stolen?"

"No," he said. "I figured that if they ever found one they believed to be one of ours, then we could use the marks we made to identify it for certain." Simon, not as gray now, furrowed his brow in thought and looked back at the painting for a moment. "Trey?" Trey again locked eyes with him. "At your mother's grave you made a promise. Do you remember what you said?"

"Of course I do," he said. "I promised I would find whoever killed my mother. Her case has never been closed."

"That's right. You did make that promise. At the time I didn't think of it as anything but the brash statement of a brokenhearted teenager who didn't really know what he should do with his life," Simon admitted. "But I don't suppose you could still try to fulfill that promise?"

"Father, I meant that when I said it, and I still mean it," he said. "I'll call one of the New Scotland Yard officers I still communicate with. I've worked on several cases since I've been a detective that involved both London and Sydney. That's quite common. Anyway, I'll call today."

"Trey, you made that promise when you were only fifteen. I didn't take it seriously, but I am going to hold you to that promise now. Find who killed my beloved Rita, Trey. I'm counting on you, or maybe I should say I'm challenging you." His father looked back thoughtfully at the painting. Then Simon said, "Trey, I am proud of the man you have become."

"Thank you. And I accept the challenge, Father," Trey said. "This is the break I've hoped and prayed for, that New Scotland Yard has also hoped for." Trey pointed at the painting. "I need to find whoever is in charge of the gallery and have this painting seized. Do you need to go up to the room and lie down? I need to go get my camera, so we could go up together."

"No, I'm feeling better now. I think I'll just wait here. I'd like to show you the marks I made on the two paintings of mine," he said.

Trey ran up, got the camera, and ran back down.

"Do you ever use the elevators?" Simon asked as Trey jogged up to him.

"Not much," Trey said. "Only if I'm with someone."

"Like me?"

Trey smiled with affection at his father. "Yes, Father, like you."

"And who else?" Simon asked. "There are some pretty girls on this ship, in case you haven't noticed. Or have you noticed?"

"What do you mean?" Trey asked. "Of course I notice pretty girls. Just because I haven't gotten married yet doesn't mean I'm blind."

"So have you met anyone in particular on the ship?" Simon smiled then. "You said you use the elevator when you're not alone. I take that to mean you know someone on this ship besides me. And I'm not referring to that Swedish fighter you've told me about. Anyway, he probably doesn't use the elevators either."

Trey laughed. "You're very perceptive, Father. You'll meet her at the auction. I think you'll like her, but don't get any ideas. I only met her last night. She's just a friend, a new friend. So don't expect too much."

Simon nodded knowingly. "Yes, I remember when I said that very thing about my Rita. Some people didn't believe me. Take the photos you need of *The Scottish Farmer*," he said. "Then let's go look at my paintings—and yours."

For the next hour, the world famous artist and his detective son studied the paintings in the ship's gallery. Simon pointed out the miniscule marks he'd made on the two landscapes that were to be sold on the cruise. Both paintings were now on display. Only one had been the previous day. Since he had his camera, Trey took photos of both paintings and the tiny marks that identified them so brilliantly, being careful not to let any of the other people in the gallery see what he was doing.

As Trey took photos, Simon said softly, "This isn't foolproof, but the odds of a thief painting over all of the marks is pretty slim, wouldn't you say? That's what your mother and I always figured."

Trey agreed. "I think I'll do the same with mine from now on, Father," he said as they continued to browse the paintings. "You know, yours really are far and away the best on the ship."

"We haven't seen the ones they haven't put out yet," Simon reminded him.

"When we do," a voice behind them said, "yours will still be the best. You must be Simon Shotwell."

Trey and Simon turned in unison. The man who had just spoken was approaching them. Trey noted a distinct American New England accent. The man was tall and slender, dressed sharply in white pants, a lavender turtleneck shirt, and a white sports coat. His short blond hair was parted in the center, framing a narrow face, striking blue eyes, and a slightly prominent nose. Four men of indistinct nationalities stood behind him.

"I'm Simon," Trey's father introduced. "This is my son, Detective Inspector Trey Shotwell." Did Trey hear a trace of pride in his father's voice? Perhaps his father truly was proud of him.

"Trey Shotwell," the man said thoughtfully. "You have a painting here as well."

"Yes, I do, but I'm not very good."

The stranger then extended a hand to Simon. "Dayton Windle. I'm the ship's art director. It is more of a pleasure to have you on board than I have words to express. We've never had an artist of your caliber on the ship before."

"It's a pleasure to be here," Simon said as he accepted the hand and they shook.

Dayton also offered his hand to Trey. "I will have to disagree with you, Detective. You do great work. I know your father lives in Sydney but is from London originally. I assume you are also in Australia now. Do you plan to someday follow in the footsteps of your father and paint professionally?"

"No, I only paint as a hobby, but I have the world's best instructor to critique my work," Trey said as he glanced at his father, who was beaming at him. "I have a full-time job."

"I gathered from your father's introduction that you are a policeman?" Dayton asked. "Where do you work?"

"I am a detective with the New South Wales Police Force," Trey said. "I'm glad you're here. I was going to look you up in a few minutes. There's something we need to discuss."

A shadow crossed the American's face. "Nothing serious, I hope."

"Actually, it's very serious," Trey said, making sure no other passengers were listening in. "Is there someplace we could have a private conversation?"

Dayton turned to the four men behind him. "You men know what to do. Let's get the paintings we need for the auction moved now. I'll get back with you in a few minutes." The men nodded and started to move away. Trey held up a hand and stopped them in their tracks. "Men," he said as he produced his police ID, "you're not to mention to anyone who I am. Is that clear? As far as you're concerned, I'm nothing more than an artist and an art collector." They all nodded with somber expressions, and Trey said, "Thank you."

"Detective Shotwell means what he said," Dayton said sharply to the four men, a very stern look on his thin face. "You do your work and keep your mouths shut. And be very careful with the paintings. They're worth a fortune." They moved quickly away, and Dayton turned to Trey and Simon. "We can meet in my office."

Simon shook his head. "I think I'll go up to our room and rest a little before the auction. The rough seas today have made me a little woozy."

Trey looked at his father with concern. "You said you were feeling better. I take it you're not."

"I am, Trey, but not as well as I'd like to feel. I just need some rest before the auction."

"Would you like someone to assist you to your room?" Dayton asked with concern creasing his brow.

"That's not necessary," Simon said. "I'm much better now than I was. I'm just a little tired—and stressed."

"What are you—" Dayton began.

"I'll explain when we get to your office," Trey said, cutting Dayton off with a wave of his hand.

After Simon had left the gallery, Dayton said, "Follow me, Trey. We'll go to my office."

"First, let me show you something," Trey said. The painting in question was several meters away. His father had proven its provenance to Trey's satisfaction, and he wanted to let the art director see it now. He led Dayton toward it, stepping around one of the men who was cautiously picking up a painting to take to the auction. Trey waited as a passenger studied the painting and then moved on. Finally Trey gestured to the canvas. "This painting is entitled *The Scottish Farmer*, and it is not what it seems."

Dayton's brow furrowed in concern. "What exactly do you mean, Detective?" he asked. "How do you know what it's called?"

"If you'll bring it, I'll explain in detail when we get to your office," Trey said.

Dayton looked Trey in the eye for a moment, and then he said, "You're serious, aren't you?"

"Quite," Trey said firmly.

Without another word, Dayton picked up the painting, handling it carefully, and led the way to his office. He leaned it gently against a wall and then sat down, offering Trey a chair. "Is this painting the reason you're on this cruise?"

"No, not at all. In fact, seeing it here was really quite a shock," Trey said, running his hand nervously across his thick, butch-cut brown

hair. He knew that what he was about to tell the cruise ship's art director was probably going to be met with some skepticism. And understandably so.

"Just a second, Detective, let me page my wife. She's my assistant
art director. I'd like her to be here when you explain the problem with
this portrait," Dayton suddenly said. He punched in a number on the
phone on his desk, waited a moment, and then said, "Coni, can you
come to my office for a few minutes?" He listened for a moment and
then said, "Yes, it is important. I know the auction begins in an hour
and a half. Tell the guys to keep at it. You need to meet me here."
Once again, he listened to his wife, and then he said, "Simon Shotwell's
son, Trey, is here with me. He has something that I believe might be
important to say to both of us." A moment later he put the phone
down. "I hope this won't take too long. We do have the auction coming
up shortly."

About two minutes later, an attractive woman, who appeared to be
in her midthirties, about the same age as her husband, came hustling in.
She had eyes that were as startlingly green as Dayton's were strikingly
blue. "This better be good, Dayton," she said sharply. "I'm very busy."

Dayton simply turned to Trey and said, "Detective Shotwell, meet
my wife, Coni. Sit down, dear."

"What is that painting doing in here?" Coni asked as she flipped
her shoulder-length blonde hair and sat down in a chair facing Trey.
"You're a police officer?"

He nodded.

"Again, why is that painting in here?" she asked sharply. "It needs
to be ready for the auction."

"There seems to be a problem with it," Dayton said. "That's what
the detective's going to talk to us about."

THREE

Both Dayton and Coni Windle leaned forward, suddenly looking quite worried. "What is it about this painting that has you concerned?" the art director asked.

"Are either of you familiar with my mother's work?" Trey asked. "Rita Shotwell?"

They looked at each other. "She's deceased," Dayton said.

"Yes, she was murdered when someone entered our home in London ten years ago," Trey said. "They stole three of my father's paintings and two of my mother's."

"That's terrible. She was quite good, I believe," Coni said. "I remember learning about her in a contemporary art class in college in Boston."

"Yes, she was good," Trey said.

"She did portraits, as I recall," she said, glancing nervously at the one propped up against the wall in Dayton's office.

"That's right," Trey responded. "So I suppose it goes without saying that the ones stolen from our home when she lost her life were portraits. They were actually a pair. She had hoped to sell them that way."

"Have either of them ever been found?" It was Dayton asking the question this time, and like Coni's, his eyes strayed nervously to the portrait he had carried into his office.

"Not until today," Trey said.

"Are you telling us that that one"—Coni pointed a slightly trembling finger—"is one of them?"

"Mother called it *The Scottish Farmer*. The companion to it was called *The Scottish Farmer's Wife*. And yes, my mother painted that."

"But that can't be," Coni said stubbornly. "It's by an English painter by the name of Ainslee Cline." She rose gracefully to her feet and knelt next to the painting. "See, she signed it right there." She poised a long, slender finger directly over the signature. "It says Ainslee Cline, as you can see."

"Yes, I see what it says, but that and a few other details have been skillfully painted over. For example, the eye color has been changed."

"Detective," Dayton said as he too rose and stepped beside his wife. "I'm afraid we must require some proof that this is your mother's work. Not that we have any reason to doubt you or your father, but, well, you know how it is. You've made a serious accusation."

"Yes, and I'm prepared to offer proof. My father recognized this painting the moment he saw it, and he pointed out that changes had been made," Trey told them. "There aren't many greater experts than him in the art world, and no one knows my mother's paintings like he does."

"I'm sure that's true, but that's not really conclusive enough to accuse someone of stealing it," he said stubbornly.

"Let me tell you something about my parents," Trey said, not about to tell them that this was something he had only learned just over an hour ago. "They keep a journal of each painting they do, and in the journal they document two or three distinctive things they do to the paintings, very small things. They also record exactly where on the painting they put their signature. In the case of this picture, my mother had not yet signed it. Unless by some rare stroke of luck the forger paints over all these marks, they will prove the identity of the painter."

Both Coni and Dayton Windle returned to their chairs. They looked at Trey expectantly. Dayton asked, "Is that true of this painting?"

"Of course it is," Trey said.

Dayton nervously cleared his throat. "Do you see any of those, uh, *secret things*, on this work here?"

"Yes, one of them," Trey answered. "There may be more, but we won't know until we can refer to her journal of this painting. It's in a safe in Sydney. My father has it secured with both his and Mother's other journals. When we get back, we'll get it and compare it to this work."

"If the painting's still available," Coni said just a bit snidely. "It's scheduled for the auction in a little while. We better get going. We still have some preparations to make."

"This painting is not going on sale. I'm seizing it," Trey said.

"We're in international waters," Dayton said. "You have no jurisdiction here."

Trey glared at him. "Get your captain in here."

"We don't need to bother him," Dayton said after exchanging glances with Coni. "If you could point out just one of those, uh, marks, we might be able to justify holding it. If you or your father can remember one and identify it."

"I'd be happy to call Father," Trey said. "He'll point one out to you."

"I hate to bother Mr. Shotwell," Dayton said. "He wasn't feeling well when I saw him." He glanced nervously at his wife, then back at Trey. "Can *you* point one out?"

"If you'd like me to," Trey said.

"Please do," Dayton said. He and Coni moved in unison toward the painting again.

"Look on the farmer's right leg, just below the knee. You'll see what looks like a tiny loose thread there."

"Oh, my!" Coni gasped. "It's right there. Do you see it, Dayton?"

"Yes," he said, his face a shade paler than it had been a moment before.

"Now, I think it would be well if we found a safe place to hold this painting. It's not only a stolen item but is evidence in a homicide investigation in London," Trey said firmly. "Now, please, the captain needs to be involved."

"I'll ring him," Dayton said. "Coni, you better go back to seeing that the auction is set up."

She left, looking quite pale and upset, and five minutes later the captain appeared. "I'm Captain Nels Johnsen," he said to Trey. "I understand we may have a little problem here."

Trey shook his hand, introduced himself, and then said, "I'm afraid it's not a small problem, Captain. It is a very serious one." He went on to explain about the theft and murder in London ten years ago.

"And you believe this painting has something to do with that?" Captain Johnsen asked in his heavily accented English. Trey guessed he was probably Danish.

"This painting is one of the ones that was stolen that day," Trey said firmly. "Let me explain how I've identified it."

The ship's captain listened and then, without argument, took possession of Trey's mother's portrait. "I'll lock this up pending a complete and thorough investigation, Detective. Perhaps when the art auction is over, you would be kind enough to come to my stateroom and discuss this matter with me further."

"I will," Trey agreed.

After Dayton had carefully wrapped the painting so that it wouldn't be recognized and would be safe, Captain Johnsen left with it.

"What now, Detective?" Dayton asked.

"I'll get back with you. I have some calls to make to some colleagues in London and to my boss in Sydney. In the meantime, you're welcome to help your wife. I'll go see how my father is doing, and then I'll see you at the auction," Trey said.

He hurried to his room and was surprised to see Aariah sitting on the small sofa beside his father.

"Ah, here's Trey now," Simon said as Trey entered the room.

"Hi, Aariah. I see you've met my father," Trey said.

She nodded. "He's been really nice."

Simon spoke right up. "This young lady has had a bit of a scare. She called our room looking for you. She didn't want to leave her room until you came for her, so I went up and escorted her down here myself."

"Thank you, Father." Trey stepped over to them. Aariah stood, and he let her enter his arms. She was trembling, and her lips quivered. "It'll be okay," he comforted, not having the slightest idea *what* would be okay. "Have you told my father what happened?"

"No," she said as she stepped back. "He asked, but I said I'd wait for you and then tell you both at the same time."

"Does it have to do with those two blokes in the stateroom next to yours?" Trey asked.

"Yes," she said. "Trey, those guys are up to something. They aren't on this trip just to have fun and relax like most of the passengers are. I'm really afraid of them."

Trey's father stood up. "You two sit there. I'll take this chair while we talk."

Trey shot him a look of gratitude and sat with Aariah on the sofa. But before she began, Trey said, "How are you feeling, Father? You're looking a lot better."

"Yes, those motion sickness pills helped a lot, and the sea has settled down too. The water's not nearly as rough. I'm fine now," Simon said.

"Father gets motion sickness," Trey said to Aariah.

"He told me," she said. "My grandmother is a little bothered too. I gave her some pills, and she's fine now too."

"Trey, did you work things out with the art director?" Simon asked.

"Yes. The captain took possession of the painting. I'll tell you the details later. Okay, Aariah, what happened?"

"What painting?" she asked.

"It's a long story," Trey said. "I'll tell you about it later. Right now, I want to know what's bothering you."

"That painting. Is it a portrait of an old farmer?" she asked.

Trey was rocked by her question. "How did you know that?"

"They mentioned it," she said.

"Okay, Aariah." Trey felt his skin prickle. "Let's hear this. I assume you overheard something."

"The men's names are Martin and Danny. I didn't hear last names." She shrugged. "I think Martin is the older one by three or four years. He's probably around forty. I recognized his voice. Anyway, Grandmother and I were seated out on our balcony when those two came out on their balcony and started talking."

"Did they know you and your grandmother could hear them?"

"They must not have. Grandmother was dozing, and I just sat quietly and listened until they went back in. Then I woke Grandmother, and we went inside. She slept through it all, but I was so shaken up that she asked me what was wrong. So I told her."

"I see."

"I can't tell you word for word, but I can tell you the gist of it."

"That's fine. Go ahead," Trey encouraged her.

"Martin said something about how Danny's sister didn't need to worry about the painting," she said. "He said it was a really good one. Then Martin left the balcony for a minute, and when he came back, he said, 'While I was mixing our drinks, I called your sister. She says we can bid up to five thousand dollars, but no more than that.' That might not be word for word, but it's close. Then Danny said, 'I think the picture of the old farmer will go for around ten thousand.' I didn't think anything of it until you mentioned it just now," she said.

Trey felt a jab of disappointment. He'd hoped they'd said something more than that. It sounded like they wanted to buy it. He asked, "So what did they say that upset you?"

With that question, Aariah's lips began to quiver again. "Martin said he was going to take me to the lounge tonight and get me drunk. I know he meant me because he referred to me as the girl with the golden hair in the next stateroom. The other guy, Danny, laughed about it. He asked Martin how he was going to do that. And then Martin said something about how he'd teach me to like him."

Trey touched her arm. "Over my dead body," he said grimly.

"That's not all," Aariah said. "Danny kept pressing Martin to tell him how he was going to get me to go with him. Martin finally said that he'd pick me up and carry me down there if he had to."

"I think we need to somehow get you and your grandmother moved to a different stateroom," Trey said. "I've met the captain. His name is Nels Johnsen. In fact, I have an appointment with him in his stateroom following the auction today. I'll have you two come with me. We'll see if he'll help us make some changes."

"Why are you meeting with the captain?" Aariah asked.

Trey explained about the painting. "I think the captain wants to ask me how I plan to go about investigating the case."

Aariah looked stunned. "It's your mother's painting?"

"Yes, she called it *The Scottish Farmer*."

"Oh my!" Aariah exclaimed.

"I suspected it was Mother's painting the moment I saw it, despite the changes that had been made to it," Trey said.

"How are you going to investigate, Trey?" Aariah asked.

"For now, I'm sort of limited because we're at sea. But I plan to call a friend in London who I talk to quite frequently. He's a detective inspector with New Scotland Yard. New Scotland Yard is the metropolitan police department for the London area. Anyway, he is now assigned to the Homicide and Serious Crime Command. That means my mother's murder is something he has jurisdiction to investigate. If I need to, I could call a couple of other officers there, but I think Willie can probably start the ball rolling. I'll also call my supervisor in Sydney and let him know what I've learned here. I think he'll have some ideas on how I should proceed."

Simon spoke up. "Aren't you going to have some jurisdictional problems?"

"Yes, but Mother's murder and the thefts of the paintings are under the jurisdiction of New Scotland Yard," Trey explained. "I'll see what Captain Johnsen thinks. I can only do what he allows me to do on the ship, but that doesn't limit Detective Inspector Willie Denning."

"What kind of experience does he have?" Trey's father asked.

"He was a uniformed constable when we left London," Trey said. "He moved up quite rapidly. He's very good, according to a couple of my other friends over there. And of course, he doesn't work alone." Trey changed the subject. "Aariah, will your grandmother be okay while we're busy for the next two or three hours?"

"All she wants to do is sit and read or watch TV," she said. "She'll be fine."

Trey, Simon, and Aariah went down to the large lounge on the seventh deck, where people were already starting to file in even though the event wasn't scheduled to begin for another thirty minutes. It was hard to get into the room as people recognized Simon and closed in around him, wanting to shake hands, get his autograph, or just speak with him. This had happened a few times when Simon had left their room to eat or to visit the art gallery or take a tour on shore. This time, however, most of the people there were art lovers, and most of them recognized the famous artist.

"Let's sit near the back," Trey suggested as he helped his father push through the crowd. "I'd like to be able to observe."

"But we can't see the paintings as well from there," Simon objected as he scribbled a signature on a piece of blank paper provided by a fan.

"We've already looked at them closely, and anyway, you aren't planning to buy anything, are you?" Trey asked.

"I guess you're right," Simon grudgingly admitted as he shook hands with a young lady who was smiling brightly at him.

They finally ended up on the back row in large, plush chairs. Each row of tables and seats was elevated, beginning with those at the main level of the lounge where the paintings were arranged. Trey had selected seats not only the highest up but right in the center as well. Aariah sat on his left and Simon on his right. The three of them could see the entire room quite easily.

Simon let out a sigh and wiped his brow with the back of his hand. Aariah leaned past Trey and said to him, "The fans love you; I feel lucky to have met you."

"Thank you, young lady."

She leaned back as Trey said, "Father loves to paint and is very successful, but he doesn't enjoy a lot of attention. He's a private person."

Simon nodded. "I get claustrophobic if I'm in crowds for very long."

"You were so nice to the people as we were coming in," she said, leaning past Trey again.

"I try, but believe me, it's very hard. I'd rather be alone in my studio painting than receiving accolades."

About ten minutes after they'd taken their seats, Dayton walked in and looked around the room. When he saw Trey and his father, he lifted a hand in recognition and smiled a welcome to them.

Five minutes after that, Aariah gasped. "There they are, Trey!"

Trey looked in the direction she was nodding and saw the two men he now knew as Martin and Danny following two people he didn't recall seeing before, a man and a woman. The man looked like he was in his midfifties, about six feet tall with curly black hair. He was stocky and walked with an air of confidence. The woman was probably ten years younger and about three inches shorter than her companion. She was a nicely built woman but what Trey would have called big boned. Her brown hair was cut quite short and accentuated an attractive face with slightly narrow-set eyes.

He wasn't sure if Martin and Danny were actually with the others until all four of them found a table on the left side of the room about three rows from the front. They sat down together and began to quietly confer with each other.

Trey had a good view of them, although he could only see the sides of their faces. Aariah touched his arm, and he looked over at her.

"It looks like there are more jerks than two," she said with a bite to her words.

"Yes, looks like it," he agreed. "Although the other two don't look as bad as your neighbors. In fact, just looking at them, they seem like they might be quite nice."

"You're an optimist," Aariah said. "I hope you're right."

Sitting there observing as everyone came in, Trey was able to recognize several people he'd seen in the art gallery. Others he'd seen elsewhere, perhaps at breakfast or dinner or even when he and Simon were taking tours ashore in Tasmania and Melbourne. Some he recognized as fans of Simon's, others just as passengers with nothing much in common. Some of the folks carried an air of wealth, both in their dress and in their bearing. Others looked more common and down to earth. Of course, he knew that dress and bearing didn't mean everything. He'd known some very rich people who went to great lengths to keep their wealth from showing, and he'd known others who attempted to look wealthy even though they weren't.

Just as the appointed hour arrived, Simon gasped. "Trey, look! That's Lukas."

Trey turned his head and spotted a man he hadn't seen for ten years. Lukas Nichols, his mother's brother, was even more overweight than ten years before. He now sported a short, pointy beard and narrow mustache, dark brown like his hair, but there was a little gray showing. "What in the world is Uncle Lukas doing here?"

"I have no idea," Simon said with a shake of his head. "But it can't be good. The guy is up to something. He was always up to something. I hope he doesn't see us."

That hope was short lived. Lukas glanced around the room, looking for a seat, and spotted Trey and Simon. He lifted a chubby hand and waved a greeting. Trey lifted his hand just a little. Simon didn't return the greeting at all. Lukas grinned, stroked his short beard, and moved toward an empty chair near the far right side.

Trey couldn't take his eyes off the man. He agreed with his father. Lukas must be up to something. It was far too much of a stretch to believe that he would be on the same cruise with family members he hadn't seen in ten years. He wondered if Lukas was alone on the cruise. He was clearly alone at the moment.

Trey finally looked away as Dayton Windle began the auction. He welcomed everyone and said, "This is the first of two auctions we will be holding. We have some great works of art to show you today, including original paintings by some of the world's premier artists. There are some oil paintings, a few watercolors, and some charcoal drawings. We also have copies of some of those great paintings for those of you who want something that is beautiful but not so expensive. And then we also have some copies that have been touched up by the original artists. Those are most likely going to be in a medium price range."

Dayton looked around the room, and then, pointing to where Simon, Trey, and Aariah were seated, he said, "We have two of the artists with us. You will recognize the name Simon Shotwell, one of the top oil painting artists in the world. Would you please stand, Mr. Shotwell?"

Simon looked at Trey a bit uneasily, and then he stood. Trey was conscious of his uncle watching, looking quite smug, which was puzzling. There was a thunderous round of applause. After the room had quieted down, Dayton said, "Simon's son, Trey Shotwell is also with us. Trey is an up-and-coming artist in his own right. He, like his late mother, Rita Shotwell, enjoys painting portraits. In a little while, you'll have the opportunity to purchase one of his paintings. Trey, would you stand, please?"

Trey stood, nodded his head in acknowledgment, and then sat back down to a polite applause.

Dayton said, "I suspect that the lucky bidders on the works of both men might be able to persuade them to give you an autograph. If you haven't already, you should find an opportunity to meet and speak with them during the next few days."

Next, Dayton introduced his wife. "Coni has one of the most critical eyes in the art world today," he said proudly. "I am lucky to have her as both my wife and my assistant on this ship. Give Coni a round of applause."

The first work was introduced. It was a rather strange work in watercolor, or at least that's the way Trey viewed it. While Dayton was giving a knowledgeable explanation of the watercolor and the artist, Aariah leaned over to Trey and said, "Did you see Martin and Danny when you were introduced? They did not look happy. The other two smiled and applauded. All four of them applauded when your father stood up."

Trey grinned. "I don't suppose I made a very favorable impression on Martin and Danny last night outside your stateroom."

FOUR

THE BIDDING WAS SLOW UNTIL the one painting of Simon's that was to be sold that day was introduced. The other one, Dayton explained, would be sold at the next auction in a few days. The lighting on Simon's painting was perfect, and Simon pointed that out to Trey. "Dayton and Coni sure know how to get the most from a painting. I'm impressed. They really make it look good."

Once again, Dayton asked Simon to stand. "Here is the chance of a lifetime to purchase a Simon Shotwell painting and to get to meet the great artist himself." After Simon was seated again, Dayton said, "Let's start the bidding on this gorgeous painting at fifty thousand dollars." There was first a gasp from the audience and then a hush settled over the lounge. "Who would like to start the bidding at fifty thousand?" A man with bright-red hair and a light-blue sport shirt raised his hand. Dayton grinned. "I have fifty thousand, who will bid fifty-five thousand?" A small woman with dyed-black hair piled high on her head lifted her hand to bid. "Thank you, ma'am," Dayton said with a large smile. "How about sixty thousand?" The redheaded man bid again.

Those two went back and forth until it reached eighty thousand. Then there was a brief pause before a bald fellow in a green shirt and tie with a tan sports coat raised his hand. A fourth bidder joined in at ninety thousand dollars. It was a man with thick black hair who was dressed down, wearing plain brown slacks and a tan sport shirt. He didn't look wealthy, but Trey suspected this latest bidder might be the richest of them all.

"Ninety-five thousand?" Dayton asked. There was a long pause. "This painting is worth every penny of that and more," he said. "Let's hear it. Who will give us ninety-five thousand dollars for this wonderful painting by Mr. Simon Shotwell?"

Aariah grabbed Trey's hand and squeezed tightly. He glanced at her and grinned. "My father's pretty popular, wouldn't you say?"

She nodded, and Trey turned back to the action. The redheaded man raised the bid to ninety-five thousand, and the little woman with the horrible hair offered an even hundred grand. In the end, the man with thick black hair in the tan shirt bought the painting for $125,000.

Then a strange thing happened. The bald man in the green shirt stood up, walked past the man in tan, glaring at him for a moment. He continued to where the lady with the horrible hair had planted her tiny bottom, leaned down, whispered something in her ear, and then left the room. There was a short period of unease before the woman rose and followed him out. Trey couldn't help but notice that his uncle was watching the pair closely. He wondered if they knew each other.

It was about an hour later when Trey's portrait of a young boy was brought to the front. "This painting is by Trey Shotwell, son of Simon," Dayton said. He talked for a few minutes, describing what he felt were the paintings strong points, and then he said, "Now, Trey, I hope you don't feel bad if I start this painting for less than I did your father's."

Trey chuckled. "Suits me fine. Father's the professional. I'm just an amateur."

There was some polite laughter, and then Dayton asked for a bid of two thousand dollars. The red-haired man who had bid on Simon's painting raised his hand. Dayton raised it five hundred, and no one bid, but on the third and final request, Aariah raised her hand.

"You don't have to do that," Trey whispered.

"But I like it, and I can afford that much."

Trey didn't know what to say. The red-haired man bid next, and once more Aariah raised her hand. "Hey, that's getting to be a bit much," Trey said.

Aariah grinned at him. "Don't tear down your own work. I know good art when I see it."

Dayton asked for another bid, five hundred higher, and pointed to Trey's left. The bid came from the woman beside Martin. He looked back at Aariah and smirked.

"They're just doing that to spite me." Aariah rolled her eyes.

"Don't bid again, Aariah. They think it's a game, and they must have money. Let them have it," Trey said.

She nodded, and Dayton asked for another bid. The redheaded man bid again, and the woman raised it. Dayton looked at the man again, but he shook his head. There were no more bids, and the lady at Martin's table bought it for $4,500.

"Ugh," Aariah said. "They probably won't even appreciate it. I really like it."

"Then I'll paint one for you, and it won't cost you a thing," Trey said impulsively.

Her eyes popped wide in response. "You don't have to do that. We hardly know each other," she protested.

"That's true, but I hope to get to know you better."

Aariah blushed, lowered her eyes, and smiled. "Same here."

"So you'll let me if I want to, right?" he asked.

"We'll see," she said.

Trey nodded. "That Martin guy looks like he thinks they've really put one over on you. But hey, it made me some money. If they don't like it, they have to pay anyway."

She gave him a fleeting smile, and the auction went on. When it was finished, people filed out. Trey just sat and watched them go. He was surprised when the lady who had bought his painting worked her way to the front of the room, her entourage of three following her. She went right up to Dayton and said something. He gave her a reply accompanied by a shake of his head. She said something else, and once again Dayton just shook his head. Finally, the woman smiled and led her group toward the rear exit. They passed near where Trey was seated. The woman with the short brown hair waved at Simon. Martin, who was bringing up the rear, paused for a moment, called Aariah by name, and then said, "Too bad we outbid you on your boyfriend's crappy painting. Guess you'll have to cozy up to me if you want to see it again." And then he scurried after the others. Trey saw the woman look back at Martin with a frown, shaking a finger at him. A moment later they all left the lounge.

Trey, Simon, and Aariah went to the front. Trey asked Dayton, "What did that lady want—the one who bought my painting?"

"She asked about the one you called *The Scottish Farmer*," Dayton replied with a frown. "She asked if it would be offered later, that she really quite liked it. She didn't seem too upset, but the one guy, a mean-looking fellow, seemed downright angry. When I told her it had been pulled, she said she was sorry because she would really have liked to bid on it. Then she said something that really threw me. She said it reminded her of your mother's painting. She said it wasn't nearly as good as Rita Shotwell's work but that it was similar enough to be worth something.

"The guy she called Martin said, 'You had no right to pull that painting.' She said, 'Forget it, Martin. I bought a nice painting from Rita Shotwell's son.' Then this Martin guy said a couple of words that I won't repeat and finished with, 'He paints crappy stuff.' The woman apologized to me, and they left."

"You're sure you didn't tell her why it was pulled?" Trey asked.

"Absolutely not," Dayton said. "But she did recognize that it was a lot like your mother's."

"Thanks, Dayton."

"She seems to think highly of your work, Trey. The others didn't say much except for Martin. But I can see he's a jerk."

Trey chuckled. "You got that right."

"Do you know the guy?" Dayton asked.

Aariah spoke up. "He's been harassing me, and Trey's helping me out. The guy scares me."

"Wow. I wonder what he's doing with a nice lady like her," Dayton said, looking puzzled.

"Did the lady happen to say what her name is?"

"She did. Let's see. I think she said Daphne. Yes, that's it. Daphne Slader. The tallest guy is her husband. I think she said his name is Gil."

"Have you ever seen any of them before?" Trey asked.

"No, not that I recall. The Sladers do seem to know their art, though," Dayton said.

"Dayton," Simon spoke up then, "thanks for doing such a good job selling my painting."

"You're welcome. The fellow who bought it, he's French. He told me yesterday that he planned to buy that one of yours no matter what it cost him." Dayton chuckled. "We don't sell a lot of paintings on the ship for anywhere near that amount."

"Do you happen to know his name?" Trey asked. "We'd like to thank him."

"Damien Latimer. I'm not sure how he made his money, but he has a lot. And he loves your work. He told me he'd bought a couple of your paintings before. They're displayed in his home."

"He doesn't look rich," Aariah said.

"No, he's not that kind. He's not stuck on himself at all. His wife's the same way."

"Was she here?" Trey asked. "I didn't notice a woman with him."

"She doesn't stand out, but no, she's not here. I met her on a previous cruise. Really nice people, and they both speak very good English. He said she couldn't come on this trip. The only reason he came was so he could buy your painting."

"That's amazing," Aariah said.

"I'm sorry you didn't get Trey's painting," Dayton said to her with a sympathetic smile. "But I do believe Mrs. Slader will appreciate it."

"Aariah will get one for free," Trey said with a grin. "We know the artist."

They all chuckled at that, and Aariah blushed.

"Yes, I suppose you could do one for her," Dayton said.

"Well, we better go," Trey said. "I have a meeting with Captain Johnsen."

When they exited the lounge, Damien Latimer approached them. "Mr. Shotwell," he said with enthusiasm and a strong French accent, "I love your work. This is my third of yours. I hope to get more."

"Thank you, sir," Simon said with a smile. "I appreciate your taking the time to come on this cruise. I'm sorry your wife couldn't be here with you."

"I came just to get that painting," Damien said. "That biddy, Mademoiselle Claudia Gaudet, she lives just to try to outbid me, but it'll never happen. I have to chuckle when I think that she and her friend Victor Krause were bidding against each other for a little while. I don't think they realized at first. Strange people, those two. Claudia pretends she has money, but she can't afford your work, Mr. Shotwell. I know it for a fact. She lives in the same neighborhood as a cousin of mine. No one cares much for her, unless it's that bald German." He laughed cheerfully.

He turned to Simon, who had a strange look on his face. "Do you know her personally?" Simon asked.

"Yes," Damian said. "She came to a party at my cousin's home a number of years ago. And of course I saw her at auctions back—"

Simon interrupted Damian nervously. "Did she ever mention me?"

"Of course she did, but it was about your art. She talked about how she plans to get some of your paintings, that she very much admires you."

"I see." Simon rubbed at his chin. "Well, maybe someday she'll be able to afford to," he said, with a strain in his voice that Trey was pretty sure no one else could detect.

"Mr. Shotwell, again, I sure do thank you," Damian said.

"Call me Simon," Trey's father said.

"Sure thing, Simon, and I'd be pleased if you'd call me Damien. Hey, why don't you and I go find a drink somewhere? If you don't mind, that is."

"That'd be great. Trey, you don't need me, do you?"

"Nope. I can handle it, Father," Trey said. "I'll catch up with you before dinner."

The two older men went off jabbering like a pair of lifelong friends.

Aariah smiled and said, "I think that's cool."

"Yeah, me too," Trey agreed. "We better move on."

"It's right kind of you to bring this pretty girl along, Detective Shotwell," Captain Johnsen said after Trey had introduced Aariah. "She certainly brightens my cabin." The compliment made Aariah blush. The captain noticed and added, "She's even prettier with that crimson face." He laughed heartily. "I take it we can talk freely around her."

"Yes, of course," Trey said.

"This shouldn't take long, Detective. Would you young people care for a beer or something stronger while we visit?"

"Thank you, but I don't drink alcohol," Trey said.

"I don't either," Aariah said, giving Trey a sidelong glance.

"How about a root beer?" he offered.

They both agreed. While sipping on the root beer, Trey and Captain Johnsen discussed the painting. "I just wanted to figure out the jurisdiction thing," the captain said. "I can commission you to do anything we need on the ship, but it's the theft of the painting, its, uh, alteration, and your mother's murder that concern me."

"That's not a problem," Trey said. "I have some good friends with New Scotland Yard. One of them is an especially good friend, Detective

Inspector Willie Denning. He's worked on my mother's case off and on for ten years. He was a constable back when she was killed and was one of the first officers on the scene. Anyway, I plan to call him a little later. It's a ten- or eleven-hour time difference there. I'm just waiting until I'm sure I can reach him. When I do, I'll tell him everything I know, and he'll take it from there."

"That's a relief, Detective. If you trust your friend in London, then so do I."

"He's one of the best," Trey said confidently.

"If you don't mind, would you check with your department in Sydney—let them know what's going on and make sure they don't object to my using you a little on the ship?"

"I'll do it right now," Trey said and placed the call. As he was sure would be the case, it wasn't a problem with his supervisor. All he asked was that Trey keep him advised of any developments.

After Trey completed his call, the captain said, "I don't know exactly what you can do, but if I think of something or if you do, consider yourself commissioned. Just let me know if you learn anything."

Trey agreed and then said, "Captain Johnsen, there is something else we need to discuss with you. It's about Aariah."

The captain scrunched his eyebrows and focused on Aariah. "What seems to be the problem?"

"There are these two guys in the stateroom next to me." She hesitated.

Trey continued, "They're harassing and threatening her. She's scared of them and for good cause."

"That kind of behavior is not tolerated on my ship," Captain Johnsen said sternly. "Tell me exactly what they've done."

Trey and Aariah filled him in on the actions of Danny and Martin.

Trey said, "Finally, when their friend outbid Aariah on a painting, Martin made some rude remarks as they left the lounge."

"Why would he say anything in front of you?" Captain Johnsen pressed.

"Well," Trey said, feeling awkward, "the painting she bid on was one I painted."

"I didn't realize you paint too," the captain said. "I'm impressed."

"I don't paint all that well." Trey sipped his root beer.

"He's actually very good," Aariah said, pointing her soda in his direction and smiling brightly. After just a moment, her smile faded, and she went on. "When they were leaving, Martin stopped, looked at me, and said something about now that he had the painting, I'd have to, you know, be his friend."

"I don't suppose he said it like that," Captain Johnson said, drumming his hand on the table next to him.

"Well, no, but—" Aariah began.

"I don't need it word for word, young lady. I get the idea. But I thought you said it was his friend who bought it."

"She did, but Martin rubbed it in Aariah's face," Trey said with disgust. "Don't get me wrong. The woman, her name is Daphne Slader, seemed to like the piece. She just doesn't have very good taste in the company she keeps."

Trey and Aariah both finished their sodas as the captain rubbed his chin thoughtfully. He finally looked at Trey. "So you're thinking that it would be best if Aariah was moved to a different stateroom?" he asked.

"Yes. Aariah and her grandmother," Trey responded. "Is that possible?"

"I'll make it happen," the captain said firmly. "We have three or four empty staterooms. I'll get someone on it now. Your cell phone obviously has satellite capability, Detective. Give me your number, and I'll call you as soon as I have something worked out. Also, I'll need both of your room numbers." After he had written down the number Trey told him, he asked, "Do you have a satellite phone, Miss Stanton?"

"No, sorry," she said.

"That's okay. Detective Shotwell, will you be in touch with Miss Stanton?"

Trey looked at her and said, "I'll be sure and stay close to her the rest of the day."

* * *

Simon and Damien had really hit it off. Over drinks they'd laughed and talked like they'd known each other all their lives. Neither of them were heavy drinkers, and both were still nursing their first drink thirty minutes later.

"As I mentioned earlier, I am now the proud owner of three of your excellent paintings, Simon. I have another one that looks a lot like yours. In fact, if I didn't know differently, I'd swear you painted it," Damien said with a grin.

Simon's mind raced. "Would you mind describing that painting?" he asked.

Damien's smile faded. "It's a desert scene. Something like you might see in Arizona or Nevada in the United States," Damien said. "It has a few plants—cactus and that kind of thing. There's a colorful sunset over—"

Simon held up his hand, cutting Damien off. "Do you mind if we finish this conversation after I find my son? I'd like him to hear."

"Your son? The detective?" Damien looked closely at his new friend. "Sure. Get him. I take it there's a problem?"

Simon, who also had a phone with satellite capability, just nodded as he sent a short text message to Trey.

Five minutes later, Trey and Aariah arrived. Aariah was out of breath. Trey wasn't. "We ran all the way," Trey said. "Is something wrong?"

"Sit down," Simon said, nodding to the two empty chairs at the table. When they were both seated, Simon said, "Damien was just telling me about the paintings of mine that he owns. He also says he has one that looks like mine but isn't."

Trey was instantly alert and turned to the wealthy collector. "Can you describe it?"

"Your father just asked me the same thing," Damien said, his brow creased and one foot tapping incessantly under the table. He gave the description to Trey, who listened intently.

Trey and his father exchanged glances, both nodding. Then Trey asked, "Who signed the painting?"

Damien rubbed his forehead with three fingers. The tapping of his foot ceased as he concentrated. Finally he said, "Ainslee Cline. I'm pretty sure that's it."

Simon said, "Isn't that the name on . . ." His voice trailed off.

"Yes, it is," Trey said. "Mr. Latimer, have you by any chance seen any other paintings signed by this same artist?"

"I think I have," he said thoughtfully. "I have a friend in Germany who also buys the best paintings he can get his hands on. The style on that painting is different from yours, but it's signed by Ainslee Cline as well. It's a portrait of—"

"It's called *The Scottish Farmer's Wife*," Trey interrupted. "It's of an old lady beside a scraggly tree holding a basket of yellow flowers."

Damien's eyes opened wide. "How did you know that, Detective?"

"My late wife, Rita, painted it," Simon answered for him.

Damien raised both hands in the air and then brought them crashing down on the table. Fortunately the men's glasses were empty, for they both skidded across the table and fell to the carpeted floor. For a moment, rage colored his face scarlet. Finally, he relaxed, and the color drained away. When he spoke, it was slowly, his French accent more prominent than before. "I will help you find this woman, this Ainslee Cline, and see what her game is," he said.

"Or man," Trey offered. "Just because the signature is a woman's name doesn't necessarily mean it's a woman who's doing this."

"Man, woman, whatever. I'll help you if I can. This is an outrage."

Just at that moment, a waiter arrived and asked if there was a problem, and if so, could he help? Four sets of eyes swiveled to his face.

Damien spoke. "Yes, there is a problem, but it has nothing to do with the service here," he said. "It is a personal matter. But thanks for asking."

The fellow hesitated, looking all four of them over carefully, and then he sidled away from the table.

"I'm sorry I got so upset," Damien said. "What can I do to help? Money is not a problem. I could hire private investigators if that would help."

Simon shook his head. "I don't feel good about you spending your money on my problem."

Damian stared across the room for a moment, and then a smile creased his face. He met Simon's eyes. "If I help you and the crooks are caught, you could do a painting for me. It wouldn't have to be a large one, but it would mean a lot to me."

Simon looked at Trey. "What about it, son?" he asked. "I'm more than willing to do the painting. In fact he could have the one I'm working on up in our room when it's finished. Would a private investigator help?"

Trey was thinking about a former New Scotland Yard investigator who had retired and was now working as a private investigator in London. He was one of the men who, like Willie Denning, Trey had been close to as a boy. He was one of the original investigators on the case.

"Do you remember Inspector Ruben Hawk?" Trey asked his father.

"Yes, I do," Simon said after a moment's thought. "He was one of the men who worked on our case when your mother was murdered."

"That's right. He retired three or four years ago and now operates his own investigation firm. Most of the people who work for him are former New Scotland Yard officers," Trey said.

"Do you know how to reach him?" Damien asked. "I'll bet he could go to Germany and take a look at my friend's painting."

"Of course I know how to contact him," Trey said with a grin. "He's a good friend of mine."

"My son always wanted to be a policeman," Simon explained to Damien. "Before we moved to Australia, he would hang out a lot with policemen in London."

"I still have contact with several of them," Trey said. "I've even worked some cases with them that had ties to both London and Sydney."

"Trey vowed that he would catch his mother's killer someday," Simon added. "I think these men will help him do that."

"I'll call both Inspector Hawk and Detective Inspector Denning tonight. At that time it will be a reasonable hour of the day in London," Trey explained.

"I'll pay all the costs associated with Mr. Hawk," Damien said. "I know you could afford to pay him, but I'd like to do this. And if we are successful, I'll take whatever painting you would be willing to give me, Simon. Does that sound fair?"

"It's a deal," Simon agreed.

"That's great!" Damien smiled and turned to Trey. "Now, Trey, let me give you my cell phone number, and you can have your friend call me. I'll work out the details with him."

Trey and Aariah left the two older men in deep conversation and went up to her room. As luck would have it, they met Martin and Danny in the hallway. The two men blocked the hallway, and Martin jeered, "Hey, pretty lady. Why don't you come with me, and I'll let you look at the painting you wanted, even though it's of *inferior* quality."

"Please step aside, gentlemen," Trey said evenly.

"And if we don't?" Martin challenged him.

"I don't think you want to find out. Now move!"

"Hey, no need to threaten," Martin said, raising his hands defensively. "Not that you scare us in the least. I just wanted to be polite to the beautiful lady. She and I are going to get to know each other much better before this cruise is over."

Trey stepped closer to them and said softly, "Move, now." He was ready to enforce his request if he had to.

It appeared that the two men believed he might be capable of inflicting some damage, for they moved to the side.

Trey ushered Aariah past them, not looking back, but he did hear Martin say, "You haven't seen the last of us, Shotwell."

FIVE

AARIAH'S GRANDMOTHER WAS SLEEPING WHEN Trey and Aariah entered the stateroom. Aariah whispered, "Let's go out on the balcony and shut the door. I don't want to wake her."

They hadn't been out there for more than five minutes when the elderly lady slid the door to the balcony open. "I didn't hear you come in, Aariah," she said. "Oh, my! Who is this handsome young man?"

Aariah and Trey both got to their feet. "This is the friend I told you about, Grandmother. His name is Trey Shotwell, Detective Inspector Trey Shotwell," Aariah said with a grin at Trey. "Trey, this is my grandmother, Charlotte Bray."

"A policeman, Aariah? How nice," Charlotte said. Trey smiled at her. She was short and slightly stooped with white hair.

"He's also a painter," Aariah added. "I went to the art auction with him and his father, who is a world-famous artist."

"My goodness, it is so nice to meet you, young man," Charlotte said. "You two mustn't mind me. I'll just stay inside and turn on the TV while you visit out here. It's such a nice day. The sea isn't rough like it was this morning."

"Actually, Mrs. Bray, would you please sit down beside Aariah?" Trey said. "I'll just lean against the railing. There's something we need to talk to you about."

The old lady sucked in a deep breath. "Are you two getting married? But you barely met."

Aariah went beet red.

"No, I'm afraid that's not it." Trey chuckled. "Now don't get me wrong. I think your granddaughter is lovely, but like you say, we hardly know each other. There's something else we need to discuss."

"It's about the men in the stateroom next door," Aariah said, pointing.

"What about them?" Charlotte asked, looking with wide-eyed concern at her granddaughter. Before either Trey or Aariah could respond, she went right on. "I believe they are bad men."

"Yes, I think that might be the case," Trey said. "And I want Aariah to be safe, as I know you do. The ship's captain has agreed to find a more suitable stateroom for the two of you, one where they won't be so close and as likely to make Aariah uncomfortable."

"You spoke to the captain?" Charlotte asked, clearly astonished.

"We both did, Grandmother," Aariah said. "His name is Captain Johnsen. He's from Denmark and is a really nice man."

"We're going to move to a different room?" the old lady asked. "Is that what you're telling me?"

"Yes, that's right. As soon as it's arranged, Captain Johnsen will let us know," Aariah said.

"Should we pack now?" Charlotte asked.

"I think you can wait until we know when and where you'll be going," Trey suggested. "Right now, I'd love to hear more about you. You're native to Australia, right? I'm an immigrant from Great Britain, but I very much enjoy living in Australia."

Aariah's grandmother relaxed, and for the next few minutes, they visited as the dark blue sea rolled by, the pleasant, salty scent of the water drifting up to their balcony. Then a knock came on the door. "I'll answer it, Grandmother," Aariah said, rising from her chair.

Trey moved right behind her just as his phone began to ring. "We'll be back in a moment, Mrs. Bray," he said and then answered the phone.

"Detective, the change has been arranged," Captain Johnsen said. "Two stewards will be at Aariah's stateroom momentarily. They will move the ladies into the stateroom next to you and your father."

"That's great. Someone's at the door now," Trey said. "Thank you for your consideration."

Trey was surprised at how quickly the move had been arranged. He was pleased that Aariah and her grandmother would be in the stateroom next door to him and his father and told Aariah about it as she opened the door to the hallway.

She invited the stewards in and then asked Trey, "Was there an empty room next to you?"

"I don't think so," he said. "I'm sure the captain asked someone else to make a shift as well, but I'm sure he made it well worth it. I'll leave you alone to pack, but I'll be back to help the stewards move your things."

"These nice men said they'll move our things," Charlotte said, referring to the stewards.

"I know they will, but I'd like to be with you when they do."

The old lady's eyes grew wide. "You want to make sure those men from next door don't cause any problems," she said. "You're such a thoughtful young man."

It took a little time for the women to pack, but once they had accomplished the task, the move went smoothly. Trey felt a measure of relief. He wasn't so naïve as to suppose that Martin and Danny wouldn't still harass her if they ran into her or try to find out where she's been moved to. He was happy he'd at least be close enough to keep the wolves at bay most of the time.

The stewards had stacked the women's suitcases near the door to their new stateroom. Trey helped lift them onto the beds. "I'll leave you two to unpack. Then why don't we all, you two and my father and I, go to dinner together a little later?"

"That would be very nice, Detective Shotwell," Mrs. Bray said. "I've stayed cooped up in my room almost the entire trip. I'd like to see some of the ship. Aariah, why don't you and I go down and admire the art a little later?"

Aariah smiled brightly at that. "I'd like that, Grandmother," she said. "I didn't know you liked art."

"Of course I do," she said. "And I especially want to see what this nice young policeman painted."

"Would you mind if I tagged along?" Trey asked. He was more worried about Martin and Danny than he wanted Aariah and her grandmother to know.

Charlotte favored him with a bright smile. "You're such a thoughtful young man." She turned to Aariah and spoke again, the smile gone.

"You see, Aariah. You can find nice young men without having to go to the Mormon Church."

"Grandmother, I like the people there," Aariah began. "Trey is—"

He cut her off with a gentle motion of his hand. "There are nice people in all churches." He winked at Aariah. "I'll leave you two pretty ladies to your unpacking. Knock on my door when you're ready to go."

* * *

Gil, Daphne, Martin, and Danny were sitting at a table in one of the bars. Daphne was glaring at Martin. "You're a fool," she said. "There are plenty of women your own age on this ship. You don't need to chase after one so young."

"But she catches my eye," Martin said, "just like you caught Gil's eye."

"The difference is Gil also caught my eye. It wasn't one-sided."

"You're the one who bought the painting," Martin reminded Daphne snidely.

"That was because the artist has a lot of talent."

"No, it's because I asked you to show that girl and Shotwell that they aren't such hot stuff," Martin countered.

Daphne glared at him. "I would have bought it with or without your request. And I also don't appreciate you being so vocal about what an awful painting you think it is. I like it, and if I decide not to keep it, it's one Gil and I could make a nice profit on. But make no mistake about it, Martin, it's my painting, not yours."

"I thought you bought it for me," Martin sniveled.

"I don't know why you thought that," Daphne said. "I would never buy anything for you."

Gil finally spoke up, the final word in the group. "You heard Daphne," he said. "The painting is hers. And you will not harass that girl anymore. You either, Danny."

Martin slammed his fist on the table. "Have it your way—this time." He got up and stormed angrily toward the bar.

"Martin, what do you think you mean by that?" Gil called after him.

"You'll see," he said, and he was gone.

Gil turned to Danny. "Danny, keep him under control. He's not family like you are. Daphne and I expect you to make sure he doesn't cause any more trouble. Don't let that hothead ruin the trip for us."

"I'll try," Danny said glumly. "But you know how Martin is."

"Yes, we know," Gil said. "But I will not tolerate his insolence. You keep him under control. He'll either do as I tell him or . . ."

Danny left the bar as Gil's words trailed off. When he turned into the hallway near their room, he could hear a loud pounding. When Danny got closer he realized Martin was pounding on the door of their neighbor. He felt a chill go over him.

"Martin, don't do that," he said when he reached the bigger man a moment later. "Gil's getting really angry with you."

"I'll do as I please." Martin lifted his fist to pound again, but the door opened and his fist hit nothing but air.

The man standing in the door was a far cry from their attractive neighbor. He stood a towering fourteen inches over Martin. The face was scowling down at them. His head was attached to a pair of broad shoulders by a neck that looked as big as an elephant's leg. The man spoke English with a strong Scandinavian accent. "Are you looking for me?" he growled in a voice so deep it rumbled.

"No, uh, I was looking for my, uh, girlfriend," Martin stammered.

The huge man reached down and took hold of the front of Martin's shirt. "Do I look like a girl to you?"

"No, I, uh, I mean the American girl. She has long blonde hair and pretty—"

"My name is Hans Olander. I am the prettiest person in this room," the huge Swede said. "If you bother me again, I shall throw you over the side of this ship and let the sharks eat you. Am I understood?"

Unfortunately, Martin had consumed too much alcohol. His judgment was seriously impaired. He opened his mouth again. "What have you done with my girl, you big, ugly hunk of dog meat?"

Hans didn't throw him over the balcony, but he did send the smaller man crashing against the hallway wall with a short punch from one of those mammoth fists. Martin slowly slid to the floor, moaning in pain.

"That was just a tap," the big man said. "Next time, I will knock you *through* the wall instead of just into it." He slammed the door with a resounding bang.

Danny stood looking down at his friend, who was missing a tooth. He spotted it lying on the floor but didn't touch it. Martin's nose was bleeding, and his lip was split. His eyes were glazed.

Danny desperately grabbed him by the shirt, dragged him to their door, and pulled him inside. "You idiot. Look what you've done now. Gil'll kill you if he finds out what you did, and you know he will. Now I get to be the one to calm him down. Get yourself cleaned up before you bleed all over everything."

Martin, through glazed eyes, looked up at Danny. "Who was that guy?"

* * *

Trey heard the commotion upstairs as he was leaving his room. He ran to the stairs, pounded up them, and entered the hallway just in time to see Danny pulling Martin into their stateroom. He waited until he heard the door close before walking down the hallway. There was blood and a tooth on the floor. He looked at it, puzzled, and then tapped lightly on the door to Aariah's former stateroom.

"I said not to bother me again," said a deep rumbling voice as the door swung open. He looked up to see the frowning face of a giant, his friend Hans from the exercise room.

"Sorry. I didn't mean to upset you," Trey said, backing away from the door. He knew how strong the man was and didn't doubt the damage he could do if riled up.

To his relief, a huge grin spread across the man's face. "Sorry, Trey. You aren't who I thought it would be. I had trouble with a couple of punks, and I figured they were coming back for more. Come on in, my friend."

"I just noticed blood on the floor . . . and this tooth," Trey said, bending down and picking it up. "The women who were in this stateroom were moved for their safety. One of the men next door threatened one of them. I take it you met them."

The Swede's smile grew broader. "I don't know all the details, but I was asked to move here by the captain himself in order to make things better for a young lady. Nice guy, Captain Johnsen, even if he is Danish. He simply asked me to keep an eye on those two. It didn't take them long to cause trouble. I'm afraid I lost my temper for a moment and poked one of them to shut him up. I might have poked him a little too hard. I need to control my temper better. I guess I should confess to the captain."

The big Swede's grin was infectious, and Trey found himself chuckling. "I guess they were a little surprised to find that the women were gone," he said.

"Yeah, they were." The giant beckoned with a hand about the size of a volleyball. "Please, come in, Trey. Maybe you can tell me more about the trouble these two have been causing." The Swede shut the door behind them and said, "Captain Johnsen told me a policeman had requested the ladies be moved, but I didn't know he meant you."

The two men visited for a few minutes about their respective professions. They had both needed a break from their work. Hans had come on the cruise just to get away for a while. He had told Trey during one of their workouts in the gym that he had a couple of matches in Sydney a few days after the cruise ended.

"I've been thinking maybe I'll get a chance to go to your fights," Trey told him as the two men walked through the stateroom and onto the balcony. As they stood looking over the passing sea, Trey spoke again. "Tell me more about yourself, Hans. I haven't heard you mention who you are traveling with."

"That's because I am alone. My wife divorced me a couple of years back. She said she loved me but hated my work. I tried to persuade her, but I failed."

"I'm sorry to hear that, Hans," Trey said sincerely.

The big man stared out over the water. "Maybe I need to be more honest with myself. I have a bad temper at times, and that was part of the trouble that caused my divorce. Don't get me wrong." He glanced down at Trey. "I never struck her or physically hurt her, but I said things I deeply regret."

"We all do things like that."

"I guess," Hans said. "You know, I still miss her sometimes, but I have moved on." He grinned and looked at Trey again. "Maybe I will meet someone on this trip. When I do—this trip or later—I have promised myself that I will work hard to treat her better than I treated my wife."

"I hope you do meet someone, Hans." The two men again looked into the distance.

"You mentioned you're traveling with your father," Hans said after a moment of companionable silence. "You didn't tell me your father is a famous artist. You also didn't tell me you're an artist too."

"How did you hear that?" Trey asked.

"I overheard it in the dining room after the art auction."

"I'm not all that good, but my father is what they call a world-class painter."

Hans again looked down at Trey. "The young woman, the one Captain Johnsen said is as pretty as a fresh lily, she is not also with you? I got the impression that the two of you were close."

Trey chuckled. "I just met her last night. But she's very nice, and you could say we have become good friends already."

"Ah, that I might be so lucky. The captain tells me you are, what would you say, working for him on a little matter? I think he said you were additional security for the young lady and her grandmother and that you are interested in some criminal act that may have occurred."

"Yes, you could say that," Trey agreed.

"I would be glad to be of assistance if you should need any help, Detective Shotwell."

"Thank you; that's nice of you, Hans. I hope, however, that things calm down now that Aariah and her grandmother have been moved and now that you've trimmed Martin's wings."

"That is the name of the big-mouth drunk who is now missing a tooth?" Hans asked.

Trey nodded. "His friend's name is Danny. They seem to have connections with another pair, a woman and a man," he said. "As a police officer, I look at them through suspicious eyes. I don't like what I see."

Hans chuckled. "I have some beer if you'd like a drink."

"Thanks, but I don't drink alcohol. I'm afraid if I did I'd become like those two." Trey pointed to the stateroom next door.

"I don't drink much myself, but I'm not quite like those Mormons, you know, the ones who don't drink at all. Like you, I guess," he said.

"A lot like me," Trey agreed. "I'm one of them."

"A Mormon, hey? That's great. You haven't mentioned that before. I believe in God, but there are many religions in the world. It's confusing."

"I'd be glad to tell you about my church sometime," Trey said, thinking of the admonition of the prophet to find opportunities to spread the word. Now, already on this trip, two opportunities had presented themselves.

"Thank you, Detective. I feel lucky to have met you. Maybe God is trying to tell me something. Maybe I need to change more than just my temper."

"He probably is," Trey agreed. The sea was quite calm, and off in the distance, a large ship, a freighter, was passing in the opposite direction. He felt suddenly inspired and said, "Many people are like that ship over there, adrift on a sea of uncertainty. Now, I'm sure that ship has a destination and knows how to get there, just like this one, but so much of the world isn't that way. They're simply drifting through life with no understanding of why they are on this earth or where they are going. I myself was that way. But now I know exactly where I'm going—or at least where I am trying to go."

"I'm intrigued," Hans said. "Please tell me more, if you have time."

"I have a few minutes, but I'm planning to go to dinner with my father, Aariah, and her grandmother. You would be welcome to join us if you like," Trey offered.

"I wouldn't be intruding?"

"Not at all."

"You want to get me outnumbered," Hans said, that huge grin splitting his massive face. "That would be three Mormons to one nonbeliever."

Trey chuckled. "Actually, the opposite would be true. None of them are Mormon, although Aariah has been studying the Church, much to her family's chagrin. But if the group setting makes you uncomfortable, I have a little time right now. I'd be glad to answer any questions you might have and share a few of my beliefs with you."

"I'd like that. But there's something I think I should do first," Hans said, walking back inside. "You wait right here."

Trey stared out to sea, watching the distant ship as it sailed toward Australia and silently praying he could help this man, this hot-tempered and yet gentle giant. A moment later, Hans came back out with a couple cans of root beer. "If you don't drink beer, maybe you'd like a root beer."

"That would be great," Trey said as he accepted the can.

"I suppose I should give up my beer. I know when I drink I get sort of mean. I know it's not good for me, but I kind of like the stuff. You'll have to work on me, I guess."

By the time Trey was ready to head back to his own stateroom an hour later, he felt great. He had enjoyed the discussion with Hans and was certain of one thing—the two of them had turned a budding friendship into one that would last a lifetime, whether Hans ever investigated the Church or not.

As he opened the door, Trey turned to his friend. "I'll meet you at the elevator for dinner. My stateroom is directly below yours, one deck down."

"I'll be waiting for you there," Hans said. "And where do we meet the women?"

"They're in the stateroom next to my father and me," Trey said. "They'll be with us when you come down."

"Ah, that Captain Johnsen, he is a good man—and a wise one, no? He will help your friendship with Aariah grow." Hans smiled knowingly. "Yes, he is good, and he is smart."

SIX

DINNER WAS A DELIGHTFUL AFFAIR. The five of them talked and laughed and told stories like they'd known one another all their lives. When they had finished eating, Hans Olander said, "Simon, I would like to see your painting, the one that sold for a lot of money today." He turned to Trey and added, "I would like to see yours too, my friend."

"I would like that as well," Charlotte said to Hans. "You are such a delightful man." It was clear that the old woman was quite enamored by the giant.

But then Hans frowned. "Will they be on display still, or will they be put away since they have both been sold already?"

"They were there earlier," Simon said. "I'm sure they'll still be on display. They just have small sold signs on them."

The paintings were there, and both Charlotte and Hans were very complimentary. The two paintings were now displayed right next to each other, and the group was discussing them when the woman who had bought Trey's painting and the man who had been with her approached.

The woman smiled and said, "Ah, we get to meet the famous artists." She held out her hand to Trey. "I am Daphne Slader, and this handsome man is my husband, Gil."

"It's a pleasure," Trey said, forcing himself to keep his dislike for Martin from interfering with the way he came across to this woman, who had smiled at him after buying the painting despite Martin's rudeness.

"Yes, indeed," she said. Then they finished introductions all around. That completed, she again turned to Trey. "Contrary to what our 'friend,' or at least the guy who likes to hang around us, said, your painting,

Mr. Shotwell, is beautiful. In fact, it is outstanding. I'm afraid I have to admit that it's worth far more than I paid for it. I will cherish it."

"Thank you, but Martin seemed to think it was his," Trey said.

"Oh, no. I bought it for me, not for him," she said. "He can be a pig at times." She turned to Aariah, smiled, and said, "I hope you can get Mr. Shotwell to paint you one of your own sometime. I know you wanted this one."

"He has already offered to do so. Thank you," Aariah said.

For the first time, Daphne's husband, Gil, entered the conversation. He looked older than her, maybe in his midfifties, compared to her midforties. He said to Simon, "We are admirers of your painting, Mr. Shotwell. It's an honor to meet a man with talent such as you have."

"Thank you very much. I'd be happy if you'd call me Simon," Simon said.

"And you may call me Gil," the man countered. "I hope that someday we are financially in a position to purchase one of your paintings. We have always admired the work of your late wife, too. Our condolences. The art world lost a great painter of portraits when your wife was so cruelly taken. Her death was a loss to all of us."

"Thank you," Simon said. "Her death left a hole in my life that will never be filled."

Daphne then said, "But I do believe your son will soon fill her shoes with his amazing portraits." She smiled, but a cloud seemed to pass across her face. "Earlier, there was a painting displayed here. It reminded me of the kind of work Rita Shotwell did. It was of an old farmer. I had planned to bid on it, but then, for reasons the art director won't divulge, it was pulled from the auction at the last minute."

"Yes, we saw it here as well. It was good, but not up to the standards of my mother's work," Trey said coolly. Then he smiled. "But I'll admit it was probably better than the one you bought of mine."

"I love the one I bought," Daphne reiterated. "And if you happen to run into Martin again, don't let him persuade you otherwise. And don't let him make you think I bought it for him. He is not one I would buy anything for." Once again she turned to Simon. "I can't wait to see what your other painting brings. It is to be sold at the next auction, is it not?"

"Yes, it is. I hope you'll like it as well," Simon said.

"I've already seen it, and I can assure you I do. We both do. We have never been disappointed in anything you've painted."

The Sladers moved on, and after they had left the gallery, Simon said, "They seem nice. I wonder why they're so much the opposite of their friend Martin."

Trey shrugged. "I have no idea, but they seem sincere enough."

"They do, don't they?" Simon nodded. "Hey, I think I'd like to go outside for a little while. The rest of you are welcome to join me if you'd like."

No one indicated otherwise, not even Charlotte Bray. But Aariah said to her, "If you're too tired, Grandmother, we'll go back to the room."

"I'm just fine, Aariah," she said resolutely. "It's a beautiful evening, and I am enjoying the delightful company. Anyway, I'm tired of being cooped up in the room."

They exited through a starboard door and moved aft toward a section of the railing where there was no one standing. Then Simon said, "I'm still thinking about the Sladers. That was strange, wouldn't you say, Trey? They seemed so nice, not at all like their friends."

Trey had continued thinking about the encounter himself. "They seem to be real fans of your painting, Father. And they were certainly polite. Not at all like Martin."

"The woman was way too patronizing," Charlotte said. "I didn't care much for her."

"Grandmother!" Aariah said sternly. "Why would you say that? She was really nice."

"I mean it, Aariah," she said. "She seemed a phony to me."

"I agree with Charlotte," Hans said. Everyone looked up at him, way up at him. "I would go a step further. I think both of them are phony. I don't mean they didn't like your art, either of you, but it was just something about them. The woman was almost gushing, and she didn't look like the gushing type, but what do I know." Then he unleashed that huge, loveable grin of his. "But I certainly prefer them to the one whose tooth I knocked out."

"What!" Aariah exclaimed. "You met Martin?"

"Didn't Trey tell you that Captain Johnsen asked me to move into your old stateroom and keep an eye on Martin and Danny for him?"

"He didn't," Aariah said in surprise. She looked at Trey. "Is that where you met him?"

"No. We met in the gym. But I did run into him again at your old room," Trey admitted. "I guess I wanted to see who the captain put next to the jerks. He picked the right guy, that's for sure."

"Tell us about the tooth," Aariah said. "Or were you even serious about that?"

"I'm serious. Martin pounded on my door, and when I opened it, he demanded to see you, Aariah. I attempted to explain that I was now his neighbor. He was quite drunk and very demanding. Our disagreement became a bit heated, and I ended up losing my temper and punching him."

"Good for you," Aariah said. "That's what I wanted to do, but I'm not big enough."

The big man chuckled. "Honestly, I shouldn't have done that. I'm a professional fighter, and I could have hurt him a lot worse. Fortunately, I didn't hit him hard, but I hit him hard enough to knock one of his front teeth out. I probably loosened some other ones too. I feel badly about it now."

"You shouldn't, Hans," Simon said. "He threatened this young lady and scared her half to death. I hope you convinced him to behave himself."

"I hope so too," Hans said, and then, looking down at Simon he spoke in a soft, though still rumbling, voice, "I'm sorry about your wife, Simon. It must be a great loss to you."

"As I said, she left a hole that can never be filled. I ache each time I think of her, knowing I will never see her again," Simon said.

"You don't really believe that, do you?" the big man asked. "I can't help but think that God will let us see our loved ones again, sometime, somehow."

"I fear that might not be the case," Simon said, dropping his eyes and then facing the sea.

Trey was just about to say something about how he knew they could see their loved ones again, but before he had a chance to speak, Aariah drew a sharp breath.

"There they are," she said, her voice breaking.

"There who are?" Charlotte asked in concern.

"Martin and Danny," she answered as the other four turned.

The two men were deep in conversation and seemed oblivious to what was going on around them until they were nearly abreast of Trey and his group. It was Danny that looked up first. He said, "Martin, let's go inside," and grabbed his friend by the arm and began tugging.

But by then Martin had focused on Hans, and his battered face filled with rage. It appeared he'd been drinking again. "You'll wish you had never met me, you big idiot."

Trey held his breath, and Aariah grabbed hold of his arm and stepped close to him. Hans, who had been holding onto the rail with one huge hand, pushed himself away. "I already wish that. You're like a pesky gnat. Don't make me slap you again." His voice rumbled, and his eyes were narrowed.

"You owe me a tooth," Martin said. "And I expect you to pay."

The giant's face relaxed into a smile. "That's not a problem." He reached one of his hands into a pocket of his pants. When he pulled his hand out, he held, between two beefy fingers, a small, ugly, brown-tinted tooth. "Is this the one?" he asked.

Martin's mouth dropped open. Hans held the tooth out to Martin, who reached and opened his fist. Hans dropped the tooth into it. "There, now you have your tooth back. Given a little time, the ones I loosened will tighten back up again. But I'd try, if I were you, to keep from getting them bumped until then." Hans waved a hand toward the two men in a shooing motion, like he was trying to get rid of a pesky fly. "Away with you now. Don't be bothering us again."

Martin was either too drunk or too stupid to do what the Swede had suggested. Instead, his eyes turned to Aariah. "Why don't you come with me now?" he said. "I'll let you look at my painting, and then I'll buy you a drink."

"I don't drink. And anyway, you don't have a painting," Aariah said as she clung tightly to Trey's arm. "Daphne bought it for herself, not for you."

"It's mine, ugly as it is, and before you know it, you'll be mine as well. Come with me now," he said as he stepped close—so close the liquor on his breath nearly made her gag.

Martin reached out a hand toward her while Danny pulled on his other arm. His hand never touched her. Faster than a striking snake, one of the big hands of Hans Olander grabbed the front of Martin's shirt and, tearing the drunken man's arm loose from Danny, picked him clear off his feet and held him a good foot above the deck. The tooth flew from Martin's fist, hit the deck, then skidded off, headed for the frothy water far below. The Swede's face was dark and his blue eyes piercing as he looked into the smaller man's face. When he spoke, his deep voice was amazingly soft and yet full of menace. "You have a choice, Martin. Either you apologize to the young lady and promise to never speak to her or even come close to her again, or so help me, I will toss you over the rail and into the sea."

The threat must have sobered Martin up for that short moment, for he whispered, "Okay." It was hard to hear him because he was being choked by his own shirt, but Hans heard him and placed him back on the deck. Trey noticed that several people had stopped nearby to watch the drama unfold. He recognized two of them from the auction—Claudia Gaudet, the tiny French woman with the dyed black hair and air of wealth, and the bald man, whose name, according to Damian Latimer, was Victor Krause. Victor still wore the green shirt and tan sports jacket he'd had on at the auction. The two of them were standing together, whispering to each other.

Martin tried to dash away when Hans let loose of his shirt, but he didn't get anywhere before the swift hand of the angry professional wrestler once again grasped him. And once again, Martin was lifted into the air, legs and arms flailing desperately.

For a moment, dead silence prevailed. Then with that one powerful arm, Hans pulled Martin toward him until Martin's face was no more than six inches from his face. For a moment, the angry blue eyes of the wrestler peered deeply into the hazy brown ones of the offender. Everyone jumped when Hans suddenly shouted with almost enough force to throw the ship off course, "Apologize and promise to stay away from her. Do it now!" He let go of Martin.

Martin's feet went right out from under him when they hit the deck, and he hit with a thump on his bottom. Hans bent down, and he lifted Martin back to his feet, depositing him, more gently this time, right in front of Aariah. "Now!" he thundered again.

"Sorry," Martin mumbled without looking at her. "I won't be bothering you again."

Once more, the giant's fist gripped Martin's shirt and lifted him from his feet. "I'll be holding you to that promise, little man. If I hear that you have so much as looked her way, I'll come after you. And when I find you, so help me, I'll feed you to the sharks."

He then placed the drunken fool on the deck and gave him a shove toward Danny, who said, "Daphne and Gil will kill you for this, Martin. You just don't learn, do you?"

The two of them scampered away like a couple of frightened rabbits, in such a hurry they weren't watching where they were going. They ran smack into the small French woman, knocking her to the deck, where she lay on her back, her feet thrashing and her mouth emitting a terrifying noise. Bald-headed Victor, who was standing directly behind her, stuck a foot out, and tripped Danny, who pulled Martin to the deck with him. The pair frantically thrashed at each other in an attempt to stand back up and get away. Victor knelt beside the French woman, took her hand, and pulled her into a sitting position. "Are you all right, Claudia?"

"No, I broke one of my nails," she said, holding her hand up for all to see. Sure enough, a long, purple fingernail dangled from her right index finger.

Other than the nail and her bruised self-esteem, Claudia seemed to be okay, but she made no effort to regain her feet. Martin and Danny, on the other hand, finally managed to get their feet back under them. As they started to back away, Victor shouted after them, "You two owe Claudia an apology. If you know what's good for you, you'll give it right now."

To everyone's surprise, Martin said in a drunken slur, "Sorry, Claudia. It was the giant's fault."

Danny said, "We really are sorry. We didn't see you."

"Well, watch closer next time," Victor said. "You could have hurt her." He paused, gave a wan smile to Claudia, and then looked back at the drunken men. "You could get yourselves pitched over the edge of the ship if you're not careful."

Martin and Danny said nothing else. Hans did, though. "Go on, you two, get out of here." He was advancing toward them as he spoke.

"We're going," Danny said. "Come on, Martin." In their haste, they again failed to watch where they were going, and another collision occurred just a few meters from the door. This time it was Trey's uncle, Lukas Nichols, who went down in an inglorious heap. It took him a while to pick his chubby self up from the deck. When he did, he shouted in the direction the fleeing drunks had gone. They were just then banging into each other in an effort to beat the other through the door and into the interior of the ship.

"I ought to kill you for this," Lukas shouted as he shook his fist at them. He stood a moment, brushing himself off, and then, without another word, he limped back the way he had come—in the same direction Martin and Danny had gone—muttering and cursing and shaking his fists. It didn't appear he'd even noticed Trey and Simon. If he did, he failed to acknowledge them.

Trey walked over to where Claudia and Victor were still huffing with anger. He asked, "Can I help you folks?"

The bald German looked up from where he was kneeling beside the petite French woman. "I can take care of it, Mr. Shotwell. We don't need your help."

Trey shrugged and backed away as Victor helped the little woman stand up. Then Trey said, "I saw you two at the auction. Thanks for bidding on my father's painting."

"Your father is a great artist," Claudia said, glancing at Simon, who was standing beside the rail, looking pale. "Someday I'm going to own one of his paintings. It's just so hard to outbid that greedy Damien Latimer. He simply won't quit bidding. He does it just to spite me. But I'll figure out a way to get one of Simon's paintings despite that despicable man. I promise I will. Victor said he'd help me. Didn't you, Victor?"

The bald German glared at her for a moment, and then at Simon, and finally at Trey. His eyes glittered with anger. "If that's what you really want, I guess I will."

Claudia spoke again. "You will help me, Victor." It sounded more like an order than a request. "When I finally obtain one of your father's paintings, it will be displayed in a place of honor in my home." She smiled at Simon, who was looking even more ill than before.

"That's very nice of you," Trey said. "I believe I heard someone say your name is Claudia. Is that right?"

"Yes, Claudia Gaudet, and this gentleman is Victor Krause."

Victor nodded, staring at Trey with dark gray eyes that held no warmth. "Claudia, I know you like Shotwell's painting, but I still don't see why," he said.

"But you bid on it," Trey said in confusion.

"I wasn't thinking," he growled. "I'd been drinking. Your father is scum. Come on, Claudia. We can find better company someplace else."

Claudia mouthed what Trey thought was, "Sorry," but he couldn't be sure. Then the two of them turned and walked away.

Trey stared after them, noting the eccentric blue shoes, pointed at the toe and with a slightly raised heel, that Victor wore. Other than that, he was dressed in expensive but fairly normal clothes. His behavior wasn't normal though. For some reason, he hated Trey's father. Trey didn't think anyone disliked his father, other than his uncle. He shook his head and let his eyes follow the odd pair for a moment. He couldn't believe Victor would be so rude.

"He's the one that's scum," Hans said softly. Then he turned to the stunned crowd of gawking onlookers. "That's all folks," he said in his normal rumbling voice, shooing them away with his huge hands. "The show's over." The crowd dispersed without a whimper. The giant seemed to have that effect on sober folks.

Simon, still looking very pale, met his son's eyes.

"Do you know those people, Father?" Trey asked.

Simon didn't give Trey a direct answer. "I guess that guy doesn't like me."

"Maybe he was just embarrassed. He did look awfully silly down on the deck like that," Trey said.

"So did she," Simon said with a slight tremor in his voice.

"Father, are you okay?" Trey asked.

"I'll be fine. I think watching the water down there has made me just a little seasick," he said.

"You should probably go lie down," Trey said.

"I think I will," Simon agreed.

Trey turned toward Aariah, who was staring silently at Hans. Finally, she said, "Thank you for defending me, Hans. You're a real gentleman."

"You are welcome, Aariah," he replied, his huge grin once more in place on a now friendly looking face. "I'm sorry I lost my temper," he said. "But I think Martin will leave you alone now, despite my outburst."

"Because of your outburst," Aariah said, and she stepped over and gave the big man a hug.

His face went red, but his smile never faltered. "I guess I should go up and spend some time in the weight room. I have to stay in shape, you know," he said awkwardly. "I have a couple of matches scheduled in Australia when I finish the cruise."

"I'd say you're in pretty good shape right now," Simon said, his color slowly returning.

"Mr. Olander," Charlotte said, "that was beautiful. Thank you for defending my granddaughter's honor." She looked at him adoringly. "You are a wonderful man."

"Grandmother, you look tired. I think it's time we go up to our room," Aariah told her.

"As a matter of fact, I am tired dear, but thoroughly entertained. I think I'll sleep very well tonight," she said with a smile.

"I'll go with the two of you, and then I think I'll put on my exercise clothes and join Hans. I could also use a good workout," Trey said.

"And I need to lie down for a few minutes, and then I'd like to do some work on my painting," Simon said. At the inquiring looks he received, he added, "I'm doing a painting while I'm on the cruise."

Aariah looked at Trey and asked, "Are you going to come back on deck and run tonight after your workout?"

"I am," he said. "I'll be here about ten."

"I'd like to come with you and read while you run," she said with a slight blush.

"I'd like that. I'll tap on your door when I'm ready to leave," Trey said.

"Do you mind if I run then too?" the big Swede asked. "I assume it's not so crowded then."

"It's just right by that time of night," Trey responded. "But I think you'll show me up just like you do with the weights."

Hans chuckled. "I know I can outdo you on the weights, but I expect that when it comes to running, I'll be the tortoise while you are the hare."

* * *

"We ought to kill you right now, Martin," Daphne raged. "Don't you have a brain left in your head?"

"It's that big man; he's the one who caused all the trouble," Martin whined. "You should see him. He's seven feet tall and built like a tree."

Danny, angry and frightened, had dragged Martin to the couple's stateroom on the tenth floor. Martin cursed all the way but was too drunk to get away from his very determined friend. When Daphne had answered the door and saw Martin's face, she'd grabbed him by the shirt, just like Hans had done, shoved him onto the sofa, and demanded to know what had happened.

He'd attempted to give a version that favored him in its entirety, but Daphne was having none of it, nor was Gil.

"I've seen that guy," she said. "He's not quite seven feet, but close. He seemed like a real nice guy though. And he was hanging around with that girl we told you to stay away from, her and the Shotwells."

Gil spoke up then, but it was to Danny that he addressed his question, "Where did you two meet this guy?"

"He was in the girl's room, right next to us," he replied. "But we didn't know she had moved to a different room. Martin knocked on her door. He just wanted to apologize. Isn't that right, Martin?" Danny's anger had died down, and he again was in *protect-stupid-Martin* mode.

Martin readily agreed with Danny's lie. That explanation, however, provoked another question from Gil. "Why was the girl given a different room?"

Both men shrugged. "How are we supposed to know?" Martin asked.

Daphne and Gil both shook their heads. "I suppose she must have asked to be moved because you couldn't keep your mouth shut," Daphne said, glaring at him. "And why doesn't that surprise me?"

"You're being a jerk, Martin. I thought I made it clear you were to be a gentleman. You're becoming an embarrassment. I ought to just throw you to the sharks before you embarrass us again," Gil said.

"That's what the giant said," Danny told them.

"What?" Daphne asked, confused.

"He threatened to throw Martin to the sharks," Danny responded.

"He sounds like a man after my own heart," Gil snarled. "And by the way, what happened to your tooth?"

Gil and Daphne kept pressing until they had pretty well extracted the entire story, warped, of course, in Martin's favor as much as the two men could manage. When the Sladers were satisfied, they sent the younger men to their room with a strict warning not to come out again until Gil and Daphne told them they could. As they stumbled from the Sladers' stateroom, Gil called after them, "If you cause trouble again, you'll wish you'd never come on this cruise."

SEVEN

TREY HAD NEVER MET ANYONE who had the physical strength of Hans Olander. Trey was strong, and for his size, he could pump weights with the best of them. But Hans's strength was in a whole different sphere. When Trey thought about the big guy punching Martin in the face, he realized Martin had been lucky there wasn't more damage.

When the two men, along with Aariah, went down to the outdoor walkway on the promenade deck, Trey was once again amazed—by two things. First, Aariah had come dressed to run, and she did amazingly well. After three miles, she called it quits, and sat down with her books. The second amazing thing was the giant. He stayed right with Trey, and it didn't seem to be any more effort for him than it was for Trey. They ran ten fast miles before calling it a night.

Aariah joined them again, with Trey carrying her bag of books, as they walked two times around the ship, cooling off and chatting like old friends. Then they sat down on the deck chairs and talked for nearly an hour. Most of the time, they talked about the Church. Aariah had her Book of Mormon with her, and she showed it to Hans. He asked if she'd read it. She said, "I'm reading it for the second time now."

"Do you believe it?" he asked.

"Yes, I do," she said.

"Then why aren't you a Mormon?"

She looked at Trey and then back at the Swede. "I guess I'm afraid," she said.

"Afraid of what?" he asked.

"Afraid that my parents and my grandmother will disown me," she admitted as tears wet her cheeks.

He nodded. "Trey faced the same thing. He told me so. And look at what good friends he is with his father now. You must never avoid doing things you want to do out of fear."

"Trey has more courage than I do," she said softly as the ship rocked gently.

"I don't think so, Aariah. You just don't realize it yet," Hans said. "If you believe in something, you should do it. If I had one of these books, I think I'd read it. I do read the Bible, you know."

"Well, my friend," Trey said. "You're in luck. I just happen to have one for you. In fact, you can keep it if you want to. I'll bring it up to you when we get back to our rooms."

* * *

Trey's father was asleep by the time the trio got back to their staterooms. Trey grabbed the Book of Mormon from his suitcase, ran it up to Hans, then hurried back to his own room and out onto the balcony, pulling out his cell phone. The number of his friend, Detective Inspector Willie Denning, was in the contact list in his phone. He dialed and waited while it rang.

"This is Detective Denning," Trey heard his friend say in his cheerful British brogue. "What are you up to, Detective Shotwell?"

"Hey, Willie, it's good to hear your voice. I need a favor, or maybe I should say I have some information for you on a case you and I are both familiar with," Trey said.

"Don't tell me, Trey. Have you finally got a break on your mother's murder?" Willie asked.

"As a matter of fact, I have."

"I don't know how you managed it, but tell me about it. I'll make some notes."

"I'm on a cruise with my father," Trey began.

"Do you mean to tell me that you and he are on the same ship? I thought he was still upset with you for becoming a cop," Willie said with a chuckle.

"Oh no, not at all. Father has mellowed over the years, Willie."

"I'm glad to hear that. But if this is about your mother's murder, how in the world could you have learned anything on a cruise?" Willie asked in puzzlement.

"It does seem rather odd, I know. Anyway, here's what I have," Trey said. "Two of the paintings that were stolen were my mother's work."

"Yes. We've been watching all these years for those and the three of your father's to appear. So far, nothing."

"Well, that's where things have changed," Trey said. "One of the paintings, the one she called *The Scottish Farmer*, is on this ship. It's been painted over some, altering it a little, but my father positively identified it by a hidden marking Mother had painted into the portrait. It's been seized and is in the possession of the ship's captain."

"That's great, Trey. Does it have a signature? As I recall your mother hadn't yet signed it," Willie said, sounding quite excited.

"It's signed by Ainslee Cline."

"I'll see what I can find out about that name," Willie promised.

"That's what I was hoping, but there's more. A Frenchman by the name of Damien Latimer bought one of my father's paintings during an art auction on the ship this morning. In talking to him later, we found out he had previously purchased two of Father's paintings and also one that looked similar. And get this, Willie. The signature on *that* painting is also Ainslee Cline."

"Ah, now that is something. Do you think your father will be able to identify that painting as well?" Willie asked.

"Oh yes. He and Mother both formed a habit of painting tiny identifying marks on all their works. They both kept—and my father still does—a journal on each painting, and in the journal is a detailed description of the identifying features."

"I assume Simon has those journals," Willie said.

"They're locked up in a safe in his home in Sydney. But there's still more. Damian has a friend in Germany who has a painting by Ainslee Cline as well. We think it is the companion piece to the one we seized on the ship. Mother called it *The Scottish Farmer's Wife*."

"So if we can figure out who Ainslee Cline is, it might take us a long way toward finding your mother's killer," Willie stated flatly.

"That's my hope," Trey agreed.

"I'll get to work on it," Detective Denning promised. "Is there anything else?"

"Yes. I know that Inspector Ruben Hawk has a private investigation agency now that he operates all over Europe."

"Correct, and that does include Germany and France," Willie said with a chuckle. "But I don't think you can afford him."

"The Frenchman, Damian Latimer, is a multimillionaire, maybe even a billionaire, and he'll pay whatever Inspector Hawk charges."

"I'll call Ruben and tell him what you've learned and see if he'd be willing to help out. If he is, should I have him call you?"

"Please do," Trey said.

"What time is it where you are right now?" Willie asked.

Trey looked at his watch. "It's nearly two thirty in the morning. And I need to get some sleep."

"I'll have him call you at a decent hour," Willie promised. "And I'll keep in touch on whatever developments I make here. By the way, where are you? I know you said a ship, but where is the ship?"

"Between Australia and New Zealand," Trey said. "We're sailing toward New Zealand."

After a couple more minutes, Trey hung up the phone and went to bed. He set the alarm on his iPhone for eight and settled down for the night.

* * *

The room's phone rang. Trey was sleeping soundly, and it took him a moment to orient himself. By then, he and his father were both awake. Trey grabbed the phone. "Detective Shotwell," the distinctive Danish voice of the ship's captain said, "I need your help."

That plea woke him up fully. "What do you need me to do, Captain?"

"Assist my security people if you can. We have a big problem."

"What's the problem?" he asked as he looked at his watch. It was a few minutes past four o'clock.

"Someone broke into the vault where we keep the paintings. One of our security officers noticed it first. He called Dayton, who checked it out. He's running an inventory as we speak. Whoever broke in was either very lucky or good with technology."

"What do you mean by that?" Trey asked.

"The first thing we did was check the surveillance cameras. Our entire system has been hacked and shut down. So we can't confirm anything from the cameras."

"This means whoever did it planned it way in advance."

"I'm afraid you're right. Anyway, we could use your expertise, Detective. Our security people, with one exception, are not trained police officers, and if it turns out that there's damage to any of the art, it will need to be handled as a crime scene. I was hoping you could advise my security team on how to secure the scene and preserve the evidence."

"I'll be right down," Trey said. He dressed in less than a minute as he explained to his father what was happening. "The art vault has been broken into. They asked for my help."

"I hope nothing is damaged," Simon said anxiously.

"Me too," Trey agreed.

When he arrived at the vault, Dayton and Coni were standing by the door, keeping the security officers at bay.

"Detective Shotwell," Dayton said with relief as soon as he spotted Trey. "I'm glad you could come down."

"I hope I can help," Trey said. "Do you know yet if any damage has occurred?"

"I don't. We only stepped in, looked around, and stepped back out. I was afraid we might disturb some evidence."

"You did the right thing," Trey said. "Let's do this by the book. First, we'll need some latex gloves."

"You," Dayton said pointing at one of the security officers, "find some latex gloves. And be quick about it."

"I brought my camera," Trey said. "Let's start by taking pictures of the door. How was it opened?" Trey looked the door over closely without touching anything. "I don't see any marks where it might have been pried."

"It was just hanging open like this when our security officer saw it."

"The captain called it a vault, but it's really just a room, isn't it?"

"I guess, but not just an ordinary room. It has only this one door, and it's a strong one, as you can see," Dayton told him. "It's steel plated."

"But you lock and unlock it with a key," Trey pointed out. "This kind of lock can be opened with lock-picking equipment if a person knows how."

"You're probably right," Dayton agreed with a long face. Just then the security officer returned with the gloves. "What now?" Dayton asked Trey.

"You, Coni, and I will wear the gloves. We'll go in, and you tell me if there's anything out of place. I'll snap whatever pictures I think we need."

Coni carried a list and checked off each painting as Dayton inspected them one at a time. The ones that had been sold at the auction were in the back of the room. The group got to them last. "So far there's nothing missing and nothing damaged, as near as I can tell," Dayton reported. "Now we'll inventory and inspect the ones we sold. I hope our luck holds out."

It didn't take long before Dayton's face went pale. "Oh, no! This is a disaster. There are two paintings missing."

Trey didn't need Dayton to point out which ones. He could see for himself—the one he had painted and the one his father had painted were both conspicuously absent. Trey felt his stomach roll. His wasn't that important, but his father's? That was another matter altogether.

After the inventory was complete and Trey had taken pictures of the spaces where the missing paintings should have been, he turned to the art director and his assistant, Dayton and Coni Windle. "For now, the only person we'll tell is the captain."

"What about the buyers?" Coni asked. "We've got to let them know."

"Only if we fail to find the paintings or they're damaged when we do find them. They've got to be on this ship somewhere. Will you call the captain or would you like me to?" Trey asked, looking directly at Dayton.

"Your father's painting was one of the most valuable ever sold on this ship," Dayton said in despair. "The captain won't be happy."

"Me or you?" Trey pressed.

"It's my responsibility," Dayton said.

Coni put her arms around him and said, "Trey's right. They're somewhere on this ship. I'm sure the captain will have us conduct a thorough search, and they will be found."

"But will they be damaged?" Dayton asked. "Any defacing of any kind would destroy their value, and the cruise line would have to make it up to the buyers. Let's lock up and call the captain from our office. We'll have a security officer stay here until the captain says otherwise."

Ten minutes later, Captain Johnsen, with a grimace and rubbing the worry from his eyes, met them at the door to the vault. "Open the door, Dayton. I'd like to see for myself."

He came out of the room a moment later cursing softly. He repeated what Trey and Coni had already stated. "They're on the ship. There have been no other vessels within miles of us. I want all the passengers back in their rooms as quickly as we can get them there. That shouldn't be too difficult since most people are in bed this time of the night. When we're certain everyone is where they should be, then the three of you, myself, my first officer, and the entire security staff will conduct a search of every stateroom. If that does not produce the missing paintings, then we will search the rest of the vessel, including the rooms of all the crew members. And so help me, if one of them is the culprit . . ."

His voice trailed off, and Dayton said, "Surely it's one of the passengers. We have a good crew. Nothing like this has ever happened before. But even if one of them did take them, there's no way they could ever get them off the ship."

Trey had disturbing thoughts to the contrary, but he kept them to himself for now. At the captain's orders, everyone was sent back to their staterooms. That wasn't a huge undertaking as it was now just short of six o'clock, and most of the passengers were still in their rooms, probably sleeping until the announcement was made into every room over the ship's speakers, waking them up.

It took less than a half hour to clear the common areas of the ship. After that was completed, Captain Johnsen told the appointed searching crew, "Check every single stateroom, even the unoccupied ones. "No guests or staff members are to leave their room for any reason whatsoever unless I personally approve it. And I won't approve it for anything less than a medical emergency."

He then made assignments, and the tedious process began. The searches were done by two-person teams as assigned by the captain. A security guard by the name of Bonnie Springer was teamed with Trey. She was from Miami, one of only two security officers from the United States and one of only three female security officers. In addition, Bonnie was the one officer who had police experience. She was tall, about six two, and strong, her two hundred pounds consisting largely of well-toned muscle. Despite her muscular body, she was quite striking in appearance with an attractive face and bright green eyes. She made Trey feel short and light when they stood together.

"I've seen you in the weight room," she said when they were introduced. "I had no idea you were a detective. I'm impressed." She favored Trey with a smile that went clear to the corners of her green eyes. "You and a great big guy work out together, don't you?"

"Yes, we do, and that's where I've seen you," Trey agreed. "I knew you looked familiar. I assumed you were a passenger. I know you're an American. Your accent gives you away."

"I'm from Miami. My father is a law enforcement officer, a captain with the police in Miami. He talked me into applying for the force there, which I did. I was hired, worked for about three years, and then decided to do what I'd always wanted to do. I love the water. I'm an experienced diver and, if I might say so, a very good swimmer. I wanted to sail the world and swim and dive in exotic places. So, much to my father's disapproval, here I am, living my dream and loving it." She smiled. "Should we begin?"

Most of the passengers were understanding and had no qualms in allowing their rooms and luggage to be searched. Some of them were dressed only in nightclothes; most of them, probably because they knew a search was imminent, had gotten dressed for the day. Captain Johnsen, when he had made the ship-wide announcement, had stated that a very serious crime had been committed, that something of great value was missing, and that he hoped everyone would be cooperative. He had apologized in advance for the inconvenience the search would cause. After listening to Trey, he intentionally didn't state what was missing. Also at Trey's suggestion, the search was to include even places where only small items, such as jewelry or *small pieces of cut-up paintings*, could be hidden.

The first hour was uneventful, but when one of the security officers reported that there appeared to be a missing passenger, Captain Johnsen called the searchers back together. He told the assembled group, "There is one passenger unaccounted for. Detective, you know him. It's Martin Talley. Would you describe him to the rest of us?"

"Martin is about forty years old and has shoulder-length, dark-brown hair. He's a couple inches shorter than I am. He probably weighs between 160 and 170 pounds. He has brown eyes and a British accent. He's also missing a front tooth and has some bruises on his face and a split lip. He is a heavy drinker and a real troublemaker," Trey said.

"Thank you, Detective," Captain Johnsen said. "We won't start the search over again if you're all sure he wasn't in one of the staterooms you've gone through. So have any of you seen him during your search so far?"

The response was a strong negative all the way around. The captain thoughtfully rubbed his chin. "I just changed my mind. We need to check with everyone in the staterooms you've already searched, but all you need to do is ask if anyone has seen him. If he'd been hiding, you'd have already found him. Use both Martin's name and the description Detective Shotwell just gave us."

Trey asked if Martin's roommate, Danny, was still in their room. Someone answered in the positive. Trey turned to the captain. "I think he needs to be questioned sooner rather than later."

"I agree, and I'd like you to do the questioning, Detective. So here's what we'll do. Bonnie, since you're the only person on my staff with police experience, I'd like you to continue working with Detective Shotwell. I'll assign a new team to take your place on the search." He again addressed the entire group. "Bonnie and Detective Shotwell will be conducting interviews with anyone you feel they should talk to. Please be observant. If anyone acts suspicious when you ask about the missing passenger, contact me right away, and I'll have Trey and Bonnie take it from there."

* * *

They interviewed Danny right in his room. "Full name?" Trey began.

"Danny Bidwell."

"Danny," Trey continued, "we need you to tell us where Martin is."

"I don't know," he said.

Trey studied his body language. Danny was extremely nervous. "Danny, don't try to mess with me. You know something. Either you tell us now or risk the anger of the captain. He does have a cell he can lock you in until we reach land, where you could then be turned over to the authorities."

Trey waited for a full minute. Bonnie, as he'd asked her to, was taking notes. Danny squirmed nervously but said nothing. Finally, Trey said, "Okay, let's take this one step at a time. When did you see Martin last? That's a question you can easily answer."

Again, he said nothing.

Trey turned to Bonnie. "I'm out of patience. Call the captain. Tell him we have a prisoner for him."

"Okay, okay, I'll tell you," Danny said, his shoulders slumping. "We were in the bar having a nightcap about two this morning. I was really tired. I tried to get Martin to come to the room with me, but he wouldn't. You've seen Martin. You know how difficult he can be."

Trey nodded. "Which bar?"

Danny told them, and Bonnie wrote it down.

"What was he doing when you left the bar?" Trey asked.

"Drinking coffee. I had told him he'd had enough alcohol," Danny said.

Trey asked, "Was he talking to anyone?"

"No, the bar was pretty much empty by then. He and I had been alone."

"I see. And he never came to the room?"

"I don't think so. I went right to sleep when I got here. When I got woken up by the intercom, I noticed Martin wasn't here. If he came in before that, he didn't wake me up, and he left again. But I don't think he ever came in."

"Did he have any arguments with anyone at the bar?"

"I didn't see one. The last argument he had was when that big idiot was tossing him around and threatening to throw him overboard," he said. "Maybe that's what happened. Maybe that big guy threw him into the ocean."

Trey ignored that, but he found himself wishing Hans hadn't said what he did. That could come back to haunt him. But he moved on. "Danny, that wasn't the last confrontation you and Martin had. If you'll remember, you guys knocked a lady down. The guy with her tripped you."

"Yeah, and he threatened Martin too. Maybe *he* threw Martin over the side," Danny suggested, his eyes watching his hands.

"And then you bumped into another passenger and knocked *him* down," Trey reminded him as he thought of his uncle Lukas, wondering again what he happened to be doing there at that time of night.

"He threatened Martin too. Maybe he did it."

"Did what?"

"Threw Martin off the ship," Danny said.

"So you *do* know what happened to Martin. You're saying someone threw him overboard," Trey said quickly, leaning toward Danny and shaking a finger in his face.

"Yes; I mean no. I mean, I don't know where he is. I don't know what he's doing. He's probably in one of the bars."

"No, Danny, he's not. We've checked very carefully. But suppose you're right. If someone did throw Martin overboard—surely someone would have seen it. There are a lot of people on this ship," Trey reasoned. "He could have been rescued if it had been reported promptly."

"Martin can't swim," Danny said. "He says he can't even tread water. He'd drown within seconds if he was thrown overboard."

Trey exchanged glances with Bonnie and then asked again, "Danny, are you sure there weren't any more arguments with anyone last night?"

"I'm sure. We went right to the bar," he said. As he spoke he kept his eyes averted. Trey was sure there was something Danny wasn't telling him—he was lying. Trey threw a few more questions at him, but he could see he wasn't going to get anything else out of Danny. Maybe later he'd question him again if he learned something that might give him some leverage.

After they left the stateroom, Bonnie said, "He's hiding something, Detective."

"Yes, I think you're right, but I have no idea what it is."

"Who do we talk to next?"

"Danny and Martin have a couple of friends on the cruise. They're a married couple, Gil and Daphne Slader. I want to talk to them, but first, I'd like to talk to the people in the rooms on either side of Danny's." Trey pointed to the door that had been Aariah's and explained about the problem she had experienced with Martin. "The captain had some stateroom assignments changed. There's only one person in that room. It's the big guy that Danny just referred to. He knocked Martin's tooth out here in the hallway. Martin provoked him. His name is Hans Olander."

"You are out and about bright and early, my friend," the big Swede said when he opened his door to Trey's knock. "Surely you didn't have all the sleep you would have liked last night, did you?"

"Not nearly enough," Trey agreed. "In fact, I had practically none."

"My, oh, my," Hans said as he looked at Trey's partner, his grin spreading. "You're the pretty lady I've noticed in the weight room. Who is this, Detective?"

Trey couldn't help but chuckle. He glanced at Bonnie, whose face had turned a pretty shade of pink. "This is Officer Bonnie Springer," he said. "She's part of the ship's security team. She and I have been given a little assignment from Captain Johnsen."

"You lucky dog you," Hans said, scarcely taking his eyes from the security officer's face. "Isn't she a little tall for you?"

"Not really," Trey responded with a wink as he stretched to his full height, knowing she towered over him.

"Well, it's nice to see a woman with some stature," Hans said. "And such an attractive one at that. Why don't you two come on in?"

They did as bidden, and after Hans had invited them to sit down, Trey said, "We need some help, Hans. It seems that one of your neighbors is missing."

Hans tore his admiring eyes from the face of Trey's partner, who also was admiring him. "Which one, Martin or Danny?" he asked.

"Martin," Trey responded.

The Swede's huge head moved back and forth for a moment as if in disbelief. "What exactly do you mean by missing?" Hans finally asked.

"He's not in his room like everyone's supposed to be, Hans."

"But Danny is?"

"Yes. We just spoke to him." Trey noticed that Bonnie had her pen and notebook out and was poised to write something, when something worth writing came along. "Danny claims he doesn't have any idea where Martin is. He says the last time he saw him Martin was drinking coffee in the Moonlight Bar. He left Martin in the bar and came up to his room. Martin never showed up there."

"What time was that?" Hans asked.

"Around two, he claims."

"Let's see, you brought me up this Book of Mormon a little after midnight, after we'd finished our run," Hans said as he pointed toward where the book lay on his nightstand. "I went right to bed after that."

"So you didn't hear any unusual noises from over there?" Trey asked, nodding toward Danny's stateroom.

"Not a peep," the Swede said. "The first thing I remember after going to bed was hearing the captain's voice waking us all up."

"Okay, we've got to keep moving." Trey stood up. "We've got more people to interview."

"Trey," Hans said as the officers started toward his door.

"Yes, Hans?" Trey said turning back.

"You know I didn't mean it when I said I'd throw Martin overboard, don't you?" he asked, his face somber, worried even.

"Of course I know that, Hans. No one's accusing you of anything. You just relax."

"Yes, of course," Hans said. "I'll do that, right here in this room under house arrest until that jerk Martin shows up and you find whatever precious thing it is that's missing."

Trey stepped back toward him. "I'm sorry, my friend. This will all work out soon, and we can hit the weights and do some more running."

The big man finally managed another smile. "You're a good friend, Trey. And you're a good man. You take good care of this partner of yours. Maybe we'll see her in the weight room again soon."

Bonnie smiled up at him and said, "I'll be there, Hans. And maybe we can get a little better acquainted then."

"That would be very nice. Okay, well, you guys have fun. I think I'll read for a few minutes in that book you gave me, Trey."

"You do that, Hans," Trey said.

EIGHT

They left Hans with a smile on his face and knocked on the door on the other side of Danny's stateroom. They didn't learn anything new there either. "Next stop, the Sladers," Trey announced when they were back in the hallway. "We need to figure out what stateroom they're in."

"I can take care of that," Bonnie said. She pulled out a small radio and spoke into it. Within a minute or so, she had the room number. "It's upstairs," she said. "Stateroom 1258." They headed for the stairway.

"Hans is a nice guy, isn't he?" Trey asked.

"As a matter of fact, he is. I can't wait to see him working out again! Wow. What a man. I should have introduced myself earlier. How long have you known him?"

"Just since the first day of the cruise," Trey responded, grinning at Bonnie.

"Is that all?" she asked, looking at him in surprise. "It seems like you two have known each other for years."

"Nope. Hans is an easy man to get to know. And he is a decent guy; I can tell you that."

"I think you're right. And tell me, Detective, who is Aariah?"

"Someone else I just recently met. Like you, she's an American. She's on the cruise with her Australian grandmother. She's a nice girl."

"And pretty?" Bonnie asked with a mischievous grin.

"Very," Trey agreed.

"And you plan to get to know her better?"

"I hope I can. She's, uh, quite a girl."

"But this Martin guy was harassing her?" Bonnie asked. "Is she the reason for the shifting of stateroom assignments yesterday?"

"That's right." While they walked to stateroom 1258, Trey explained what had happened.

"He sounds like a real creep," Bonnie said.

"You could say that," Trey agreed.

She paused a moment then said, "You gave a Book of Mormon to Hans. I take it you're a Mormon."

"I am. I have been for about seven years."

"My cousin joined that church about five years ago. I've gone with her a few times," she said. "She gave me a Book of Mormon. I have it on the ship with me, but I have to confess I haven't read it yet."

"Are you going to?" Trey asked.

"I hadn't thought about it for a while, but if that cute hunk of a Swedish guy is going to read it, then I guess I can too." Suddenly, Bonnie looked concerned. "Trey, do you know if Hans has a wife?"

"Not anymore," he said.

"Good," she said softly.

Trey smiled to himself but said nothing further. They reached 1258, and Trey knocked on the door.

"What's going on?" Gil asked when he opened the door. "This lockdown of the captain's is highly unusual, and I, for one, do not appreciate it. We've already been searched, so you don't need to do it again, if that's why you're here." His eyes darted to Bonnie and back to Trey. "*She's* ship security, but you're just a passenger. What are you doing here? Shouldn't you be in your room like the rest of us?" His tone was brusque. He was clearly irritated. He'd be more irritated if he knew that the painting his wife had purchased had been stolen from the art vault, Trey thought.

Daphne joined Gil at the door. "What do you need?" she asked. She also appeared to be out of sorts.

"We need to talk to you about your friend Martin Talley," Trey said.

"What concern is he of yours?" Daphne asked. "If it's about his harassing your girlfriend, we already told him to quit it. What more do you want us to do?"

"I'm not here for personal reasons. And Aariah is just a friend, someone I met on the ship. I'm working under the authority of Captain Johnsen. I am a criminal investigator with the New South Wales Police

Force. This is Officer Bonnie Springer of the ship's security team," Trey said. "We need a moment of your time."

The couple looked shocked upon learning that he was a police officer. Daphne said, "I thought you were an artist."

"That's my hobby. I'm a police officer by profession."

"Well, I suppose you can come in." Daphne opened the door and led them inside. She stared at Trey for a moment then asked, "What's this about Martin? Has he caused more trouble? We know about the altercation on the promenade deck. Danny told us. But we sent the two of them to their room after that. I suppose they're still there."

"Danny is, but not Martin," Trey said. "He seems to have disappeared. He's either hiding somewhere on the ship or he isn't on it at all."

Daphne gasped, and Gil's face grew grim. "If he isn't on the ship, that would mean he fell overboard," Gil said. He turned to Daphne. "He and Danny obviously didn't stay in their room last night like we told them to. I told you Martin's drinking would cause him trouble someday. It looks like that day has arrived."

"Are you saying you think he might have fallen off the ship?" Trey asked.

"With drunks like Martin, anything's possible," Daphne said, pulling a face in disgust.

"He could have been thrown off the ship," Gil suggested. "Martin certainly had a way of making people angry. Maybe he pushed someone a little too far."

"I suppose that's possible, but I can't believe my brother would have let that happen," Daphne said. "Danny's more responsible than that."

"Danny's your brother?" Trey asked with a raised eyebrow as he noted in his mind that Gil used the word *had*, past tense, instead of *has* when he spoke of Martin.

"Yes, he's my younger brother. He and Martin are friends. Danny insisted that we bring Martin on this cruise with us. I regretted it as soon as he hit the first bar," Daphne said. "I didn't know he was such a drunk. He's a waste, that guy is."

"I take it you don't like him too well," Trey observed.

"That's right, but I don't hate him," she said quickly. "I certainly wouldn't want anything bad to happen to him. He is Danny's friend, after all."

When Trey decided there was nothing more to be gained by talking to the Sladers, he signaled Bonnie with a nod of his head, and they left.

Out in the hallway, they were again headed for the stairs when Bonnie got a call on her radio. The captain's voice was soft. "Are you and Trey with anyone at the moment?"

"No," she said.

"Good. I need both of you in my cabin as soon as you can get here. No need to knock. Just come right in."

NINE

THEY LOOKED AT EACH OTHER. "Now what?" Trey asked.

"I don't know, but the way this morning is going it can't be good."

"That's what I'm afraid of," he said with a sigh.

She looked at Trey. "Elevator or stairs?"

"I prefer the stairs. I can make it quicker that way."

"Same with me."

They found the captain pacing his cabin floor and mumbling to himself. "Just got a troublesome report," he said to them without preamble. "A young girl claims to have seen someone fall overboard from the railing on the promenade deck. She says it was directly below her balcony."

"And she didn't report it until now?" Bonnie asked. "That's strange. And how did she see it at that time of night?"

"She apparently napped a bunch during the day and couldn't sleep. She says she took a blanket to the balcony and was standing by the railing watching the water," Captain Johnsen said.

"Where is she?" Trey asked.

"My first officer is escorting her and her parents down here as we speak. That's why I asked you two to hurry. I wanted you here before they arrived."

"How old is she?" Trey asked.

"I've told you all I know. I'm hoping you can get more from her and her parents."

"I'll do my best," Trey promised. While they were waiting, Trey brought him up-to-date on the interviews they had conducted.

"Anything stand out to either of you?" Captain Johnsen asked.

"Danny Bidwell was lying," Trey said. "For one thing, his sister and brother-in-law had told both him and Martin to go back to their room and stay there after the problem on the walkway; we know that didn't happen. But there's something else. I'm just not sure what he might have been trying to hide or why. And when we were with the Sladers, they seemed uneasy," Trey continued. "And they did express anger over Martin's behavior."

Bonnie, who was looking at her notes, said, "They didn't seem happy to learn you're a cop, Trey. Also, Gil Slader used the past tense when he referred to Martin."

"I noticed that too," he said.

"What did he say?" the captain asked, resuming his pacing.

Bonnie looked down at her notebook and read, "Martin certainly had a way of making people angry." Then she looked up and added, "Gil also said that maybe somebody threw him into the ocean. I didn't write down exactly what he said that time."

"Maybe he's right," the captain said as he looked toward his door. "I wonder what's keeping them." It was clear he was referring to the first officer and the little girl and her parents. "You said you talked to Hans Olander. Did he hear or see anything that might be helpful?"

Trey couldn't resist. "Mostly he admired Officer Springer."

The captain chuckled. "He's a great young man. Did he tell you that his father is a ship's captain?"

"No, he didn't," Trey said in surprise.

"He and I have known each other for years, and I've known Hans most of his life. He's a right decent sort. He didn't bat an eye when I asked him to move to Aariah's stateroom and keep an eye on those two rascals," he said. "I would trust that man with my life."

"He didn't see or hear anything from the guys next door after he went to bed," Trey reported.

"What time was that?" Captain Johnsen asked.

"He and I went to the weight room and lifted weights. Then later we went running. It was shortly after midnight when we went to our rooms."

"He was worried about one thing," Bonnie ventured hesitantly.

"And what was that?"

Trey told the captain about the altercation on the promenade deck and what Hans had said about throwing Martin overboard if he didn't stop harassing Aariah.

"Good for him!" the captain thundered. "But don't worry, Bonnie. He would never do anything like that. He's a professional wrestler—and a very good one—and he does have a bit of a temper, but he's really a gentle giant. You should get to know him better. You'd like him."

Her attractive face went pink. "He's a professional wrestler?"

"That's right, and he'd be a right good catch; I can tell you that for sure," the captain said with a grin.

Bonnie was rescued from further embarrassment by the door opening. The first officer ushered in a young girl and two adults, made a quick introduction, explained that the couple didn't want to speak with anyone official and had resisted coming with him. Then he excused himself to go back to the search.

The couple's names were Julius and Blanca Schmitt. And one thing was clear. They were too old to be the little girl's parents. Elsie Schmitt was the child's name. She spoke very good English, but the adults did not. The only way to talk to them was to have the little girl translate into German. That was painstaking, so he gave up on it for the time being and concentrated his efforts on little Elsie.

"I am a police officer," he told her. "You know what a police officer is, don't you?"

"Yes," she said. "A cop."

"That's right, Elsie, I am a cop. Do you like cops?"

"Yes, I do. They took my mommy and daddy away," she said with a frown. "Mommy and Daddy were mean to me, but now I have them." She pointed to her grandparents. "And I love them," she added, looking at the elderly couple with affection. "They're good to me."

Trey was stunned by her answer. "Where are your parents now?" he asked.

"I don't know," she said. "My grandparents say they're looking for me, but they won't let them find me. It would be dangerous for me to live with them."

The grandparents simply sat there, looking uneasy. Trey glanced at Bonnie, who also looked worried. The captain cleared his throat. Trey turned back to the little girl and asked, "Elsie, you said your parents were mean. Did your father or mother ever hurt you before the police took them away?"

"Yes," she said, dropping her blue eyes and staring at the floor.

"What did they do to you?"

For a long moment, she just kept staring down, and finally, without looking up, she said softly, "They hit me a lot. And they locked me in my closet and made me stay there—sometimes for a long, long time."

Trey was feeling sick inside. Another glance at Bonnie told him she was equally disturbed. "Do you want your parents to find you?" he asked.

She looked up, her eyes wide with fear. "No. I'm afraid of them. They'll hurt me again. They were mad when the cops came, and they shouted at me when they were taken out of the house."

"What did they say when they shouted?" Trey asked.

She looked at her grandparents for a moment, and then she said, "They said they'd make me wish I hadn't told on them."

"Did you call the police?" he asked.

She nodded her little head. "I had to. They hurt me a lot."

"Do your grandparents take good care of you?" Trey asked as he attempted to shift the focus from the parents.

"Yes, they love me." She glanced at them. "They don't understand English. We talk only in German."

Trey was trying to get a feel for the little girl before he got to the big questions, the ones about a person being thrown from the ship. "Are you having fun on this ship?" he asked.

Her eyes misted up. "No. We don't do anything. My grandmother isn't well, and so we mostly stay in our room. I watch some TV. We read books. But I get bored. I want to have fun."

Bonnie leaned forward, her eyes misty, and said, "If it's okay with your grandparents, maybe you would like to do something with me."

Those little blue eyes lit up. "Really?"

"Yes, really."

Trey sat back and let the two of them chat about what kinds of things they could do, but finally he broke in. "Elsie, there are a few other things you and I need to talk about. By the way, you speak really good English. Where did you learn it?"

"My mother is from America," she said. That was answer enough.

Trey finally turned to the matter at hand. "I understand you saw something during the night from your balcony," he said.

"Yes, I did," Elsie answered, looking him in the eye.

"What were you doing on your balcony so late at night?" he asked, glancing at Bonnie, who was busy taking notes again and didn't look up.

"I had a long nap yesterday, and I couldn't sleep. I took my blanket and wrapped it around me to keep me warm," she said. "I didn't want to wake them." Elsie nodded toward her grandparents.

"Were you sitting on one of the chairs on the balcony?" he asked.

"No, I was standing up and was looking through the railing," she responded. "I was watching the water. I love watching the water go by, even when it's mostly dark."

"What was it that you saw that upset you?"

"Somebody fell into the water," she said.

"You saw a person fall?" Trey asked.

"I think he got pushed," Elsie clarified.

"So the man fell from somewhere below your balcony? Where were the people you saw standing when he fell or was pushed?"

"They were on the place where people walk around the ship," she said.

"I see. Can you see that walkway very well from your balcony?"

"Just the outside edge of it."

"But you could see the railing?" Trey asked.

"Yes, I could see that."

"Tell me again what happened. Start when you first saw someone down there," Trey encouraged her.

"I was looking way out when I heard somebody shout. I looked down then. I could see some people, but I couldn't see them very good, so I pulled a chair to the railing and stood on it. Then I could see a lot better. But I was careful not to lean too far. I didn't want to fall."

"I'm glad you were careful," Trey said. "What did you see when you were on the chair?"

"There were three people shouting at each other. Then one guy fell."

"Think really hard now, Elsie. How did he fall? What was happening when he went over the railing?" Trey asked.

Elsie closed her eyes tightly and rubbed them with her fists. Finally, she moved her hands and opened her eyes again. "One of them, the one that fell, was leaning against the railing. The other two were sort of pushing on him. Then they grabbed him by the legs and lifted him and threw him over. So I guess they really didn't push him; they threw him in."

"Did the man that fell have his face toward the water or toward the other people?"

She closed her eyes again, rubbed them, and then opened them. "He was facing the ocean."

"And they picked him up and threw him over the railing?" Trey questioned her.

"I think so," she said.

"You seem pretty sure that the one that fell was a man, is that right?" Trey asked.

"I think so. But I couldn't see very good."

"What about the others. Could you tell if they were men or women?"

She shook her head. "I was mostly watching the guy they threw in the ocean. It might have been a man and a woman, but I'm not sure. I'm sorry. I didn't do very good, did I?" Elsie asked, her eyes filling with tears.

"You did great," Trey said. "I'm proud of you. You're a very brave girl."

"Thank you," she said softly.

"Do you need a drink of water or anything, Elsie?" Trey asked. "I do have some more questions for you."

"I'm thirsty, and I'm tired," she said.

"I'll get you some water," the captain said.

They all relaxed while Elsie drank the water—all but the grandparents, that is. They were wringing their hands and constantly wiping perspiration from their faces. Trey once again began to ask Elsie some questions. "Did you see the man again after he fell into the ocean?"

"No. But I couldn't see the water very good close to the ship," she said.

"Okay, now, Elsie, tell me how long you watched the other two people."

She shook her head. "I got off the chair and pulled it back. I didn't want them to see me."

"Can you tell me anything about what they were wearing?" Trey asked.

Elsie thought for a minute. "I think they were wearing black stuff."

"That's good, Elsie. Were their heads covered?"

She scrunched her eyes and then said, "I think so. I think they had hoods over their heads. Black hoods."

"How was the man dressed that went over the edge?" Trey asked.

"He had black too, but he didn't have a hood. I saw his hair."

"You were very observant, Elsie, and you have a great memory."

"Thank you," she said.

"Did you see the two people do anything else before you got off of the chair?" Trey asked.

"No," she said, shaking her head.

"How long did you stay on the balcony, Elsie?"

"I went back inside after that. I was afraid."

"Did you wake your grandparents then?" he asked.

"I tried to, but they wouldn't wake up," Elsie said.

"Did you try very hard to wake them?"

"I did, but they take pills to help them sleep. So I sat on my bed until I fell asleep."

Trey sat back, looking at the captain and Bonnie. He shook his head. "The poor kid," he mumbled.

The interview with Elsie continued. Trey asked what she did when she woke up. She said, "I woke up when the captain's voice—his voice," she said pointing at Captain Johnsen, "told us to stay in our rooms."

"Did your grandparents wake up then too?" Trey asked.

"No, but I woke them up," she said. "I guess their medicine wasn't working anymore."

"And did you tell them what you'd seen?" he asked.

"Yes, but they told me I'd had a bad dream and to go back to sleep," she said.

"Did you have a bad dream?" Trey asked her.

She slowly shook her head. "No, I was awake when the guy fell in the ocean," she said with a stubborn set to her jaw. "But they didn't believe me. So I laid down, but I couldn't sleep."

"How did you finally convince your grandparents?" he asked.

"When the two officers came to search our room. I told those men, and they believed me because there was a man missing."

After a few more minutes, Trey decided he had learned all he was going to from Elsie, but he had her translate some questions for her grandparents. They were of little help, so he terminated the interview. Bonnie escorted the three of them back to their stateroom, but Trey stayed and talked things over with Captain Johnsen.

"Detective, do you think that the little girl's version of what she saw is correct or do you think she may have made some of it up or remembered wrong?" the captain asked.

"I think what she told us is what she saw," Trey said as he slowly nodded his head.

"That is my assessment as well, Detective. That means we won't find the missing man on the ship, for he is overboard and dead."

"Murdered," Trey said.

"Yes, I would say so. The question now is who the two people were who threw him off the ship. I wish the cameras hadn't been tampered with. It makes me wonder if the theft and the murder are related. If not, we have two separate incidents to worry about. And that means more criminals at work." Exhaustion showed on his face, but he didn't let it divert him from what he knew needed to be done. "Okay, the search will continue. But I don't think we should tell any of the staff that we know where our missing man went. Someone else might have seen something and mention it to the searchers."

"What would you like Officer Springer and me to do now?" Trey asked.

"Just keep investigating. Maybe find out who might have had something against the victim," Captain Johnsen said.

"There were several people who were angered by Martin to the point of threatening him. I think we need to talk to them," Trey suggested.

"Great," the captain said. "But both your interviews and the search must be hurried along. If we don't get food available to our passengers soon, we could have a revolt on our hands."

Bonnie still wasn't back when Trey's phone rang. "Detective Shotwell, this is Ruben Hawk. I just got off the phone with Detective Inspector Willie Denning. He tells me you're in need of my services."

"He told you what it's about, didn't he?" Trey asked.

"Yes, your mother's murder. It appears you might have finally gotten the break we've searched for the past ten years. What would you like me to do?"

Trey explained, "There's a wealthy Frenchman on board who bought one of my father's paintings at an auction on the ship yesterday. He thinks he has a stolen one in his home in France and that his German friend has one in his home. It's the Frenchman, Damian Latimer, who would like to hire you."

"How do I get in touch with him?" Ruben asked.

"Just a moment, Inspector," Trey said. He turned to the captain as he held the phone away from his mouth. "Do you mind if I go talk to Mr. Latimer about hiring the private investigator I am on the phone with?"

"Go right ahead, as soon as Bonnie gets back," he said even as Bonnie opened the door and stepped in. "Looks like she's here. So go ahead, and if Mr. Latimer will promise to keep it to himself for now, you can tell him about his missing painting."

Trey spoke to Hawk for a moment more before he ended the call. Then he and Bonnie went directly to the Frenchman's stateroom. "What in the world is going on, Detective?" he asked. "I'm hungry, and I'm sure everyone else on the ship is too." He appeared to be frustrated.

"I'm afraid you're right," Trey told him. "I'm assisting the captain this morning. This is Officer Bonnie Springer of the ship's security staff. We need to talk to you."

"Come on in," he invited them. They stepped in, and he had them sit on the sofa. He pulled a chair out from the desk and sat down opposite them. "What do you need to speak with me about?"

"Two things, Damien," Trey began. "First, I've made contact with Ruben Hawk, the former New Scotland Yard inspector who now is a private investigator."

"Excellent," Damian said. "Is he willing to work for me?"

"He is, and I told him I'd put you in touch with him."

"Can we do that right now?" the wealthy Frenchman asked. "I'm clearly not doing anything else."

"Yes, but first, we wanted to advise you about the purpose of all the disruption this morning."

"Something was stolen," Damian said. "I've gathered that. Can you tell me what it is?"

"Yes, something very valuable," Trey said. "And I'm afraid it's not good news for you. The painting you purchased yesterday is missing."

Damian burst to his feet, his face turning dark. "How could that have happened?" he demanded. "I was told it would be kept totally secure."

"We don't know how it happened," Bonnie broke in as she and Trey also stood up. "It had been placed in the vault for the night, but the vault door was found hanging open. Your painting and the one Trey painted have both been taken."

"Surely you've checked the surveillance cameras," Damian said, pacing back and forth in front of the officers, his wiry body as tight as a violin string. "If you haven't, you must do so now."

"We tried, but the camera system was hacked and isn't working," Bonnie said, looking down at Damian from her considerable height. The Frenchman was only about five six while Bonnie stood six two, but he didn't shrink in the least under her overpowering physical presence.

He did stop pacing and ran one hand through his thick black hair. "This is more than a crime of opportunity, Officer," he said. "It was planned by an expert. Perhaps a professional thief with a lot of technical knowledge and hacking ability."

"Yes, we agree," Bonnie responded.

"Now I'm confused, though. If it's stolen paintings you're searching for, why are the ship's officers searching in every drawer and suitcase? The painting won't fit in those small spaces."

Trey creased his brow. "We hope that the paintings haven't been damaged. But just in case, we're checking everywhere that pieces of them could be hidden."

The Frenchman's dark brown eyes narrowed. "They better not be damaged," he said slowly, drawing his words out. "To cut up a work of art by your father is unthinkable."

"The art is insured," Bonnie said, hoping to quell the building anger evident on the rich man's face.

"I don't need more money, young lady," he said hotly. "I have money. What I want is my painting back. Simon Shotwell is my favorite painter, and that work I bought yesterday is irreplaceable."

"I'm sorry," Bonnie said, her eyes looking at her shiny black shoes.

"Tell Captain Johnsen I'll offer a reward for the return of the painting," Damian suddenly said. "People are more likely to speak up if they think there's something in it for them."

"Human nature," Trey agreed. "Why don't you come with us, and we'll talk to him in person right now. When we get there, I'll see if I can reach Inspector Hawk and let you work out whatever arrangements you want to with him."

The captain was on his phone when they knocked. "Come on in," he shouted.

As the three of them stepped through the door, he waved them to a seat. As soon as he had completed his call, Captain Johnsen said, "Mr. Latimer, I'm so sorry about what's happened. Be assured we are doing everything we can to find your painting."

The two men shook hands, and then Damian came right to the point. "Captain, I would like to offer a reward of twenty-five thousand American dollars for information that leads to the return of my art." He looked over at Trey and then added, "I'll also make an offer of five thousand for the return of the one Detective Shotwell painted."

"Are you sure?" Captain Johnsen asked, taken aback by the offer.

"Money is not an object to me, Captain. It is beautiful art that matters to me. Yes, I am serious about the rewards," he said.

"Do you have a suggestion on how to get the word out?" the captain asked.

The little Frenchman chuckled. "The same way you woke me up this morning," he said. "Make an announcement on the ship's PA. Repeat it a few times. I want those paintings found."

The captain looked at Trey. "What do you think?" he asked.

"I say do it," Trey responded. "But it's your call, Captain."

"All right," the captain said decisively. "I'll do it."

He stepped over to his sound system and grabbed the mike. Trey pulled out his phone and began to search his contacts list for Inspector Hawk's number. A moment later the captain's voice boomed over the speaker. "This is Captain Johnsen. May I please have everyone's attention? I am sorry for the inconvenience this morning. I would like to explain what is happening. Two pieces of art were stolen during the night." He then described the art and the value of each piece. Then he said, "I am authorized to offer a cash reward for information leading to the return of the paintings. For the Simon Shotwell painting, an offer of twenty-five thousand American dollars has been made. For the Trey Shotwell painting, the offer is five thousand American dollars. If you have any information, please call the following number from the phone in your staterooms." He gave the number, thanked the passengers again, and ended the announcement.

In the meantime, Trey had reached Inspector Hawk. They talked for a minute before Trey handed the phone to Damian. When Damian finished working out the terms of the investigation with Hawk, he handed the phone back to Trey.

Inspector Hawk said to Trey, "I'll get right on it, Detective. And I'll keep both you and Mr. Latimer advised of my progress. I'll also work closely with Detective Denning. It's time we solve your mother's murder and bring the killer to justice."

"Thank you, Inspector. I'll let you know anything I learn that might help you," Trey promised.

As soon as Trey was off the phone, Captain Johnsen said, "Now that we've told everyone what's missing, I think we better take a slightly different approach to the search. The crew members need to get food ready before we have a revolt." He smiled. "Not a mutiny, but, well, an angry bunch of passengers could cause a lot of trouble. While the crew is working, we'll search their quarters down on the lower decks."

"How close to being finished is the initial search?" Trey asked.

"I had a report while you were on the phone. It's pretty much finished. All passengers and crew are accounted for except for Martin Talley. So I think I'll allow the passengers to go where they please at this time. And we'll hope that the reward Mr. Damian has so kindly offered will soon bear fruit."

"Captain, do you have anyone who can fix the cameras?" Damian asked.

"I have my top computer specialist working on the problem right now. It may take him a while though. I'm afraid that's the best I can do." The captain turned to Trey. "I'd appreciate it if you and Bonnie would assure Daphne and Gil Slader that we're doing everything we can to find their missing painting and that if we fail, the cruise line will reimburse them. We're insured, so they won't be out any money."

"We'll do that right now," Trey agreed, although he wasn't excited about it. Despite the compliments about his painting, he felt uneasy around the Sladers.

When he and Bonnie went to the Sladers' stateroom, there was no response to Bonnie's loud knock. They checked the restaurants and the lido deck, where the buffet was quickly being set up and hungry passengers were already beginning to eat. The ship was big, and if someone was moving around, it would be hard to find them, so Trey said, "We'll have to check their room again later. Right now, I'd like to go out and take a look at the spot where Elsie saw someone thrown overboard."

They arrived at the location Bonnie thought would be the right place and looked carefully around. They found nothing, and after a half hour, they gave up. "I guess that was a waste of time," Trey said. "Let's go see if the Sladers are back at their stateroom yet."

Daphne answered the door. "What now?" she asked sharply. "We haven't seen Martin and neither has Danny. And we know our painting is gone. It's a nice painting, but it's not exactly irreplaceable."

"Actually, we did come to discuss the painting. May we come in for a moment?" Trey asked.

"I guess, but Gil's in the shower," she said. Trey thought that was a bit strange, considering all the hours everyone had been confined to their quarters. He also noted that Daphne's hair was wet, like she'd just had a shower as well.

"Thank you, Mrs. Slader," Trey said as they stepped in and waited while Daphne shut the door behind them.

"Give me just a moment. I need to let Gil know we have company so he won't step out of the shower and embarrass himself." It only took her a moment, and then she said, without inviting them to sit, "What did you need then, Detective?"

Just then, the captain's voice again came over the sound system. They all listened as he repeated the offer of a reward for the missing paintings. Trey waited until the announcement was over, then he said, "The captain asked us to assure you that everything possible is being done to find the painting you bought, but in the event that it isn't found, the cruise line will fully reimburse you."

Her face lit up. "That would be great. I doubt it will be found if it hasn't already, but we'll accept the money," she said. "Thanks for coming by." She moved toward the door.

Trey followed. "Do you have any idea who might have wanted that painting bad enough to steal it?"

"Your girlfriend, maybe," she said with a forced chuckle. "I know she likes it. But of course, she can get all the Trey Shotwell paintings she wants. No, I seriously don't have any idea. But if I think of someone, I'll be sure and let you know."

"I could use a shower too," Bonnie said when they were walking down the long hallway. "Unlike the Sladers, I haven't had a chance yet."

"They must have come back from wherever they were earlier and decided they needed a shower. It strikes me as strange. I take it that bothered you as well," Trey said.

"Yes, it did." Suddenly her radio came to life. She answered it quickly.

The captain's voice said, "We just got a report of some kind of problem on the tenth deck, around where Trey's stateroom is. Would you two check it out as quickly as you can?"

TEN

TREY'S HEART WAS IN HIS throat as he ran to the stairs and pounded up as quickly as his legs would carry him. Bonnie was right with him every rapid step of the way. He entered the hallway and saw a small crowd of passengers and a steward standing outside Aariah's door. The steward was trying with little success to keep the people back. Trey couldn't see beyond the crowd. He stopped and demanded, "What is going on here?"

Before anyone could answer, the crowd parted, and he saw Aariah lying very still on the hallway floor. Her long golden hair was spread across her face and the carpet. Blood was dripping from her mouth. "Aariah," Trey choked as he dropped to his knees beside her and pressed a finger to her carotid artery.

"Stand back," Bonnie ordered, and the crowd moved down the hallway, eyes wide and dismay evident on their faces. "Is she alive?" Bonnie asked as she joined Trey on the floor.

"She has a pulse. Make sure the ship's medical team is on the way," he said urgently as he began to check her arms and legs. He was conscious of Bonnie as she spoke into her radio, but mostly he concentrated on Aariah.

Her eyes fluttered. "Trey?" she asked in a weak voice.

"Yes, Aariah. It's me. I'm here. You're going to be okay."

"I got hit," she said as her eyes opened and she attempted to focus on his face. "Your father . . ." Her voice trailed off.

"What about my father?" Trey asked as panic began to grip him.

"He's . . . he's . . . hurt," she managed to say.

"Bonnie, stay with her. I'll check on my father." Trey rose to his feet, the beat of his heart pounding in his temples.

The door to his stateroom was shut. He inserted his key and pushed on the door. He instantly spotted his father's easel lying in a heap on the floor. The painting he'd been working on was lying upside down just beyond it. He could see his father's feet hanging over the end of one of the beds. Trey stepped in only to have his world come crashing down around him.

Simon Shotwell was lying on the bed on his back. The hilt of a knife protruded from his chest. Blood was pooled all over him and the bed. Trey stepped near. His father's eyes were open, staring at the ceiling, unseeing. Trey knew death when he saw it. He heard a strangled cry and realized it was coming from him.

"Father, I'm so sorry," he said in a choked voice. "I should have been with you." Trey leaned down and put his finger over his father's carotid artery, knowing he would find no beat. It was what he'd been trained to do. He removed his hand and took a deep breath in an attempt to gain control of his emotions. Someone had murdered his father. He had a job to do. "Father," he said, his voice broken as tears poured from his eyes, "I *will* find whoever did this. You have my word."

He was aware of someone pressing close behind him. He turned to find Aariah, steadied by the muscular arms of Bonnie, reaching for him. He took her in his arms and held her tight. "Is he . . ." Aariah began as she looked up at him. She couldn't finish.

"Yes, Aariah, he's dead," he said between bitter sobs. "And I'll find out who did it if it's the last thing I ever do."

She dropped her head against his shoulder and sobbed with him. Bonnie, meantime, was once again on her radio, calling for assistance. "Is your grandmother okay?" Trey asked Aariah.

"She's upset, but I don't think they hurt her," Aariah answered without moving her head from his shoulder.

"I'll check on her," Bonnie said and moved away from them. When she returned three or four minutes later, she was accompanied by Hans.

The Swede laid a large hand on Trey's shoulder and said, "I was hungry and went down to eat. I'm so sorry, Trey."

Trey looked up, his eyes blurred with tears he just couldn't seem to stop. "Whoever did this planned it carefully, Hans. I just don't understand why anyone would do this to my father. He never hurt anyone in his life."

"Again, I'm so very sorry, Detective," he said, his deep voice filled with emotion.

"Thank you, Hans."

"Aariah," Bonnie said, "your grandmother is okay. She's resting. Two members of the medical team just got here, and I had them go in and check on her. The doctor's on his way."

"Thank you, Bonnie," Aariah said.

"They'll check on you, too," the officer added.

"I'm fine now," she said. "I have Trey."

"Yes, you do," he said softly, caressing her long hair.

The doctor came and was ushered into the Shotwell's stateroom. Captain Johnsen arrived only a moment after the doctor had pronounced Simon Shotwell dead. "I'm so sorry, Trey," the captain said.

Trey nodded. "I'll find out who did this."

"I'm sure you will, but you'll have help. I've already ordered that the ship turn around, since we're still closer to Sydney than New Zealand," the captain said. "We'll have a lot of unhappy passengers, but we have no choice. The safety of the passengers must come first. There are killers on board. The sooner we get additional help, the better."

"I'll do what I can in the meantime," Trey said.

"Be careful, Detective," Captain Johnsen said. "You could be a target too."

Trey had already entertained that thought, but it didn't matter to him. What mattered was that he'd lost his father, a man he both loved and admired. His heart was broken. He wanted to get to work, both to keep his mind occupied and to find who did this horrible thing.

He was anxious to speak with Aariah in the hopes of getting a solid lead. They sat on the balcony of her stateroom a few minutes later. Bonnie and Hans sat inside with Charlotte. The seventy-five-year-old lady was extremely upset over the murder, and the two were trying to engage her in pleasant conversation while Trey questioned Aariah.

"Grandmother didn't want to go out of the room to eat until you could go with us," Aariah said. "And I agreed. I did go next door and talk to your father for a couple of minutes after the captain told everybody we could leave our staterooms. Simon was busy painting. He told me he would wait for you to return and then the four of us could go eat together."

"How did he seem?" Trey asked. "It must have been a blow to him to learn his painting had been stolen."

"He said he was quite sure you would find it, Trey. He told me you're a very good artist but a *great* detective," she said.

Trey felt a rush of emotion at her words. "My father was a great man," he responded, choking on his words. He had to take a moment to compose himself, and then he asked, "So what happened after you went back to your room?"

"Grandmother and I sat and talked. She was worried but not unduly so. She just seemed so surprised that someone would steal the paintings," Aariah told Trey. "I'd been back about ten minutes when someone knocked on your door. I got up to see who was there, but Grandmother wanted me to stay with her. So I sat down again. A moment later, I heard your father shout. I'm sure it was his voice; it was very loud. Then, after a moment, the door slammed. I wanted to see who had upset your father. I guess that was stupid. I opened my door and looked into the hallway. This guy started to walk past my door. I tried to go back inside, but he jumped and grabbed me. I tried to scream, but he slapped my face and told me to shut up.

"I was scared, and I didn't know what to do. I didn't have time to think much about it. The last thing I remember before his fist hit my face was the thought that he was going to kill me. The next thing I remember is you touching and speaking to me."

"Tell me what he looked like," Trey requested.

"I can't," she said, her eyes dropping.

"You mean, you don't remember? Think really hard, Aariah."

She shook her head and looked up again. "I mean, I didn't see his face. He had something pulled down over his head, a stocking of some kind. I couldn't even tell you the color of his hair since he was also wearing a hoodie," she said. "It was a black hoodie."

"But it was a man, not a woman, and he was alone, is that right?" Trey asked

"Yes . . . well, I think it was a man."

"Because of his voice?" Trey asked.

"Yes. He was talking funny, like he was trying to disguise his voice, but I thought it was a man's voice," she said with a look of uncertainty on her face.

"Aariah, are you telling me it might not have been a man?" Trey asked gently.

She looked out over the sea for a moment and then looked back at Trey. "I think it was a man, but maybe it wasn't. I'm not sure. But whoever it was must have been alone. At least I didn't see anyone else."

"Could there have still been someone in my room with my father?" Trey asked.

She shook her head. "I don't think so."

"Is that because you heard the door close?" Trey asked. "Remember, if you let go of the door it shuts itself."

"So maybe whoever hit me came out and let the door go, and then someone else might have come out after," she reasoned. "That could have happened. I don't know. I'm sorry, Trey. I'm a terrible witness."

"You're a great witness. You can only tell me what you saw and heard," he said. "Now, tell me how tall he was and how heavy."

"If it was a man," she said. "I'm not sure how big he was. It all happened really fast. Whoever it was might have been about your size. Maybe a little bigger. Maybe not. I'm just not sure. It wasn't someone a lot bigger than you, I'm sure of that."

"Okay, good. Did you see his eyes? We'll assume a man for now, knowing it might not be," Trey said.

She shook her head. "The stocking was pulled over his eyes. It was sort of sheer material, so he could see through it, but there was no way to tell his eye color."

"Did you see any hair?" Trey asked.

She shook her head.

"What about his hands? Did you see his hands?"

She thought for a moment and then said, "There was blood on them. I mean, there was blood on the gloves. He was wearing gloves, black gloves."

"What color clothing was he wearing, and what kind?" he asked.

"It was all black," she said. "That's all I remember for sure."

Someone in black, Trey thought. This wasn't the first time someone in black had committed a crime on the ship. "If you think of anything else, let me know," Trey said, and Aariah mutely nodded.

Trey was tired and hungry but didn't feel like eating; his friends convinced him to try anyway. Charlotte was far too upset to leave the stateroom, so Aariah ordered her a light breakfast to be brought to the room. A few minutes later, Trey, in company with Aariah, Hans, and Bonnie, picked at a light lunch. All he could think was how much he already missed his father. To Bonnie, he eventually said, "The Sladers had just showered. I wonder if they have bloody black clothes."

"I was thinking that, too," Bonnie said. "Maybe we should try to search their stateroom."

As they were finishing lunch, Trey was again summoned to the captain's cabin. "Bring your friends with you, including Officer Springer," he said.

The captain was stressed and tired, like Trey, but he was very much in command. "I've had some folks strongly resist my decision to return to Sydney," he said. "I think you might want to talk to some of them."

His interested stirred, Trey asked, "Who are they?"

"A woman by the name of Claudia Gaudet made it clear she didn't want her trip disrupted. So did the man who seems to be a friend of hers."

"That would be Victor Krause. He made Martin apologize to Claudia, and then he also threatened Martin," Trey broke in. "Actually, I guess he threatened both of them."

"That's right. The Sladers were also upset. They said they paid for the trip and now it's being cut short. They demanded I keep going. They also demanded I return the money for the painting that was stolen, which I agreed to do," the captain said, "but not until we are absolutely certain it won't turn up."

"Has anyone responded to the offer of a reward?" Trey asked.

"A few, but none that have any credibility. We'll see if something more comes of it," the captain said.

"Are there any others who complained?" Trey asked.

"Several, but most were not ones I would worry about. However, there was one man who was especially vocal. He was also quite threatening toward me. That's what bothered me."

"What's his name?"

"Lukas Nichols," Captain Johnsen said.

"That I can believe," Trey moaned.

"Do you know him too?" the captain asked in surprise.

"I'm afraid I do. He's my uncle—my mother's younger brother. He's a world-class jerk."

"Is he dangerous? Would he do anything to sabotage the ship if he doesn't get his way?"

"I don't know, to be quite honest, Captain. But I know this. He's not a nice man. When I saw him on the ship, it was the first time I'd seen him in ten years," Trey explained.

"So it's just a coincidence that he's on the same cruise as you and your father?" the captain asked, cocking his eye.

"I'm sure he'd say it was, but I think he came to cause my father trouble." Trey rubbed his temples. He was getting an intense headache. "What I don't know is what kind of trouble he might have had in mind. He may have planned to disrupt one of the auctions. He was at the first one, but he didn't do anything. He might have been planning to do something at the next one."

"Detective, someone murdered your father. Could it have been your uncle?"

It was like the captain had read his mind. Trey definitely suspected his uncle, but again, he didn't know what the motive would have been. Lukas didn't like Simon, but did he hate him enough to murder him? Trey asked himself. To the captain, he said, "I hate to say it about my own uncle, but yes, I think that's possible."

"I'm so sorry about all this, Detective. Now for the main reason I had you come talk to me." The captain rubbed his head and frowned. "I have been overruled by our corporate office. They said they'll send a team of investigators to meet the ship but that I'm not to go back to Sydney. I have been ordered to once again proceed toward New Zealand."

Trey stared at the captain. "They want you to do that with unidentified killers having the run of the ship? That's crazy."

"I agree, but as I said, I've been overruled. It's out of my hands. I'm sorry. Now, here's the next question that I have for you, Detective. Your father's body has to be taken off the ship. We can have a helicopter pick it up and take it to Sydney, unless, as his next of kin, you want it taken somewhere else."

Trey's head was spinning. Aariah took hold of his arm. He looked into her eyes and forced a smile. He looked back at Captain Johnsen. "Sydney, for sure. That was his home."

"Would you like to fly with the body?" the captain asked next.

"Yes, I must. But I won't abandon the search for his killer," he said. His mind was whirling, but suddenly a calm settled over him and a clear thought came to his troubled mind. Could his father's killer be the same as his mother's? Could the thieves who stole from his mother and father in London ten years ago be on this very ship right now? If so, who were they? His uncle's face swam before his eyes. Trey blinked to clear it away but said nothing of his thoughts to the others. He also thought about the Sladers' showers, taken so quickly after the murder. And yet he couldn't think of a possible reason they would have done it. They seemed to have thought highly of his father.

"When will the helicopter be here?" Trey asked as he shoved the thoughts aside for the time being.

"It will take a little while, but the corporate office is already working on it. I suspect it will be here by early tomorrow morning, maybe even during the night," Captain Johnsen told him.

"I'll be packed and ready to go," Trey announced. "Where's my father's b-body at now?"

"It's in the infirmary, packed in ice, but for obvious reasons we can't keep it there for long."

"I understand," Trey said. Even now he was thinking ahead, thinking of how he would proceed in the hunt for the killer.

"Detective, there's one more thing," the captain said. "It's about your father's other painting, the one we were to sell at the next auction. Are you the heir?"

Trey had a ready answer to that question. He was Simon's sole heir. It was in writing in the form of a trust and was filed at a solicitor's office in Sydney. He supposed his father had a copy of it somewhere as well. "Yes, I'm his only heir. The painting is mine."

"What would you like me to do with it?"

Trey thought for a moment. What would his father want him to do with it? He pictured his father's face, could almost hear his father's voice. Suddenly, he knew what to do. It was almost as if his father was telling him what to say. "He consigned it to sell, so sell it," Trey said firmly.

"Very well, that's what we'll do."

"Before you leave the ship, are you going to talk to your uncle?" the captain asked.

"I wouldn't miss the chance," Trey said, his voice cold and bitter. "Do you know if there's anyone traveling with him?"

"I don't know, but I'll try to find out," the captain promised.

"Thank you." Trey walked to the door and opened it. When the captain spoke his name, he stopped and turned back. "Yes, sir?"

"I'll see that the cost of the trip for both you and your father is reimbursed."

"Don't worry about it. None of this is your fault. I appreciate everything you've done," Trey said. "I just hope the investigators can solve my father's murder."

"I wish you could stay, but I know you need to go and take care of a funeral and whatever other matters need to be attended to in Sydney. I'll keep you apprised of every development in the investigations—your father's death, the theft of the paintings, and the murder of Martin Talley."

"Thank you," Trey said as he once again turned to the door, but he was again stopped short.

Aariah said, "Captain, is there room on the helicopter for my grandmother and I to go to Sydney? I don't think she can complete the trip with all that's happened. She's very distraught. And I would like to be there to support Trey."

"It's more than okay with me," Trey said, putting his arm around her and pulling her close. His father was the only person Trey was close to, and now he was gone. Aariah, even though he'd known her for only a short time, would be a great support in this time of intense grief. He both wanted and needed her, more than he would have ever thought possible.

"Then I'll arrange it," Captain Johnsen said. "And I'll also let my art director and his assistant know that the sale of the second Simon Shotwell painting will proceed as planned. And I'll make the announcement over the intercom that we'll proceed as originally planned after all."

ELEVEN

TREY WANTED TO GO TO the Sladers' stateroom and search for black clothing, but he didn't have the authority. The captain had assured him the staff would watch the laundry and let the official investigators know of Trey's suspicions.

Trey spent the afternoon with Aariah, who made it her mission to comfort him. His sorrow at the loss of his father was almost stifling. At first they mostly talked about the murders and the missing art, but Aariah attempted to shift their conversation to things that wouldn't cause him so much hurt. They began to talk about themselves—details of their childhoods, their families, and their hopes and desires for the future. They discovered they had a lot in common and enjoyed many of the same things.

Hours later, as their conversation wrapped up, he told her he had work to do. "I've got to do what I can to help find the person who did this to my father—and to my mother."

Aariah accompanied him three different times to knock on his uncle's door, as that was something the captain felt like he could legally do. But there was never an answer.

She followed Trey around the ship, searching for Lukas when he didn't respond to the knocks. They finally gave up, and Trey took her to dinner, where they were met by Hans and Bonnie. The four of them were like lifelong friends. Bonnie was out of uniform, dressed casually and looking quite attractive. The conversation at dinner was about the Mormon Church, Trey's painting, and Aariah's grandmother's health. She had declined joining them for dinner, citing an upset stomach.

Nothing was said about the violent death of Trey's father. And that made it easier for Trey to enjoy the time with his new friends.

They had just finished dinner and were leaving the dining room when Trey's phone rang.

"Trey, it's Willie," his friend from New Scotland Yard announced.

"You're up and about early," Trey said.

"I have a few things to report," Willie responded. "I hope this is a good time for you. How are things?"

"Things are terrible," Trey said with a catch in his voice. He took a deep breath and continued, "My father's been murdered."

It was totally silent on the line for a drawn-out moment. Finally, Willie said, "Trey, you can't be serious."

"I'm afraid so," Trey responded. "He was stabbed right in our stateroom while I was out helping the captain."

"I am so sorry. Do you know who did it?"

"I'm afraid not." He spent a moment giving Willie further details, and then he said, "Martin Tally was thrown overboard during the night. His friend says he's a nonswimmer."

"Was that murder too?" Willie asked.

"You tell me," Trey responded. "And that's still not all. There was an art theft during the night. My father's painting—the one sold to Damian Latimer—is missing and so is the one I painted that was purchased by Daphne Slader. We've searched the ship, but they haven't yet been found."

"Oh, my good friend, I'm so sorry about your father. I'm also sorry about the loss of the paintings. But frankly, I don't think there will be a lot of tears shed over Martin Talley's burial at sea," the London detective said. "What do you plan to do now?"

"I'll be flying by helicopter to Sydney with my father's body. I need to arrange for his burial. But I'll keep looking into my father's and my mother's murders," Trey responded. "Now, you called with a report. Let's have it, Willie."

"Okay, here's what I've learned," Willie began. "Gil and Daphne Slader appear to be legitimate art dealers. They buy and sell regularly. Daphne's actually not a bad artist in her own right. She had a few paintings on display at several locations in the country and has sold a number of them for modest amounts. But her main interest appears to be buying and selling. She apparently has a great eye as does her husband. I can't find anything that sheds a bad light on either one of them. Both have clean records—not so much as a parking ticket that I can find—and are well respected."

That information did nothing but make Trey feel more strongly about his uncle. He was not well respected.

"Daphne's little brother, Danny Bidwell, is another matter," Willie went on. "I can't find any connections between him and their business, which is a positive thing for them. Danny has a record of several petty thefts, a burglary, and even a couple of assaults. He spent a year in prison. There hasn't been anything within the past couple of years, though. He's either cleaned up his act or has learned to keep from getting caught."

"What about Martin Talley?" Trey asked.

"I'm not sure what the connection is between him and the Sladers," Willie responded. "Martin's a crook, pure and simple. He's been in and out of jail since he was in his midteens. He's always looking for the easy buck," Willie reported.

"Like stealing paintings and selling them to dealers like the Sladers?"

"I guess that would be possible, but there's nothing to indicate they've ever purchased any stolen paintings from Martin or anyone else," Willie said. "But get this, Trey. Martin has been suspected of stealing jewelry in house burglaries. He may be able to pick locks, as that's thought to have happened in a couple of cases he was suspected in."

"I see," Trey said. "I take it he's never been convicted of any burglaries."

"That's right. He was only suspected; no one could make a case."

"But he does have a criminal record?" Trey asked.

"Yes. One of his convictions was for stealing artifacts from an old ship that was being salvaged from the bottom of the sea about ten kilometers off shore," Willie said. "He and another fellow dove in and took the items right out from under the noses of the salvage crew. But they both got caught when they tried to sell a couple of gold pitchers."

"Did you say he dove in and stole the stuff from the floor of the ocean?" Trey asked. "I was told he didn't know how to swim."

"He is a good swimmer. That's for sure. And he's a certified diver. Of course, his diving is all done with tanks and all the related equipment. He would be in trouble if he was thrown into the ocean like he apparently was from your ship," Willie said.

"This is interesting," Trey said thoughtfully. "You see, his roommate and friend, Danny Bidwell, is the one who told me that Martin didn't know how to swim."

"That's a lie. But even though he's a good swimmer, that probably wouldn't have saved him. Even if he survived the fall from the ship, he wouldn't have been able to swim far enough to reach shore. No one would. If hypothermia didn't get him, the sharks would."

"Yes, I'm sure that's true," Trey responded.

"There's one more thing: he's a heavy drinker. And that, Trey, is about all I've got for now."

"That's a lot."

"I hope it'll help," Willie said. "Although with Martin gone, I'm not sure how it will. Or was your father killed before Martin went overboard?"

"No, Martin was gone hours before my father was killed," Trey said. "So it couldn't have been him. Thanks for the information. You mentioned Martin had a partner on the thefts from the sunken ship. Do you have his name?"

"I do, and I can e-mail or text you a mug shot if you want," Willie offered.

"I would like it. What's the name?"

"His name is Andrew Remington. He is now thirty-eight years old. He's a small guy, just barely over five feet. And he couldn't weigh a hundred pounds soaking wet. No pun intended. He has blue eyes and light-blond hair, which he keeps short. The mug shot should give you a better visual."

"Any idea where he is now?" Trey asked.

"Not yet, but I'm trying to find out. Anything else you need?"

"Yes, would it be possible for you to check on another person?"

"I'm here to serve," Willie said cheerfully.

"My uncle, my mother's younger brother, is on the ship. His name is Lukas Nichols. He's about forty-five and hasn't been in touch with me or my father since my mother's funeral. Then out of the blue, he showed up on this cruise ship," Trey said. "I'd like to know what he's been up to the past ten years."

"I remember him," Willie said. "He created a bit of a scene at your mother's burial."

"How did you know that?" Trey asked. "You weren't there, were you?"

"No, but a couple other officers were," Willie informed him. "As I'm sure you know, killers often show up at their victim's funerals. We always have someone present at funerals, wakes, and burials."

"We do that in Sydney as well. I just never thought about it. Did you check into my uncle's activities at the time?"

"Yes, we did. Apparently it was a dead end, Trey, but now I wonder."

"So do I," Trey agreed.

"I'll look into his activities and get back with you," Willie promised.

Trey put the phone in his pocket and spoke to his friends. "I guess I'll go look for my uncle Lukas again. I really need to talk to him."

"Do you need help?" Bonnie asked. "I'm off duty unless there's another emergency."

"I'm off duty too," Hans said with a big grin. "No fights scheduled until after the cruise is over. So I'd be glad to help Bonnie find Lukas."

Bonnie was staring at Hans. "So you really are a fighter?" she asked.

The big Swede chuckled. "Of course I am. I'm a pro wrestler."

"I remember that being mentioned, but you told me you're an engineer," Bonnie said, her hands on her hips, her eyebrows drawn together.

"Actually, I told you I have a degree in civil engineering, which I do. And someday I'll work in that field. But right now, I wrestle, and I make very good money doing it. Is there a problem with that?" Hans looked a little uneasy.

Bonnie was still looking at him with a suspicious glint in her eye, but gradually, she began to smile. "Well, it depends, I guess," she said.

"Depends on what?" Hans asked hesitantly.

"It depends on how good you are," she said.

His face relaxed into a lazy smile. "I just said I make good money doing it."

Trey and Aariah were watching their new friends with interest, smiles playing on their faces. "I think she means do you win fights and not get beat half to death in the ring," Trey said, trying to sound serious but unable to hide a grin.

"Well, when you put it that way . . ." Hans began and then paused.

Bonnie spoke up before he could finish whatever he had in mind. "So what you're telling us is that you get paid to get beat up. Is that how it is?"

The big man began to chuckle. "No, it is not, little lady."

Trey looked at Bonnie, who did not look like a *little* lady. She looked like she could also be a professional fighter. "Then explain," she said firmly.

"I usually win," he said. "In fact, I mostly win. I have had a bad night or two, but I'm really pretty good."

Bonnie's face blossomed with a huge grin and sparkling eyes. "In that case, it's fine," she said. "When do you fight again?"

"I have a couple matches in Sydney just a few days after this cruise ends," he said.

"Will you be in shape for it?" she asked.

"That's why I work out so hard." He nodded. "Now, Detective Shotwell, can you use the help of me and the pretty little lady?"

Bonnie caught him with a playful elbow to his ribs. He didn't even flinch. Trey said, "I'm not sure what I'm going to do except see if Lukas is in his room now or in any of the public areas. Aariah and I couldn't find him before, but maybe he's somewhere we can find him now."

"We could divide up the decks and look through them," Bonnie suggested. "That would make it faster."

"If you guys are sure you want to help," Trey said.

"Of course we're sure," Bonnie said, looking up at Hans and catching his eye. He nodded in agreement. "In fact, we'd be glad to do it *for* you so you could go and relax."

"I can't relax," Trey countered. "If I'm not busy, all I do is think about my father." He cleared his throat and rubbed his eyes.

"Of course," Bonnie said. "Then we'll help you while you stay busy."

"I think we should check his stateroom again," Aariah said logically.

They did exactly that, but Lukas wasn't there. So they divided the decks and went to work looking in all the places where the passengers were permitted to go. They came up empty again.

"It's a big ship," Hans said when Trey expressed concerns about their failure. "He could be moving between decks or even from one end of the ship to another and we might not see him."

"Or he could be overboard like Martin," Trey said. "Something's wrong. We should have found him." He looked at Bonnie. "Bonnie, do you know if the security cameras are working now?"

"They were up and running a little while ago," she said. "Not quickly enough to help with your father's . . ." She trailed off, not wanting to finish the sentence.

Trey pushed aside the pain at the mention of his father's death. "I'd like to know if the system has been working continuously since it was fixed. And if possible, I'd also like to know if there are any clues to what caused it to fail in the first place."

After checking, Bonnie reported, "It is working again and has been continuously since it was fixed three or four hours ago. But the guys that worked on it have no idea what happened to cause it to fail. They suspect it was hacked somehow, but they can't tell for sure. Did you want to see if there's any sign of your uncle since it was fixed?"

"That would be a huge undertaking," Trey hedged.

"Come with me; we'll at least see if he's been to his stateroom," Bonnie invited.

* * *

When the group arrived in the security office, one of the technicians checked the camera focused on the hallway of Lukas's stateroom. "Is that him?" Hans asked when a picture of a man entering Lukas's stateroom appeared on the screen. Trey nodded. They watched him enter the room, and then, after what the technician explained was about twenty minutes, he left again.

The time he had left his stateroom was when the group was about halfway through their hour-long dinner. Trey asked if the technician could follow Lukas's movements by switching from camera to camera now that they'd located him. It was not only possible, but quite easy. The four watched as the technician tracked Lukas from his room. He went from his room to the elevators, got on, descended several levels, and ended up in a bar. He was in there for a few minutes, the time it took him to consume one drink, and then he was on the move again. He went from floor to floor, entered the library, and accessed one of the computers there. After twenty minutes there, he was once again on his way. At last, after drinking some more and ignoring everyone around him, Lukas ended up back in his room. They fast-forwarded an hour and were almost up to the present time, which was, according to Trey's watch, 8:45 p.m.

"Let's go. He's there right now," Trey said, surging to his feet.

"Whoa, what's going on?" Bonnie said. The screen they'd been watching had gone black.

The technician didn't have to answer. The video surveillance system had just gone off again. The fellow worked furiously with the mouse and keyboard but to no avail.

"Let's go," Trey said again, and the four of them left the puzzled technician trying to restore the surveillance system again.

The group literally ran to the stairway, up to Lukas's floor, and then down the long hallway to his stateroom.

Hans, with the biggest fists, pounded on the door, shaking the walls. There was no response. He shouted, "Hey, Lukas, we need to talk to you." Still nothing. He pounded again.

When Lukas still failed to answer the door, Trey said, "Bonnie, what would it take to get a peek in there, just to make sure he's not there?"

It took the presence of Captain Johnsen and an on-duty security officer. After ten minutes of waiting in the hallway, Trey saw the captain approaching. It took five seconds for the officer to open the door, and another ten seconds to determine that Lukas Nichols wasn't there. In another fifteen seconds, they confirmed that the surveillance system was still down, and five seconds after that, the captain said glumly, "There's going to be another crime."

Bonnie was ordered back on duty, as was the rest of the security team.

Trey, discouraged, said, "I need some exercise to get me going again. I think I'll go change my clothes and run for a while."

"I'll join you," Hans offered.

"Me too, for a while, and then I'll read," Aariah told them. "Let's meet at the door by the elevators on the promenade deck—on the port side—in fifteen minutes."

* * *

When the three of them exited the interior of the ship, the running commenced.

Trey set a punishing pace, and soon left both Aariah and Hans behind. On his third lap, he caught up with them on their second lap and slowed down. "Thanks for staying with her, Hans," he said as the three of them moved in sync toward the front of the ship. "I needed to run off my frustrations. I'm better now."

"Somebody needed to keep this girl company when you took off like a rabbit," Hans teased.

The three of them continued ten more times around the ship before Aariah said breathlessly, "I'm going to stop and read now." She'd left her bag on a lounge chair near the door they'd come through earlier.

"See you the next time around," Trey said, flashing her a smile, and he and Hans continued on.

The next time around, Trey saw that Aariah was engrossed in her Book of Mormon. She looked up, waved a greeting, and went back to reading. Five laps later, she had switched to a novel. Two laps after that, she had company. "Hey, Bonnie, why don't you join us," Hans shouted as he and Trey passed. Bonnie, in uniform, was sitting in the chair next to Aariah.

"Can't," she said. "I just came to check on you guys."

Bonnie was still standing beside Aariah's lounge chair their next time around. "The surveillance system is still out," she said as the men passed by. "They can't figure it out."

One lap later, Aariah was alone again. The few passengers who had been walking or jogging had thinned to only two or three by then. Aariah was engrossed in her book again. She looked up. "When you're ready to cool off, I'll walk with you."

"Okay," Trey said, and once again the men pounded around the ship.

They ran for ten more minutes when Hans said, "Trey, you've picked up the pace. This is tough for a big guy."

"It's tough for a not-so-big guy too," Trey responded. "I'm just trying to help keep you in shape for your matches in Sydney."

"This should do it," Hans said with a laugh, and the two men fell silent again.

"One more lap, Aariah," Trey shouted when they passed her a short time later. She smiled and waved.

They didn't see anyone else still outside on that final lap. As they pounded up the deck, Trey felt a knot of worry form in his stomach when he noted the empty deck chair. "She's not there," he said to Hans. The men rushed forward then stopped beside Aariah's empty deck chair.

The Book of Mormon was lying on the deck three feet in front of the chair. The novel was on the deck the same distance in the opposite direction. The bag was on the chair next to where Aariah had been sitting. "Blood!" Trey inhaled sharply, spotting a few drops just outside the door. "Something's wrong!"

TWELVE

Trey was angry at himself for not staying with Aariah. "Someone took her to hurt me. I should have just walked so she could stay with us." He was fumbling for his phone as he and Hans studied the area, spotting more blood just inside the door.

The captain answered on the first ring. "Captain, it's Trey Shotwell. Aariah is missing."

It was evidence of the tragedies of the day when the captain didn't so much as ask if Trey was sure, he simply asked, "Where are you?"

Trey told him and then added, "There's blood on the floor. I think she's been hurt."

Bonnie and another security officer were the first crew members there. The captain and first officer weren't far behind. A frantic search was launched immediately. Trey was beside himself with worry. And he was angry.

"I want to tear someone's head off," he growled as he and Hans accompanied Bonnie to Aariah's room. Trey carried Aariah's bag with her books in it. Bonnie tapped on the door. There was no answer. She tapped again and put her ear to the door. "I can hear the TV," she said as she inserted a master key and swung the door open.

Charlotte Bray, her white hair mussed, was sitting on the sofa, leaning back, a pillow behind her head, her eyes closed. Bonnie was the first one to reach her. She touched the old lady's forehead, and Charlotte's eyes sprang open. She gasped, but Trey said, "It's all right, Mrs. Bray. We just wanted to make sure you were okay."

"What did I do?" she asked. Then she answered her own question. "I fell asleep on the sofa. I was watching the TV. Where's Aariah?" Her eyes darted from one to the other of the three. "She isn't with you." Panic filled her eyes, and she put a hand to her mouth, muffling her next words. "Something has happened to her. Where is she?"

"We aren't sure where she is right now, but we're looking," Bonnie said. "Don't worry. We were just making sure you were okay."

"Well, I am worried," Charlotte said, angrily struggling to her feet. "I need to help find her."

"No, you stay here," Bonnie said. "It's late, and you need your rest."

"As if I can rest now," she huffed. "Go then. Find my granddaughter."

"We'll check on you every little while until Aariah is back," Bonnie promised as she and Hans moved toward the door.

Trey laid the bag of books on the small desk and started to follow them, but Charlotte suddenly said, "No, don't you go too, Trey. Please, stay here with me. Please, please don't go. I'm afraid to be alone."

Bonnie looked at Trey and nodded. "Why don't you stay," she said.

Trey took a deep breath. "Okay, but keep me informed." The last thing he wanted to do was be sidelined while others looked for the girl he had become so fond of, but he didn't have the heart to leave that same special girl's grandmother alone and afraid. After the others had gone, Trey reassured Charlotte, "I'm sure Aariah's fine. You should be proud. Your granddaughter is a wonderful person."

"Yes, she is, and despite your religion, you seem like a wonderful young man. Please sit down and let's talk."

Trey was surprised but tried not to let it show. Aariah must have told Charlotte that he was a Mormon. She didn't seem too upset about it though. "What did you want to talk about?" Trey asked, his mind more on Aariah than on her grandmother.

"I want to talk about that Mormon book Aariah has been reading."

Trey retrieved the bag from where he'd placed it when he came in. "This one?" he asked, pulling out the Book of Mormon.

"Yes, that one," Charlotte said with a bit of a frown. "Tell me what it's about."

With an effort Trey forced himself to focus and began to tell her about Joseph Smith and how he had obtained the gold plates and then translated them. Charlotte frowned throughout the entire explanation, but Trey didn't let it bother him. Then he opened the Book of Mormon and said, "Now I'll tell you what it contains."

He'd been talking for about ten minutes when there was a tap on the door. Trey sat the book down, darted over, and looked through the peephole. What he saw caused his heart to miss a beat. He swung the door open, and Aariah fell into his arms, sobbing. He quickly pulled her inside and slammed the door shut with his foot. She clung to him, and he stood there, relishing her closeness and the gentle smell of her perfume. She was trembling, but gradually she became a little calmer.

Charlotte patted her granddaughter's shoulder. "Aariah, are you okay, dear?"

Aariah shifted her head slightly from Trey's chest and said in a soft voice, "I'm fine now, Grandmother."

"You don't look fine. There's blood on your face," Charlotte said, her voice choked with worry. "We need to tend to your injuries."

Aariah pulled slowly away from Trey, and he got a good look at her face. There was blood smeared on it, but he didn't see any cuts. He held her hands up. They too were covered with blood, dried blood. He couldn't see where she was bleeding.

Charlotte also looked her over closely. Then she asked, "Where are you hurting?"

"I'm okay. But I'm afraid for Trey. Trey, they hate you. Your life is in danger. We can't let them hurt you." She choked up and once again melted into his arms.

"You like this young man a lot, don't you, Aariah?" her grandmother said with unmistakable tenderness Trey had not heard before. "Who is he in danger from?"

Again, Aariah pulled away from him and said, "I don't know, but they sent this." She pulled a paper from the front pocket of her jeans and handed it to Trey. "I better go wash the blood off my hands and face," she said, suddenly appearing self-conscious.

"And change your clothes, my dear," Charlotte added. "They're bloody too. Then you can tell us what happened."

"No, let me tell you first," she insisted.

Trey and Charlotte listened as she recited the events of the past hour or so. When she finished, Trey's head was spinning.

"I'll go clean up now," she said after a moment of silence.

Trey watched her head for the bathroom to clean up and change clothes. Then he looked at the paper she'd handed him. He set it down without reading it and put his hands over his eyes. It had been a difficult day. Aariah was safe now, for which he was very, very grateful, but his father was gone. The pain of that loss sucked the energy from him.

Charlotte stepped over to him. "It gets better, Trey. I still mourn for my husband, but the pain isn't as bad as it was."

Trey looked up at her. Despite himself he began to sob. He wasn't able to say a thing.

Charlotte continued to stand beside him. "I'm so sorry, Trey," she said.

After a couple of minutes, Trey got his emotions under control again and said, "Thank you."

The old woman smiled. "Should we see what that paper says?" she asked, pointing to where Trey had put it down.

"I guess we should." He stood and picked it up. The note had been folded over four times. It was printed on a standard piece of computer paper. All Aariah had said was that it was a threat. He stared at it, skimmed through it, and then read it more slowly, his hands trembling. *Trey Shotwell, your life is not worth anything. You are the product of greedy, evil parents who have paid for their misdeeds, and you also need to be removed from the face of the earth before you pollute it more. This is not a warning. It is a notice of your impending death. Prepare to die!*

Trey moved to the chair he'd been sitting on only a moment ago and sank down again, still staring at the note. Finally he shook his head and said, "I better let them know she's here." He pulled out his phone and dialed the captain's cell phone.

"This is Captain Johnsen," the captain said only seconds later. "What do you need, Detective?"

"Aariah's safe. She's in her room with me and her grandmother," Trey reported robotically.

"Detective, I can tell from your voice that something's wrong. May I talk to Aariah?" the captain asked.

"She's in the bathroom cleaning the blood off her face and hands and changing her clothes," he responded.

"I'm on my way to the stateroom. Tell me the number again."

"It's number 1086," Trey said.

"Stay there and I'll join you shortly."

When the tap came on the door, Trey again looked through the peephole. The captain wasn't alone—Hans and Bonnie stood with him. Trey opened the door and invited them in. "Is she still cleaning up?" Captain Johnsen asked.

"Yes," he said. "I think she'll be out in a moment."

"Where has she been?" Bonnie asked.

Trey shook his head. "I'll let her tell you. But she doesn't appear to be hurt." Trey had gotten himself under control again. The fear the note had instilled in him had turned to a slow-burning anger, not because of the threat to him but for the terrible things it said about his honest, hardworking, *murdered* parents. He still held the note in his hand and handed it to Captain Johnsen. "Here, look at this. She gave it to me. It's from whoever had her."

They all crowded into the room, closing the door behind them. The captain then read the note, his face going dark with wrath. He then handed it to Bonnie. She and Hans read it together. Then all three of them stared at Trey, who had again hidden his face in his hands.

Charlotte was sitting on the sofa, her hands folded on her lap. "May I read the note?" she asked.

"We've already gotten too many fingerprints on it," Trey said, realizing he hadn't been as careful with it as he should have been. But he said, "I'll hold it for you, and you may read it."

The old woman read as Trey held the note. Her face, which was already pale, went chalk white. "Did your parents have enemies?" she asked with a trembling voice as she looked up at Trey.

"It appears so, but I didn't know it," he said. "They were wonderful people."

Just then, Aariah joined them. The blood was gone, her golden hair was neatly brushed, and she had on fresh white slacks and a lime-green blouse. She forced a small smile. "Hello, everyone," she said. "Did you all read that terrible note?"

Trey stepped beside her and put a protective arm around her shoulders. "We've all read it," he said. "But it's a lot of hot air."

"They mean it, Trey," Aariah said. "You've got to be careful."

"I will be, I promise," he said, even though he knew that wasn't entirely true. If he were truly to *be careful*, he would go into hiding somewhere until this lunatic was caught. But that wasn't his style. He owed his best effort to his father and mother. He had every intention of pursuing whoever was behind these evil deeds. He'd use caution, but he wouldn't hide.

"Miss Stanton, can you tell us where you've been and who you were with?" Captain Johnsen asked.

Aariah nodded. "Should we all sit down?" She curled her legs beneath her on the bed and patted the mattress beside her. Trey sat where she indicated. Charlotte moved to one end of the sofa, and Bonnie joined her there. The captain sat on the desk chair while Hans brought a chair in from the deck and planted his huge frame on it.

"Okay," Aariah said when everyone was settled. "Here's what happened." She took hold of Trey's hand as she spoke. He squeezed gently, and their eyes met. "After Trey and Hans went past me that last time, I watched until they were out of sight near the front of the ship."

She paused.

"I was going to put my books back in my bag, but just then the door opened." She turned to the captain. "I was sitting on the deck chair closest to the door that leads back into the ship. It's on the port side." He nodded an acknowledgment, and she went on. "Two people came through the door."

"Who were they?" the captain asked.

She looked him in the eye again and shook her head. "I don't know. They were wearing black hoods over their faces, black gloves, and black pants and shirts, or rather, jackets. They were loose fitting. One of them could have been the one I saw out in the hallway, the one who hit me earlier."

"My father's killer," Trey muttered.

"Yes, that's what I meant," Aariah said.

"Men or women or one of each?" Captain Johnsen asked.

"I don't know that either. The jackets were so loose I couldn't tell. Anyway, they grabbed me. I tried to keep hold of the books, but one of them swatted my hand, and when they did, the same hand struck my nose and it started to bleed. That's where all the blood came from."

"Tell them what happened next," Trey pressed.

"I tried to scream, but one of them clamped my mouth shut, and the other one grabbed both my arms and pushed me through the door.

I tried to bite the hand that was over my mouth, but then that person shoved a rag in my mouth, nearly gagging me. I was kicking as much as I could, but then one of them held up a piece of white paper with large letters typed on it. It read, *Don't fight us, and we won't hurt you.*"

"What happened to that paper?" Trey asked.

She shook her head. "I don't know. Maybe he put it back in his pocket."

"Did you quit struggling then?" Trey asked.

"Yes, I wasn't accomplishing anything anyway. They still didn't talk to me, just held me by the arms and pulled me into the restroom near the door."

"Men's or women's?" Bonnie asked.

"Oh, it was the men's," she said. "Anyway, I was shown a second note. It read, *You are to take a message to Trey Shotwell. If you behave, we'll let you go.* That might not be word for word, but it's close."

"Not a word was spoken by either one of them? That's what you told me earlier, right?" Trey asked.

"That's right. Maybe they thought I'd recognize their voices."

"I understand. So what happened then?" the captain pressed.

"I thought they would let me go right then, but they didn't. Instead, they shoved me in a stall, tied my hands and legs together and then tied me to the toilet. Then one of them shoved that note in my pocket," she said, nodding toward the threatening paper Trey had set on the bed. "They left me sitting like that, and both of them went out of the stall and shut it."

"They still hadn't spoken?" Bonnie asked.

"That's right. Still not a word," she confirmed.

"Then they left the restroom," Trey prompted.

"I think so. For a long time I just sat there and listened for them. I was afraid they'd come back. I guess I expected them to, because they'd told me I was supposed to take a message to you, and I couldn't very well do that tied up and all."

"Unless they expected that sooner or later someone would find you and then you'd be able to get the message to me," Trey said.

"That's what I was hoping. Anyway, someone came in a few minutes later and shouted my name. I couldn't answer, and whoever it was left again," she said.

"Sloppy searching," the captain growled. "I guess I need to do some training. You should have been found right then."

She nodded. "But after a little while, I realized I needed to quit feeling sorry for myself and see if I could get myself untied."

"And you did," Trey said, forcing a gentle smile for her benefit.

"Yes, but it wasn't easy. I was tied with strips of sheets. I guess they had them when they grabbed me. Maybe they both had their pockets filled. When I got to looking down at the knots I could see, I thought they didn't look too tight. Like I said, I was sitting on the . . . ah, toilet, with my hands tied in front of me," she said, demonstrating by clasping her hands together. "My legs were tied together and then tied around the bottom of the toilet. Another strip of sheet was around my stomach and arms and also tied around the toilet. After a few minutes, I was able to get my hands out from under that strip of cloth that went around the toilet, and then with my teeth, I pulled the knot on my hands loose."

"And all the while you had a cloth stuffed in your mouth?" Bonnie asked.

"No. Once my hands were free, I grabbed the rag and pulled it out. It had been choking me, and I kept thinking it was going to make me throw up." She shuddered, but then she went on. "It wasn't very big. It was a small white hankie. Anyway, once it was out of my mouth and I wasn't afraid of choking, I used my teeth to pull the knots loose on my hands. It took a few minutes, but like I said, they weren't terribly tight. Once my hands were untied, I was able to work on the rest of the knots."

"How long did it take you?" Trey asked.

"A little while," she said. "The knots on my legs were a lot tighter, and I had to stoop over to reach them. That part was slow. I guess it was at least fifteen minutes or more."

The captain said, "Did you leave all the pieces of cloth there?"

"Yes, I just dropped them by the toilet as I got them loose," Aariah answered.

"Bonnie, go get them," he ordered the security officer.

"Yes, sir," she said, and left immediately.

"Was your nose still bleeding?" Trey asked.

"No, and I wasn't worrying about it. There was blood on my hands and face, but I didn't take time to clean up, as you saw. I did read the note they shoved in my pocket. Then I just got out of the restroom and headed to my room as fast as I could. I had to warn you."

"Did you see anyone while you were coming up?" Trey asked.

"No, I used the stairs, and I ran as fast as I could. But then I remembered that my card was in my bag, so I couldn't open the door. I see you brought that up." She gestured to the bag Trey had dropped on the bed. "I was hoping I could wake Grandmother up. She sleeps pretty soundly once she falls to sleep. I was so relieved, and surprised, when it was you that opened the door. Thank you for being here, Trey."

"Thank your grandmother. She's the one who insisted I stay with her," Trey admitted.

"I was afraid to be alone after I found out you were missing," Charlotte explained.

It was only a couple minutes before Bonnie returned—empty-handed. "There's nothing there, Captain," she reported. "No strips of cloth and no blood that I could see."

"They must have gone back, and when they found that she was loose, they cleaned up behind her," the captain said, shaking his head.

Aariah turned to Trey again. "We've got to keep you safe," she said, her eyes misting and her voice full of emotion. "I care a lot about you."

He might have told her the same thing, but instead he sent her that message with his eyes. She nodded in understanding.

THIRTEEN

WHATEVER THE KILLERS HAD DONE to the surveillance system cameras was beyond the ability of the technicians to repair. They reported to the captain when he called from Aariah's stateroom. After taking the update, the captain said, "They even called and consulted the cruise line's headquarters. At this point, it looks like we'll be without it for a while."

The loss of the camera system was a big blow. People were free to move around the ship with no accountability. It definitely made Trey realize he needed to use extreme care.

Aariah realized it too. "You need to have someone with you all the time."

"She's right, Detective," the captain said. "From now until you leave this ship, I want either Bonnie or Hans to stay with you constantly."

The big Swedish wrestler chuckled. "I always wanted to be a bodyguard."

"I need to go to my room and clean up," Trey said.

"I'm afraid your stateroom is still a bit of a mess," Captain Johnsen said. "I was told by my corporate office to leave it as is until the investigators get a chance to check through it. They would have preferred to have your father's body left there as well, but of course, that wasn't possible. I'm sorry about all this, Detective."

"It's not your fault, but I will need a place to stay," Trey said.

"That will be with your bodyguard." Hans smiled. "I have a spare bed."

"Thanks, Hans, that's great. I'll also need some of my things from the room if possible. My camera's in there. If I take a few pictures of the room first, before I touch anything, then I should be able to get my stuff from the closet and bathroom. It didn't appear to me that the killer went beyond the bedroom anyway."

"That should be all right. Bonnie can go with you and record what you take, if that's okay," the captain said.

"Sure. And I'll even download the pictures to your laptop, Bonnie. That way they'll be available to the investigators," Trey suggested.

The captain agreed, and then he said thoughtfully, "Aariah, I think maybe I'll have Bonnie stay in your room with you and your grandmother. Just because they didn't hurt you this time doesn't mean you might not still be in danger. I'll trust Hans to take care of Trey."

"I will," Hans said soberly.

"Okay. We should probably all get some sleep as soon as possible."

Trey gave Aariah a hug and a very tender kiss before he left her room. When he was stepping through the door, Charlotte called after him. "Trey, you and I were having a serious discussion before. I expect to finish that sometime. Will you promise me?"

"You have my word," he said as Aariah looked at him with a question in her eyes. "She can explain, Aariah. I need to go."

Stepping into the room he'd shared with his father brought a sharp pang of anguish to Trey's heart. For a moment, he just stood staring at where his father had died. They had shared some great hours in this room. His friend said nothing as Trey wrestled with his emotions. Finally he went to work gathering up his things. All he wanted to do was get out of this room as quickly as he could. After he had his baggage moved to Hans's room, Trey needed to make a call halfway around the world.

* * *

After hanging up the phone, Detective Inspector Willie Denning rubbed his chin thoughtfully. He read the notes he had taken while talking with his Australian colleague. From what Trey had told him, it seemed likely that whoever had killed Rita Shotwell ten years before had killed again. That being the case, the killers were on the cruise ship with Trey. Willie spent the next five minutes locating a phone number to the corporate headquarters of the cruise line Trey was sailing on. Next he talked to his supervisor, who knew all about the murder of Rita Shotwell. It didn't take much to convince him to let Willie catch a plane to Auckland, New Zealand, where he had already been promised a helicopter flight to the cruise ship. There, working with investigators from the cruise line, he hoped to solve the case and make the appropriate arrests. While a secretary made his travel arrangements, Willie went back to his office.

He had been busy for the past few hours, ever since he'd talked to Trey earlier in the day. With the assistance of several other officers, he had learned a lot about Rita Shotwell's younger brother—and none of it was good. He held a picture of the man in his hand. Lukas Nichols stood about eight inches over five feet. He was chubby, and although he was only in his forties, his dark-brown hair already had gray showing in it. His beard was dark and pointy, and he wore a narrow mustache. His eyes were brown and set close together in his round face.

Willie had spoken to a number of people who knew Lukas, and every one of them agreed that Lukas considered himself a dapper man, elegant in dress and manner, but they all considered him lazy as an old dog. No one claimed him as a friend, just an acquaintance. He always flashed money around, but no one seemed to know where it came from.

One person Detective Inspector Denning had been unable to speak with was the woman people described as his occasional girlfriend. Laying the picture of Lukas aside, Willie picked up a photo he had obtained from a local newspaper. Vanie Velman was the daughter of a member of parliament, a prominent man with a great deal of wealth. Vanie had never married, but not because she wasn't an attractive woman. She occasionally championed causes such as global warming, the protection of endangered animals, and other things that managed to put her in the spotlight. The picture Willie now held was taken while she had been at a meeting with her father in which they had both spoken about the dangers of the melting icecap, a subject neither of them had any firsthand knowledge of but which both spoke loudly about, asserting an expertise they did not possess.

The picture in the newspaper had been black and white, but the one the office had faxed to him was in color. She had green eyes, was five-three with a slightly heavy build that she hid nicely with what looked to Willie like expensive designer clothes. She wore her brown hair short but stylishly cut.

He put her picture on top of Lukas's and thought for a moment. He had obtained a phone number for her, but when he'd called, the person who answered—a woman who sounded quite prim and proper—told Willie that Miss Velman was out of the country. When he asked what country she was in, the prim lady said that was a private matter and refused to speak further with him.

Willie sat back in his chair, thinking about what he had learned so far. He felt like he was finally getting somewhere. If Lukas was alone on the cruise, then he wasn't a likely suspect in at least two of the crimes there. Two people had been seen shoving Martin Talley over the edge of the ship. Two people had accosted Trey's friend, Aariah. Yet Trey hadn't identified anyone who might have been on the ship with Lukas or had been seen with him. But Vanie Velman was supposedly out of the country. Willie had a feeling that she was the main source of Lukas's money since she had a wealthy father and he had no job. Willie decided to look further into Vanie's whereabouts.

Another call to the corporate headquarters of the cruise ship netted him the information he sought. Vanie Velman was indeed a passenger on the very ship where all the chaos had occurred. He was tempted to call Trey right then but hesitated. It was very late there, and Trey was probably trying to get some sleep. Still he felt it important for Trey to know that Vanie Velman, the girlfriend of Lukas Nichols, was on the ship.

Having assisted with the Rita Shotwell case and following up on it in the years that passed, Willie had several contacts in the art circles of London. Instead of disturbing Trey, he called one of them. The information he obtained was enlightening. When he confirmed that information from a second contact, he decided he had better call Trey, regardless of the hour. Willie's friend deserved to have the information sooner rather than later.

* * *

Trey was tossing and turning on the bed next to his large Swedish roommate's. Hans was sound asleep, snoring lightly. Trey's phone rang. He grabbed it, slid out of bed, and headed for the deck, hoping not to disturb his sleeping friend. "Hello," he said quietly into the phone.

"Did I wake you?" Willie Denning asked.

"I wish," Trey moaned. "I can't sleep. But I'm assuming since you didn't know that and called me anyway that you have something important for me."

"You read my mind," Willie said with a chuckle. "I do indeed have some information I thought you should have. First, though, I'm now working full-time on your mother's murder."

"That's great," Trey said. "I tell you, Willie, I feel like we're getting close."

"I'm going to get even closer, Trey. I'm flying to Auckland, and from there I'll be taken by helicopter to your ship to work with the officers that the line's corporate office is sending down." Without waiting for a response, he went on. "I know you'll be gone back to Australia by then, but I'll take over for you on the investigation."

"That is good news, Willie," Trey said. "I was torn between leaving the ship and whoever killed my father, and doing my duty as son and heir of my father. Anyway, my mind is in such a state that I'm not sure how productive I can even be."

"You're doing the right thing, Trey," Willie assured him. "Now, there's another reason for my call, the reason I didn't wait for you to get some sleep. We've been working hard here to learn all we could about your uncle, Lukas Nichols."

"You told me quite a bit when we talked a little earlier," Trey said. "I take it you've learned more."

"Have I ever," Willie said. "First, your uncle has a lady friend. Her name is Vanie Velman. Her father is a member of parliament and very wealthy."

"So this Vanie person could be the current source of Lukas's money," Trey deduced.

"That's what I think. Anyway, like her father, Vanie is an animal rights activist and global warming enthusiast. She and Lukas are often seen at art galleries. She's purchased a few paintings over the past few years and claims to be an expert on art."

"Oh my goodness," Trey mumbled. "What a connection."

"I thought so," Willie said.

"So why are you telling me this now?" Trey asked, knowing there was a good reason for the late-night call and that what he'd already learned wasn't it.

"Vanie Velman is out of the country right now," Willie revealed. He paused, and Trey waited breathlessly for the punch line. When it came, it hit him right between the eyes. "Vanie is on your cruise, Trey."

"Describe her to me," Trey said with rising excitement. "She and Lukas are in this together. My father always said he was a no-good, lazy, sleaze of a man."

"I'll do one better than that," Willie said. "I'll e-mail you a copy of a recent picture."

"What's up, Trey?" a deep voice spoke from over his shoulder.

Trey stood and faced Hans, raising one finger on his left hand as he continued to hold his phone to his ear with the right. He quickly concluded his conversation with Willie then ended the call. "That was my friend Willie Denning of New Scotland Yard," he said.

"What's he doing calling at this time of night?" the wrestler asked with a sleepy growl.

"He was dropping a bombshell that he felt couldn't wait, and he was right," Trey announced. "My uncle has a girlfriend whose father is a member of the British Parliament. She's also a wealthy, self-proclaimed connoisseur of art and does in fact frequent art galleries, shows, auctions, and so on in company with my esteemed uncle."

"The inspector couldn't wait a few hours to call with that information?" Hans asked.

Trey shook his head. "Not considering the circumstances. You know, the murders, the thefts of art, and most especially the threat against my life. He felt I should know now that this woman, this Vanie Velman, is a fellow passenger."

"She's on this ship?" Hans asked, his eyes growing wide.

"She's on this ship." Trey nodded. "And I intend to find her." He looked at his watch. "Perhaps we might have better luck finding Lukas as well. He was probably in her stateroom when we couldn't find him. What do you say we do a little sneaking around, my good friend and bodyguard?"

"Let's do it," Hans said with enthusiasm. "Do you know what she looks like?"

"As soon as the e-mail comes from Willie, I will. He's sending a picture," Trey told him.

It was only a matter of minutes before the picture came through. The two men looked closely at the image on Trey's cell phone. "She should be easy enough to recognize," Trey said, noting the green eyes and short brown hair. "Let's go knock on dear old Uncle Lukas's door."

Hans grinned. "I guess if you're going, so am I since I'm the one that has to keep you safe."

There was no response at the door of Lukas's stateroom. "Why am I not surprised?" Trey grumbled.

"So I guess it's back to bed now?" Hans asked.

"I'm afraid not. I just thought of something I want to do before the helicopter that's coming to take Father's body and me to Sydney gets here."

"Your Scotland Yard friend can do it, can't he?" Hans asked.

"Yes, but I don't want to wait that long." Trey was already walking up the hall toward the stairs.

"Let me guess," Hans rumbled. "You want to find out which room this Vanie Velman is in and see if Lukas is with her."

"That's a great idea and we'll get to it, but I have something else in mind. There's a room with a bunch of computers for passengers' use, sort of a computer lab. They even have printers. We'll go there first, and then we'll see about finding Miss Velman and my uncle."

"You're the boss." Hans shrugged. "What do you want to do in the computer lab, get the picture of Miss Velman printed?"

"That too, but I also want to see if I can figure out if the note was printed on one of the printers there," Trey explained. "I don't know if I can tell for sure. It might take a lab to check that out. And we happen to have a lab in Sydney that can do it."

"Won't you need the printers there?" Hans asked.

"No, I'll just take a printed sample from each one and have the lab compare each to my note."

"I see. And if it wasn't printed on one of the ship's computers, then what?"

"It'll only prove it wasn't printed in the computer lab," Trey said. "Then all I'll have done is eliminate those printers. It could still have been printed on the ship, on a private computer or some other one somewhere."

As he suspected, Trey was unable to determine if any of the computers matched his threatening note. He was able to get the same font, so he printed a sheet from each of the several printers. In order to make sure he used all the letters contained in the note, he simply typed the same words. When that was done, he opened his e-mail on one of the computers and printed several copies of Vanie Velman's picture.

Trey was just stapling the papers together and documenting which one came from which printer when his phone rang.

"Detective Shotwell, it's Captain Johnsen," a very tired voice said on the phone. "The helicopter is landing in about ten minutes."

"Oh, shoot," he said. "I needed a little more time."

"To do what?" the captain asked.

Trey quickly explained about Vanie Velman, and then he said, "I was hoping I'd find her and my uncle in her stateroom."

"Others will have to work on that, Detective. You need to get your stuff together and go up to the top of the ship to the helipad. And I'll need you to awaken Miss Stanton and Mrs. Bray too. I'll send some stewards to move the luggage. Just meet my people outside your doors," Captain Johnsen said. "Your father's body is being taken up right now."

"All right," Trey said. "What about the painting you're holding, the one of my mother's?"

"I hadn't thought about that," the captain admitted. "I'll have it sent with you if you want. Is there anything else?"

"Yes, my father had been working on a painting in our room. And his personal effects are still there. What happens to all of that after the investigators are finished in there?"

"After the investigators are through with everything in the room, it will be returned to you."

"Is there any chance I can take the painting now? I plan to finish it myself, and after all that's happened, I don't want to lose it."

The captain didn't respond for a moment. When he did, he said, "I'll have the art directors take both paintings up to the helicopter. All I ask is that you take a picture of the unfinished one and send a copy to me via e-mail or text so I can let the investigators look at it."

"I already photographed it in the room, but I'll do it again and get that to you as well. And thanks for all you've done, Captain," Trey said sincerely.

"And thanks for what you've done as well," the captain responded. "I trust that our big Swedish friend is with you?"

"He's hovering over me as we speak," Trey said, grinning up at Hans.

"Good, then let's get moving. I'll meet you at the helicopter."

After finishing the call, Trey said, "It appears a lot of people are going to be losing sleep tonight." As they headed for Aariah's room, he explained what the captain's call had been about.

"Good," Hans said, quite cheerfully. "Let's get you and your girl off this ship and to safety." He grinned and then added, "So I can get some shut eye."

FOURTEEN

AARIAH HAD BARELY MANAGED TO get to sleep when Trey began pounding on her door. It was Bonnie who opened the door. Trey announced, "The helicopter's almost here. Stewards will be here for the luggage in a minute."

Aariah was rubbing her eyes as she approached Trey and gave him a hug. "How soon do we need to be ready?"

"Five to ten minutes," Trey said. "Hans and I will meet you back here then."

Simon's body was loaded first, then the two paintings, and the luggage went on after that. "This helicopter is huge," Aariah said as she, Trey, and their bodyguards, watched the loading taking place.

Trey forced a grin. "With all that luggage you ladies brought, we needed a big one."

She punched him playfully on the shoulder. "It takes a lot of stuff for women to travel," she responded.

The captain approached them. "Detective, let me know what you learn. I know it's not easy for you, but I'd like to see the autopsy report on your father as soon as you get it."

"I'll see that you do. And Captain, I'll be in close contact with Detective Inspector Denning after he gets on the ship. You'll like him," Trey said. "He's a very capable investigator."

Security Officer Bonnie Springer hugged Aariah, her grandmother, and even Trey. "I'm sorry this trip was such a disaster for the three of you. And Trey, I'm especially sorry about your father."

The art director, Dayton Windle, and his wife and assistant, Coni, finished storing the two pieces of art on the helicopter before they too expressed their condolences to Trey. "I'll get the best price I can for your father's other painting, Detective," Dayton said. "And I promise we'll keep it secure. I'll even sleep in the vault if I have to."

"You won't need to do that, Dayton," the captain said. "I'll keep security on it until it leaves the ship, legally and in perfect shape."

"Thank you, Captain, and you too, Dayton. I'll be in touch," Trey said.

Five minutes later, the large helicopter lifted off, banked steeply to the left, and then headed for its destination in Sydney.

* * *

Three days had passed since their arrival in Sydney. Trey spent most of the time grieving and taking care of his father's affairs. He tried not to dwell on the ongoing investigations. Simon Shotwell was buried on the third day back in Australia. Aariah and her grandmother returned to Melbourne right after the funeral.

Detective Inspector Willie Denning and the three investigators sent by the corporate headquarters were slowly working the homicide cases on the ship without much progress, but Willie had said he'd be in touch if something important came up. Trey hadn't heard from him.

The day after his father's funeral and burial, Trey opened his father's vault and examined his parents' painting journals. He photographed the appropriate pages showing the identifying marks on both the painting Damian possessed in France and the one Damian's wealthy German friend had purchased. Trey believed the one in Germany was one of the ones that had been stolen when his mother was murdered. He also suspected that the one Damian had in France had been stolen at that same time. Both paintings, if they contained the tiny marks his parents had recorded in the journals, would prove to be stolen. Both had the signature of Ainslee Cline, which was all it took to convince Trey that they would, in fact, turn out to be the stolen paintings.

Trey e-mailed the pictures of those journal pages to Ruben Hawk, the former New Scotland Yard inspector who'd been retained in his capacity as the head of a private investigation firm by Damian. The one thing Trey had done prior to the funeral was to take the pages he'd printed on the cruise ship and personally deliver them to the crime lab for analysis.

Trey missed his father fiercely. The two had become close during the years they'd been in Australia, and the few days on the ship had further strengthened that friendship. It would be a long time before the aching in his heart eased.

Aariah hadn't been gone but a few hours when Trey realized how much he already missed her. He had been shocked when he realized how important she had become to him in such a short time. But even though she'd wanted to stay with him in Sydney, she felt obligated to return to Melbourne with her grandmother. He'd had a hard time sleeping after she left, his restless mind on Aariah as well as on his dead parents. He was more determined than ever to find the perpetrators of those heinous crimes and bring them to justice.

Even though his vacation time hadn't been anywhere near used up, he was allowed to go back to work the morning of his fifth day back in Australia. So far it had been a busy day. Back at his desk in Sydney, Trey spent the morning going over everything he knew about the thefts and the murders. He carefully organized his notes and studied them for clues he might have overlooked. He thought about the ideas, farfetched though they were, that he had discussed with Aariah on the ship. The more he thought about them, the less farfetched they seemed.

Shortly after noon, he got a call from the lab about the printed pages he had submitted for comparison. The ink on the threatening note was the same as that on one of his test pages. The author of the note had used a computer and printer in the ship's computer lab.

That prompted Trey to call Detective Inspector Denning on board the cruise ship. "Willie," he said when his friend answered the phone, "how are things going there?"

"Slow," Willie said. "Have you returned to work at your department?"

"I have, and I have some information for you," Trey reported. "The threatening note Aariah's captors gave her was printed on one of the printers in the computer lab."

"That's good to know, but I'm not sure how it'll help," the New Scotland Yard detective said.

"Maybe it won't, but if it was before the surveillance system was brought down the second time, it might be possible to see who might have used that printer," he suggested.

"Lots of people could have used that printer," Willie reminded him.

"But it could also be one of the people who might be a person of interest. Could you check for me?" Trey asked.

"I'm afraid that's not possible right now," Willie reported. "Whoever took the system down did a thorough job of it. Until new equipment arrives at our next port of call in New Zealand, the system will continue to be down."

"Once that new equipment is installed, it should be possible to recover at least some of the past footage, right?" Trey asked.

"I asked the technicians on the ship about that. They don't think so. They think everything was wiped clean," Willie said.

"They said that? I doubt it very much," Trey responded. "Experts can usually recover quite a bit from a computer hard drive no matter how much erasing has been done. And that's where all the camera footage would have been."

"These guys on the ship probably aren't the best experts around," Willie admitted. "I hope you're right, but it'll be a while before we know."

"If those guys can't do it with the new equipment, get it to me here in Sydney. We have people here who can do it," Trey said.

"It may come to that," Willie agreed.

Trey tapped his pen on his desk for a moment. "You told me earlier that you were going to question Lukas. I know you said you'd only get back with me if you had something important to report. I guess there's nothing?"

"I talked to Lukas," Willie responded. "He insists he has no hard feelings toward you or your father. He claims to have been brokenhearted when your mother was murdered."

"Do you believe him?" Trey asked.

"No. I need proof, but I don't have any."

"What about Vanie Velman?" Trey said.

"She and Lukas are definitely a couple even though they have separate staterooms. They claim to have been in one of the bars around the time your father was killed."

"Are there any witnesses that can confirm that?"

"Lukas and Vanie claim they'd been drinking heavily and weren't sure which bar or lounge they were in. Several bartenders remember seeing them at various times, and we even found a couple of other passengers who claim to have seen them, but no one can be specific on the times," Willie said. "In my mind, they're viable suspects, but we need a lot more to make arrests."

"What about when my mother was killed?" Trey asked.

"Lukas is very vague about that. He claims he hadn't been around your family's home for a long time, but again, since it was ten years ago, he's unable to establish an alibi. We know he can't have been too far away because he showed up at the cemetery."

"What about Vanie?" Trey asked.

"Same thing, but some of my colleagues are pursuing that in London. It's all we can do," Willie said. "Now, there's something else I was going to call you about. Yesterday, two passengers who had gotten off the ship for the day, failed to come back last evening."

"Anyone I know?" Trey asked as he felt the hair rise on the back of his neck.

"I am afraid so. Victor Krause and Claudia Gaudet," Willie said. "We've asked the local New Zealand Police to look for them. They haven't had any relevant accidents reported. And they haven't been contacted about anyone missing the ship."

"Did they take bags with them? You know, something that might have had at least a day's worth of clothes."

"Most of their luggage is in the room, but they did have some small bags with them according to the staff members who checked people off the ship. Victor and Claudia were supposed to catch a bus, but they didn't. One of the other passengers said there was a taxi waiting for them, and they left in it before the bus pulled away from the port," Willie reported.

"I don't like the sound of it," Trey said. "We need to learn more about those two. I can't help but wonder if they had some kind of dealings with my father or mother sometime in the past. My father didn't mention it if they did, but I'm sure there's a lot I don't know about him and the people he associated with over the years."

"I wondered the same thing. I agree we need to learn more about them. We have investigators working on that too. And Inspector Hawk told me his agency is pursuing that angle as well."

The two officers talked for a couple more minutes and then terminated the call.

Late that evening, Trey received a call from Ruben Hawk. He had a report for Trey.

"Detective," Inspector Hawk began, "it took a while, but I finally got a look at both of the paintings in question. The owner of the one in Germany was out of the country, and no one else was able to let me see his painting. He finally returned last night, and I examined it closely. As you told me, the signature on it is Ainslee Cline. The photos of the journal pages you sent me list three distinct marks your father painted into the picture. Two of the three are still there. It appears that the thief painted over the third one. But we had enough to request that the painting be seized by German authorities."

"Thank you, Inspector," Trey said. "What about the one Damian Latimer has in his collection in France?"

"I looked at that one yesterday morning before flying to Germany. It was painted by your mother. There's no question about that, and it's now in the hands of French authorities," he said. "Damian has been extremely helpful. And he tells me he plans to outbid all others and get the other painting of your father's that's coming up for auction on the ship."

"I believe he will. The other one he bought was stolen, and I know how much he wants another of Father's paintings; otherwise I would have brought that one back to Sydney with me. But I want him to have it, so I left it on consignment. I also have the one Father was painting on the ship. It won't take much for me to finish it, and when I do, I'll give it to Damian. It's the least I can do for all the expense he's going to. Anyway, what's your next move, Inspector?" Trey asked.

"I'm going to try to locate Ainslee Cline," Hawk said. "Of course, that's probably not her real name. Who knows, it might not even be a woman. But whoever it is has several paintings that are pretty decent, most of them in the London area. Finding out who that person is won't be easy. But Damian has instructed me to spare no expense, so I and my people intend to pursue it until we find the suspect."

"I was talking a little earlier to Detective Denning. He told me that you're going to see if you can find any connections with my parents, Victor Krause, and Claudia Gaudet," Trey said. "I asked my father if he knew them, but he didn't answer at the time and was acting . . . well, a little strange. I was going to ask him again later, but I never got around to it."

"I've had a couple of my agents working on that. We have yet to find a connection, but we have learned something interesting. Claudia has a seething hatred of my client, Damian. It turns out she has a brother who owned quite a large estate in a rural area in the south of France. He got in a bit of financial trouble, and Damian bought the property to help the bloke out."

"That doesn't sound like something to hate someone for. Anyone with enough money could have bought it."

"That's true, but Damian later sold it to, now get this, Claudia's ex-husband. She hates the guy and is convinced Damian did it just to make her angry."

"Did he?" Trey asked.

"I don't think so. He claims he didn't even know the ex-husband before the sale," Hawk said. "He had no idea he was selling it to someone who would make Mrs. Gaudet angry."

"Did he know Claudia at the time?" Trey asked.

The inspector chuckled. "Yes, as a matter of fact, he had met her at a party at one of his cousin's homes. He also outbid her on a couple of paintings at art auctions in France. One of the paintings was one your father did. She apparently hates him for that as well. So there's bad blood between Claudia and Damian over those two issues."

"I assume this all happened after my mother died?"

"Some did," Inspector Hawk responded. "But he outbid her at an auction in Germany about a year before your mother was killed. So it is conceivable that she could be responsible for the paintings stolen from your parents' house and your mother's murder. She could have hired someone. Frankly, I don't think that is the case. Now, if *Damian* had been murdered, then I'd suspect her." Hawk chuckled.

"So she doesn't like Damian, and maybe she wanted to steal the paintings to spite him, but I don't see how that would make her hate my father."

"I'm not sure she does, but there could be a more sinister motive. I suppose she could have such a warped fixation on Simon's work that she simply wanted him removed so no one else could buy any of his paintings in the future. I've heard stranger motives for murder," the inspector said.

"So have I," Trey agreed, "but I have a hard time with that one. Where does Krause come in?"

"That we don't know yet, but we're working on it. And that, my friend, is all I have for you at the moment."

Trey quit for the night and went to his apartment. He heated a can of soup for dinner and then brought out the painting his father had been working on just before he was killed. Trey studied it for a long time. Looking at the distinctive brushstrokes made his heart ache for his father. He intended to finish it and then put both his signature and his father's on it, but as he studied it, he felt very inadequate. He was still looking at it, trying to decide how to go about finishing the painting in a way that wouldn't detract from his father's work when his phone rang.

"I'm lonely," the voice of the girl he adored came into his ear.

"Me too," he said. "How's your grandmother?"

"She misses you too. She's reading my Book of Mormon. I didn't think that would ever happen. You had quite an effect on her. She really likes you."

"I like her too. Please tell her for me," Trey said.

"I will," she promised. "How are you doing, Trey? I know you must be having a hard time with your father gone."

"I'm just taking it day by day. I was just looking at the painting he was doing on the ship. I can't stand the thought that he'll never be able to put a brush to a canvas again. No one can ever replace him." He felt his emotions bubbling to the surface.

"I'm sorry, and I know you are right; although you'll come closer than anyone else. How's the investigation coming?" she asked. They had talked once or twice a day since arriving back in Australia, and each time she asked that question. He was touched that she cared so much.

He told her what he could, not mentioning the missing passengers. He was feeling some discomfort over that. He kept thinking of the threatening note he'd received and asked himself several times if it might have been written by those two. He knew that if he mentioned it to Aariah, she would worry too, and he didn't want her to. He sure wished the camera system was working again.

They talked for a long time before his phone beeped, alerting him that he had another call coming in. When he saw who it was from, he said, "Aariah, I have another call. It's from Willie Denning. I think I better take it."

"Let me know what it's about," she said. "Call me back when you finish talking to him."

"I'll do that," he promised. Then he took Willie's call. "Hey, Willie, what's happening? I hope you have some good news for me."

"I'm afraid I don't," the Scotland Yard officer said. "I'm afraid it's bad news."

"Don't tell me my father's other painting has been stolen," Trey said with an uncomfortable twist in his gut.

"The captain just contacted me. In fact, I'm in his cabin right now."

"Get to it. My stomach can't take the suspense."

"Two more passengers are missing. Just like yesterday, two people failed to come back on board this evening."

"Who?" Trey asked with increasing trepidation.

"Lukas and Vanie," Willie said.

Trey broke out in a cold sweat. "You've got to be kidding."

"I wish I was."

"Has anyone checked their staterooms to see if they took anything that might indicate they were planning on leaving?"

"We have. Most of their clothes and so on are still on the ship, but they were both carrying small bags when they left to go catch a tour bus this morning."

"Did they catch the bus?" Trey asked as he wiped the perspiration from his brow.

"Yes, and they were on it all day, until the last stop. They didn't show up that time. The bus driver waited a few minutes, but he couldn't wait too long or the rest of the passengers on the bus would miss the ship themselves. The driver told the police on shore that he assumed they'd found their own way back to the port. That happens all the time; people change their minds and find their own way back to the ship. But Lukas and Vanie never did get on the ship. And again, there are no accidents or anything else that the cops were able to discover to explain why they might not have made it," Willie said.

"Just like yesterday," Trey said morosely.

"Almost, except that Lukas and Vanie *did* go on their scheduled tour. They just didn't finish it. Trey, you need to be very vigilant. Who knows where all these AWOL passengers are going or what they have in mind. Don't forget the threat on your life."

"Believe me, I haven't," Trey said. Both men were silent for a minute, but then Trey suddenly said, "I have an idea, Willie. Would it be possible to search their staterooms, of all four of the missing people, I mean? If any of them used the computers and printers in the computer lab, they may have left something in their rooms that I could get to my lab and see if it happens to be the same printer that the threat was printed on."

"What would that accomplish?" Willie asked. "It wouldn't prove anything."

"No, but it might narrow down the suspects."

"Okay, we'll get on it. And, Trey, again, watch yourself."

"I will," Trey promised.

With a heavy mind, he called Aariah back. He wished he hadn't promised he would, but he had.

She answered with worry in her voice. "What did he want?"

"He just wanted me to know that some passengers missed the ship. They stayed in New Zealand," Trey said. "I expect they'll be contacting the ship soon and wondering how they can get back on board."

"Trey, who didn't get back on the ship?" Aariah asked with uncharacteristic firmness. "He wouldn't have called if it hadn't been someone we know."

Trey decided to be honest with her. With his father gone, there was no one he cared for as much as her. He was in danger if any of the four suspects came to Australia, but so was she, even though she was clear over in Melbourne. She had a right to know. "Last night, Claudia Gaudet and Victor Krause never came back."

"Last night?" Aariah asked. "Why did he wait until now to tell you?"

"The ones who disappeared last night were only the first. Tonight a second couple didn't return. This time, it was my uncle and his girlfriend, Vanie Velman," he said.

"They could fly here, to Australia!" Aariah exclaimed with a trembling voice.

"Yes, they could. You've got to be careful. Lock your doors, Aariah, and don't go anyplace alone."

"It's you they are after, not me. And I'm a long way from Sydney. Please, be careful. I'm so scared for you."

"Not any more than I am for you. My carelessness got you hurt on the ship. I can't let that happen again, Aariah. I wonder if it would be safer for you and your grandmother to return to the ship, especially since my uncle and his girlfriend are no longer on it," Trey suggested.

Aariah shot right back with, "There's no way I'm going back. I just wish you were here with us."

"How about if you and your grandmother come to Sydney? You could stay in my father's house, and I could do more to protect you," he said. "It has a state-of-the-art security system."

Aariah was silent for a moment, and then she said, "I would like to be closer to you. Let me talk to Grandmother and see if she would be willing to do that."

"Please talk her into it. I'd even come and get you. I'm worried about you, and I miss you."

"I'll call you back," she promised. "I miss you too."

FIFTEEN

TREY SPENT THE NEXT DAY moving Aariah and Charlotte to Sydney and helping them get settled in his father's huge house. Out of an abundance of caution and at their urging, he moved in as well, but he only brought a few of his things. It was hard for him to make that move; everything about the house reminded him of Simon, and it kept the hurt in his heart from healing as quickly as he wished it would. But the temporary move did make sense. There were enough bedrooms for them all to have one to themselves and more to spare. He couldn't bring himself to sleep in his father's room, and he didn't. The state-of-the-art alarm system Simon had installed a couple of years back made all three of them feel safer.

Once they were settled in, Trey began to go through some of his father's papers with Aariah's help and comforting company. As he expected, most of it was stuff that simply needed to be discarded. He did find a copy of his father's trust, but he'd already spoken to the solicitor about that. He put it back. When he came to a file marked *Lukas*, Trey had a feeling he might find something important. With all the bad blood that had existed, he was surprised his father would keep anything about the man. The fact that he did was what caused Trey to go carefully through the file.

More than half the papers were IOUs signed by Lukas for money he had received from Trey's mother, Rita. Not one of them had been marked paid. Trey didn't doubt that nothing had been repaid, but he did wonder why his father hadn't mentioned that the money given to Lukas had been recorded. He'd always been under the impression that his mother had simply given Lukas money with no strings attached, but that wasn't the case.

"How much money do you think she lent him?" Aariah asked as they thumbed through the IOUs.

"Let's find out. I'll read the amounts, and you add them up on the calculator."

So they did, and when they finished, the total, when translated by Aariah from British pounds to American dollars, was slightly in excess of an astounding $350,000.

Trey whistled when Aariah told him the total. "Wow. That guy really did take my folks for a lot of money."

"Yeah, and he apparently promised to pay it all back." Aariah gestured to the IOUs.

"I don't think he ever intended to pay any of it back," Trey said. "I certainly don't think Father expected to get it. And I know he didn't need it. So if he ever attempted to get Lukas to repay him, it would have only been because it was the right thing to do."

"Well, I guess with your father gone, the debt is erased. How is that for a motive, Detective Shotwell?" Aariah asked with a glint in her eyes. "A 350,000-American-dollar motive."

Trey suddenly felt himself go pale.

"What is it?" Aariah asked in alarm.

"I'm Father's sole heir. I'd have to look at Father's trust a little closer and maybe talk to his solicitor again, but I'm almost positive that I inherited not only his possessions but also anything owed by creditors. So it could be that Uncle Lukas owes me the money."

Aariah went white. "So maybe he killed your father over the debt but knows that now he has to get rid of you too."

"Hence the death threat," Trey added ominously. "Okay, so we know about the debts; let's see what else is in here."

A thick letter-sized envelope with an inscription on the front was the next item of interest. "This must be something to do with my maternal grandparents," Trey said. "When my grandparents died, my parents spent quite a bit of time in court over the estate. I was only seven or eight at the time, so I don't really remember much else."

He opened the envelope and carefully removed the contents. It was a photo copy of an original that Trey suspected he was yet to find in his father's papers. It was several pages long, so he skimmed through it as Aariah watched him closely.

"What does it say?" she asked when he finally set it down on the table in front of him.

"My grandparents disinherited Lukas," he said. "He got nothing from the estate. Nothing."

"Does it say why?" she asked.

"Well, yes, I guess it does in a way. There's reference to the fact that he'd already pilfered more than his share before this document was drawn up. I guess he'd stolen from his own parents," Trey said sadly. "What scum he is."

"More motive for killing your father," Aariah stated flatly.

"Yes, and my mother, even though I don't think either of them had anything to do with this. My grandparents disinherited him, not my parents." Trey had picked up the photocopied document and shook it gently for emphasis. "But he probably doesn't believe that, so he stole the paintings, justifying it in his own mind as repayment for the fact that he got nothing from the estate. And he killed my mother in the process." He paused thoughtfully for a moment. "It makes me wonder about my grandparents' deaths. I was young then and don't remember much about it, but I can't help but wonder if they might have died under less than ordinary circumstances."

"You think it was him then, that he's the one?" Aariah asked.

"Don't you?" he asked in return.

"Yes, and now he's coming after you." She was still pale, and her hands shook. "Trey, what are you going to do?"

"I'm going to see what else is in here," he said with more calmness than he was feeling inside. He set the document down and pulled another one from the same envelope. He looked at it, read it, and then said, "This is a letter from Lukas, demanding that my parents pay him half the value of the estate. It's dated just a couple months before Mother's murder."

She nodded numbly. Trey retrieved the final paper from the large envelope and read it. "And this, Aariah, is my mother's answer to him. She told him in so many words that since he'd already stolen more than half the original estate that he had his share and that she didn't want to hear from him again."

"Trey, he's coming here after you. You've got to leave until he's caught. Surely there's enough here to get a warrant for him, isn't there?"

"This only goes to motive. If this was enough, I think my father would have already had him arrested. But I don't think it is. We've got to have more than what we've found here. Let's see what else is in the file." Trey returned the documents to the envelope and then began to examine further papers. A couple of them seemed innocuous, so he just shifted them to the pile he had already checked. But another gave him serious pause. "This is a letter from Father to Lukas," he said. "Actually, it's a copy of a letter." He read it through, his blood pressure rising.

"What does it say?" Aariah asked.

"This letter was written about six months ago," Trey responded. "My father says that he's decided to call in the debts, the IOUs. He demanded that Lukas contact him and set up a repayment schedule. There is nothing in the letter that explains why he decided to do that now. Let's see if there's a response from Lukas."

He found one, and it wasn't pretty. A letter from Lukas back to Simon was short: *Simon, who do you think you're kidding? You aren't going to get a single thing back from me. As you well know, you still owe me. So get off my back, or you'll wish you had. Lukas.*

After reading it to Aariah, Trey said, "I don't understand why my father didn't tell me he had demanded repayment of the money."

"Have you looked at that last paper?" Aariah asked, pointing her finger to the last one from that file.

"No, but I can't imagine how this could be any worse," he said, making no move to pick it up.

Aariah reached in front of him. "Do you mind if I look at it?"

"Go ahead," he said. His mind was trying to wrap itself around what he had learned from this one astonishing file.

She picked the paper up, unfolded it, and began to read. Trey turned his head toward her. He hadn't thought she could go any paler, but she did. "What is it, Aariah?" he asked.

She handed it to him. "I think it's the answer to your question. I think it explains why your father called in Lukas's loans."

Trey read it. Then he nodded his head. "Lukas wanted two hundred thousand British pounds from Father. He didn't even ask; he demanded," he said. "This is too much. My poor father. Can you imagine how he must have felt? I don't blame him for demanding repayment on all those previous loans."

Aariah asked, "Trey, do you think Lukas might have stolen those paintings from the ship?"

Trey shrugged his shoulders. "Who knows," he said. "And if he did, where are they?"

"Remember what you said to me on the ship?" Aariah asked. "You told me what you think may have happened to them. Maybe you were onto something."

"I have some investigating to do, don't I?" was Trey's response.

* * *

The next morning, Aariah fixed breakfast in Simon's kitchen. "I've got to get to my office even though it's Saturday," Trey said as he began to clear the table. "There's a lot to do. But I'll help with this first."

"We can do the dishes, Trey," Charlotte said firmly but with a smile.

"Yes, you go," Aariah said. "We'll be fine here. And we'll keep the door locked and the security system on, I promise."

"That's not enough," Trey said. "I want to make sure you have some way to protect yourself just in case the need arises, which it probably won't. Do either of you know how to shoot firearms?" he asked.

"We both do," Charlotte answered for the two of them.

"Pistols?"

"Yes," the elderly lady said without hesitation.

"Good. Let me get a couple of my father's pistols out for you." He went to his father's gun locker in a backroom and brought back two pistols. "These are revolvers," he said. "They're easy to use. Do you need me to show you anything?"

"We can handle it, Trey," Aariah said.

Her grandmother, elderly and stooped though she was, nodded in agreement. "Those are .357 magnums. I have one at my house. I'm really quite good with it."

"Great. Here's a box of ammo. You ladies load those pistols and keep them with you. Use them if you have to." He turned to Aariah. "Please keep the doors and windows locked and the alarm system activated. Call me if anything out of the ordinary occurs. Otherwise, I'll be back this evening."

He was on his way to his office when he got a call from Willie Denning aboard the cruise ship. "Good morning, Willie," Trey said. "I hope you're calling to tell me the AWOL passengers have been located."

"I'm afraid not, but I do have something for you. Along with one of the cruise line's investigators, I spent a few minutes with Daphne and Gil Slader this morning. They've been quite cooperative. In fact, they let us check their stateroom out. We didn't find any black clothing. Anyway, today, they dropped a bombshell on me."

Trey wasn't sure how many more bombshells he could endure after what he had learned the night before. "Just a minute, Willie," he said. He shifted in his seat, looked for an opening in the traffic, and pulled to the side of the road. "Okay, what do you have?" he asked.

"They admitted they hadn't planned to buy the Ainslee Cline painting because they already owned it. They're the ones who consigned it to the ship for sale," Willie said.

"Whoa! That is strange. Where did they get it?"

"They claim to have purchased it from—get ready for this—*Victor Krause*."

"The *missing* Victor Krause?" Trey said. "Do they know where he got it?"

"Oh yes, he told them he bought it from your dear Uncle Lukas about a year ago. They said they got it for a good price and figured it might sell for more on the ship," Willie explained. "Anyway, they didn't think anything about the fact that there might be a problem with it until it was pulled from the auction. And then, after buying your painting and studying it, they said they could see some of your mother's traits in your painting. And that, according to Daphne, was when they realized that those same traits appeared in the one you seized."

"Interesting," Trey said. "But Victor isn't where we can question him, is he?"

"So far, at least," Willie agreed. "But we have officers in London working on the matter. Maybe they'll find out where Victor got the painting if it didn't come from your uncle. I also let Inspector Hawk know, and he'll have his agents in France and Germany see what they can dig up about Victor and Lukas and how either of them might have come up with the paintings."

"Okay, well I have something that might give us a clue to that," Trey said. "I think it is very likely Victor got it from Lukas." Then he told Willie what he'd learned about his uncle and the motives.

"Okay, so Victor may have told the truth to the Sladers," Willie said. He was silent for a moment, and then he went on. "I find it interesting that your uncle and Victor are both missing. They didn't abandon the ship at the same port, but they're both in New Zealand. It wouldn't take them long to meet up again and fly to Australia," Willie said. "It's looking more likely that Victor bought the painting from Lukas. I wonder, could Lukas be the shadowy Ainslee Cline? I mean, he is part of a very artistic family, Trey."

"I don't think he can paint," Trey said, but then he considered it for a moment. "Maybe he does paint. My father never gave me an indication that he could, but who knows? My mother painted, and so did her mother. You may be right."

"There's one more thing you need to know," Willie said. "It comes from one of the detectives working the case in London. Martin Talley's close friend and fellow diver, Andrew Remington, left London about two weeks ago."

"Don't tell me he was coming to Australia," Trey said.

"You're a quick study, Trey." Willie laughed. "Yes, and we've confirmed that Remington did in fact arrive in Sydney two days after leaving London. So there's one more element in this whole thing that we need to consider—what is he doing there?"

"I have an idea," Trey said.

"Tell me about it," Willie requested.

For the next couple of minutes, Trey explained his no-longer-so-farfetched idea to Detective Denning. It was an idea he'd discussed with no one but Aariah to this point, but it seemed like something that was actually possible, unlikely as it was. "Keep it to yourself for now," he told Willie. "I might be way off base, but it's worth thinking about."

"Yes, it is. But I'm afraid there's nothing I can do to help you on that," Willie told him. "You and the others from your department will have to work on it."

"I've been cleared to work on nothing but this case, or these cases, as that might be what we have. Anyway, my partner went on vacation the same day I did. We were both off three weeks. I came back early, but he didn't. So I'm working alone for the time being."

"I don't like that," Willie told him. "Your life's in danger."

"As I'm well aware, but it is what it is. I'll be careful, but I intend to do my part to bring these killers to justice," Trey said.

"Oh, there's something else I was supposed to tell you," Willie said. "The painting your father was working on while he was on the ship is no longer considered of importance to the murder investigation. And when it's finished, Damian Latimer tells me he'd love to have it."

Though there were no officers who could be assigned to work full-time with Trey, the police department did make sure that everyone on the force and on other forces in surrounding states was on the lookout for the suspects who were no longer on the cruise ship—as well as the short and wiry British ex-con, Andrew Remington, now believed to be in or around Sydney.

There wasn't a lot more Trey could do to protect himself except be watchful, and he was that. He stopped by his apartment and packed a few more items he thought he might need before heading back to his father's house. He planned to completely move in there eventually, but he felt awkward about doing it so soon after his father's death. Trey put his things in his car and looked at the apartment for a moment. Suddenly, he felt there was something else he needed to do.

He went back inside and entered his small art studio. He gathered up his painting supplies and carried them to the car. Then he did the same with the painting his father had been working on in the ship and a couple he'd been working on before the cruise. Trey thought about a few other things he'd like to take, but the car was full. So he locked up his apartment and headed for the house in one of the more upscale neighborhoods of the city.

The delicious aroma of a simmering kangaroo roast teased his olfactory senses as soon as he opened the door. Aariah heard him come in and met him in the living room.

"That smells like kangaroo," he said.

"It is. We found it in your father's freezer," she said. She reached up, and her lips brushed his lightly. He pulled her into a tight embrace. "I've missed you today," she said.

"And I've missed you," he admitted. He was anxious to let his relationship with Aariah grow, but until he had all the threats resolved, he simply couldn't give her the attention he wanted to. He pulled away and said, "I need to fill you in on what I've learned today. There's more reason than ever for us to be cautious."

· She smiled and nodded. "And we will be. Dinner will be ready in half an hour."

"That'll be just right. I brought some things from my apartment, and I decided that Father's painting should be here rather than there. This house is far more secure than my little apartment."

"You told me you had some of your own paintings there. I think you should bring them too," she said.

"They're in the car," he said. "I'll put them all upstairs in Father's studio."

"If you want to wait until after dinner, I'll help you," she offered.

"I accept," he agreed.

SIXTEEN

THE NEXT MORNING, SUNDAY, TREY announced that he was going to go to church before he followed up on some things at work. "I'd like to come," Aariah said. He was hoping she'd say that, and he was pleased. "But maybe I shouldn't leave Grandma here alone. I guess you better just go." That did not please him.

"You go with your young man," Charlotte said. "And if you two don't mind, I think I might just tag along."

"Really, Grandma?" Aariah asked in total surprise. "I thought you disliked Mormons."

"That was before I met Trey; he told me a little about the Mormons," she said. "I think I've been misled. And you, young man, still have more to tell me."

"And I will, I promise," Trey said.

The three of them walked into the chapel ten minutes early. Even though no one in the church knew his father, the word of his death had spread, and Trey was greeted with sympathetic overtures from everyone he talked to. The ward members fussed over Aariah and her grandmother like they were long-lost friends.

When they got back to the house shortly after noon, Charlotte said, "Trey, I feel so terrible. I misjudged the Mormons. I've never met nicer people. I guess I've learned a lesson in my old age. I shouldn't have listened to all the people who tore down the Mormons without even meeting them. I hope I can go again soon."

"I'll make sure you do," Trey said.

Aariah, so happy she could shout, hugged Trey. "As soon as this is all over, I'd like to begin meeting with the missionaries again."

"When do you think you'll have time to tell me more?" Charlotte asked.

Trey thought about what he'd planned to do that afternoon and decided it could wait. "Why don't I fix us some lunch, and then I'll answer whatever questions either one of you have."

"Didn't you have some work to do?" Aariah asked cautiously.

"Nothing that can't wait until tomorrow."

There were, of course, no objections, and they spent a wonderful afternoon and evening together. Charlotte went to bed early, but Trey and Aariah stayed up late and talked. There was no doubt in his mind about Aariah. He didn't mention to her that he had fallen in love, but he resolved to do so soon.

The next morning, Trey left the ladies armed and alone in his father's house and went back to work. He was acting under the assumption that his enemies were now in the area. He was watchful everywhere he went—and he went some places that his fellow officers would have considered strange. He visited several pawn shops and art galleries. He spent much of the day at a variety of docks and ports around the Sydney area. About four o'clock, he hit pay dirt.

He was visiting some small, privately owned docks several miles south of the city, showing the picture of Andrew Remington to several people. A tough, crusty sailor in his early sixties by the name of Joe Gibbons said, "Let me see that again." Trey handed it over. "Just a little bloke, is that right, mate?" the old fellow asked.

"About five feet tall is all," Trey agreed.

"I've seen him," he said. "I did business with him. He had diving gear with him. At least he looks like this bloke. He's British or I don't know my accents. Yours is British too, but not as pronounced as his."

"I came to Australia ten years ago," Trey said.

"That explains it, then. But he told me his name was Mark Silmer. Are you sure you have the right name?" Joe asked.

"It could be Silmer," Trey said as his heart began to race. "This guy's a diver." He tapped his finger on the photograph.

"I think that's him," Joe said. "He's a foot shorter than me, but he was a wiry little fellow, looked pretty strong for his size. Had a foul mouth. Worse even than mine, and that's saying a bunch. I didn't much care for the guy, but his money's as good as the next guy's. I rent boats out, some pretty big ones, you know, forty footers and the like."

"And he rented one?" Trey asked.

"Sure did. He didn't need much in the way of instructions either. He seemed to know plenty about boats."

"Did he pay you in cash?" Trey asked.

"He did at that, mate. Peeled just what I asked off a role so big he could hardly stuff it back in his pocket."

"You said he had diving gear. Can you describe it?"

"Deep water gear," Joe said. "Ordinary stuff, but good quality—tanks, a body suit, and so on."

"Did he say what he was doing?" Trey asked.

"Looking for sunken treasure," Joe responded.

"Did he say where?"

"No, he was pretty secretive about that. He went out a couple times. The first time he left early in the morning and came back just before dark. The second time, he hauled a bunch of supplies on board and was gone for several days. "He told me he was going north to do some exploring. That was the extent of it," Joe said.

"He only went out those two days?" Trey asked.

"That's right. Then he unloaded his gear and turned the boat back to me."

"Mr. Gibbons, can you tell me what day he left for his long trip?"

"Come on inside my office." He turned and started toward the building. "I'll figure it out for you, Detective. Is the guy up to something illegal?"

"That's what I'm trying to figure out," Trey answered.

"What about the other guy?" he asked.

"What other guy? I thought you said he was alone."

"He was, but when he came back from the long trip, he had some other guy with him. I guess he picked him up somewhere," Joe responded as he opened the door to his office, which was nothing much more than a large shack.

He sat behind a cluttered, dusty desk, opened a thick ledger and thumbed back a couple of pages. He ran his finger down a column and finally said, "Here it is. Step over here and see for yourself."

Trey looked over Joe's shoulder. A gnarled finger was poised over a line where the signature of Mark Silmer was scrawled. "This is the day he left." His finger moved across the page. "And he turned the boat in then. Is that what you need, Detective?"

"That's helpful," Trey said, looking closely at the dates on the page. Remington, or Silmer, had left the same day the cruise ship had sailed from Melbourne and returned the day after Trey flew into Sydney from the ship. He set that information aside in his mind to consider more later. "Tell me about the other man."

"I didn't get a good look at him." He poked his finger on the page again. "See? It was almost ten at night when he brought the boat back. It was dark, and those lights out by my docks don't light things up too well."

"But you did see a second man?"

"Oh, yeah, but he didn't come to the office. He just lugged stuff over to the parking area."

"What kind of stuff?" Trey pressed.

"Diving equipment, mostly." The fellow grinned, exposing yellow, rotting teeth. "I was kind of watching to see if he had any treasure. I even asked Silmer, but he told me in no uncertain terms that it was none of my business."

"Did you see something besides equipment?"

"Well, there was some trash and leftover supplies. They dumped the trash in my big trash bin out there, down past the last dock, on the far side of the parking area. They took everything else to their truck. Silmer didn't actually do much of the hauling; he was in here with me most of the time." Joe lifted a finger and wiggled it as his eyebrows drew together. "Now that I think back, Detective, it was like he was trying to keep me distracted."

"That could be, I suppose. Is that all you saw being taken from the boat?" Trey asked.

"No, the last thing was a large, flat package of some kind. The other guy had it, and never even came close to the office. I couldn't see too well, but he did walk under that light over by the dock where Silmer's rental boat is tied," Joe said, pointing to a light elevated on a pole about fifteen or twenty feet in the air.

"You saw him walk past that light?" Trey asked.

"Sure did, but he wasn't too close."

"How big was the package he had?"

"About five feet by maybe three feet," Gibbons answered. "It was probably eight inches thick, something like that. The guy was lugging it like it was really awkward."

"But you couldn't tell what it was?" Trey asked.

"No. Silmer said something to me, and I had to look away. Like I say, I think he didn't want me to watch what the other bloke was doing. So I never did get a good look at him or what he was lugging." Joe rubbed his chin and then shut the book. "It was wrapped in something. I mean, you know, it was entirely enclosed. It was dark brown or black or something. I can't say for sure."

"Can you describe that other man at all?"

"Taller than the little guy by several inches, I'd say. Had a hat on. He never did look toward me. That's all I can tell you," he said. "If I'd known it was important, I might have tried to look closer, although I don't think Silmer would have let me if I'd tried."

"That's okay. This is helpful," Trey said as his mind raced through the possibilities that presented themselves by this rather extraordinary story.

"Did you see the truck they were driving?" Trey asked as Joe got up from his desk.

"It was parked right over there for several days. I did walk over and take a look one day, but I never looked inside. I didn't want to snoop or anything. It was a fairly new truck, a Ford—gray colored. It was a rental outfit. I'm sure of that. It had a sticker on the bumper."

"Did you notice the name of the rental company on the sticker you saw?" Trey asked, mentally crossing his fingers.

"Let me see; I did, but I didn't write it down or anything. I think it was Travel-a-Lot. Yeah, that's what it was. It's a small outfit. I don't think it has very many locations. Maybe only one. I honestly don't know. I've seen cars and trucks with that same sticker on them, but not a lot," Joe said.

"Did it have license plates?" Trey asked.

"Yep, local ones, but I didn't write the number down."

"Let me give you my card, Mr. Gibbons," Trey said. "If you see Silmer again, I'd appreciate a call. This number right here is for my cell phone."

"Can you tell me what this is all about?" the fellow asked.

"Sorry, it's police business. But if you do see him, or especially the two of them, don't question them or anything. They could be very dangerous," Trey said. "That's why I need to hear from you if you hear from Silmer again."

"Sure thing, Detective," Joe said as a worried look filled his eyes. "I'll call you if I see or hear anything."

Trey found the rental company in less than an hour and was able to confirm that a very small man, using the name Mark Silmer had rented a gray Ford pickup almost two weeks previously and, as yet, had not returned it. When Trey inquired concerning an estimated return date, the attendant said it was supposed to have been returned a couple days ago, but the renter had called and asked for an extension of one week. Payment had been made by a credit card in Silmer's name, and the payment had come through without any problem. When Trey asked for the address of the renter, he was given the name of a hotel on the outskirts of Sydney.

That was his next stop. It was a second-rate place, but when he checked, Trey learned that a British man going by the name Mark Silmer had checked in on the same date that Trey believed Remington had arrived in Sydney, but Silmer had checked out the same day he'd left for his extended trip on the rented boat. The same credit card had been used.

Next Trey asked that the description of the truck, which he now had a license number for, be given to every police officer in the state of New South Wales. After that, all he could do was wait and see if the truck or Andrew Remington was spotted. He gave instructions to call him if the truck was located, no matter what time of day or night it was. That was the exact same instruction he had given in the event that any of the missing people from the ship were seen.

Trey returned to his office and spent a half hour writing up a comprehensive report of the day's events. Then he called Willie and reported everything he had learned, carefully following his typed notes to make sure nothing was left out.

When he'd finished, Willie said, "Wow! So it sounds like your farfetched idea might be spot on, hey?"

"Maybe," Trey agreed.

"If you find the truck, you may be able to find the mysterious package, which you and I both hope is the stolen paintings," Willie said. "This is amazing."

"If that's what was in the package," Trey said. "I might be completely wrong, you know."

"Maybe, but I doubt it. And if you're right about that, then it's a good chance that the man who returned to the dock with Remington is in fact your first 'murder' victim on the ship, Martin Talley, who *miraculously* survived being thrown into the ocean," Willie said.

"Or who was simply being helped into the ocean and was promptly picked up by his diving buddy."

"This is stranger than fiction," Willie said.

"And it may be fiction," Trey again cautioned him. "However, if Martin *did* somehow survive—if in fact equipment had been left in the water at a specific GPS coordinate, which is the only thing I think could have happened—then whoever his helpers were are probably on the ship right now."

"Or not," Willie said. "It could be either one of the missing couples."

"True, but so far we don't know of any connection between any of them and Martin," Trey pointed out.

"But that doesn't mean there isn't one."

"If it wasn't them, then that leaves the Sladers and Danny Bidwell." Trey paused for a moment, thinking. "My money's still on my uncle. I'd almost stake my life on him being involved."

"Which you may be doing right now. I hope you're being careful."

The two officers ended their conversation with a promise to speak again in the morning after they had both had a chance to think about everything.

Back at his father's house, Aariah and her grandmother had prepared another excellent meal, but after they were finished eating, Aariah said, "We're going to need some groceries soon, Trey."

"Make me a list, and I'll go get what you need," he said.

"We'd like to go with you," Aariah said as her grandmother nodded in agreement. "It can't be any more dangerous than it was to go to church yesterday."

"Every day it gets more dangerous," Trey said. "Every day it's more likely that my uncle is in Sydney looking for me."

"For us," Aariah said.

"Yes, for us," he agreed.

"Please, Trey, let's all go."

Trey relented. They purchased the groceries and were home in less than an hour. He was relieved when his car was back in the large garage, all the doors and windows were secured, and the alarm system was activated.

At about nine, after Charlotte had retired for the night, Trey sat on a sofa in the living room with his arm around Aariah, her head resting against his shoulder. "Tell me about your day," she said. "Did you learn anything?"

"Did I ever," he said. "I think I might have been right all along."

But as he began to tell her about his discoveries at the dock, the loud and musical doorbell rang. "Who in the world could that be?" Trey stood up, pulled his gun, and cautiously approached the door.

SEVENTEEN

IT WASN'T NECESSARY TO LOOK through a peephole to see who was on the other side. Simon had installed a small video camera and TV screen near each door, which displayed what was on the outside. After what had happened to his wife in London, he had been extremely security conscious upon his move to Australia. He had changed systems several times. Each time a better system came on the market, Simon had upgraded.

Trey glanced at the front door monitor and grinned. The figure he saw was so large it filled the screen. He quickly deactivated the alarm, opened the door, and welcomed Hans Olander to his father's house—to his house.

"Why aren't you on the ship?" Trey asked. "I can't imagine Bonnie is too happy about that."

"Bonnie is the sweetest and most understanding woman I've ever met. And when we heard of the danger you may be in, she told me I should come watch after you. After all, I am your bodyguard," he said with his signature grin.

"Thanks for coming, Hans," Aariah said as she hugged the big man. "You are such a thoughtful guy. I just wish Bonnie could be here too."

"She has a break coming after the ship docks in Auckland in a few days. She's coming then." Hans laughed. "She wants to see me get beat up."

"You won't get beat up, Hans. I feel sorry for whoever has to fight you," Aariah said.

"Do you have a sofa I can sleep on?" Hans asked, glancing down at a huge suitcase.

"Come in, Hans. This is a very big house. We have lots of room."
After shutting the door and activating the alarm again, Trey said, "Let's
find you a room, and then we can talk. Some crazy stuff has happened."

"I'll fix you a snack," Aariah said. "You must be starved."

"Thank you, but you don't need to go to all that trouble," Hans said.

"It's no trouble, and I insist," she said. "You're the one who's gone
to a lot of trouble."

Hans turned to Trey. "I must make a slight correction to what I
said a moment ago. Bonnie is actually one of the *two* sweetest women
I have ever met. We're both lucky guys, aren't we?"

"I'll say," Trey agreed. "This way, Hans."

After Hans's luggage was stored, he said, "Trey, would you mind
giving me a tour of the house? I'd like to be familiar with it. I'm happy
to see you have good alarm and camera systems in place."

"My father, as you can imagine after what he went through with
the loss of my mother, was very security conscious."

"He was a smart man. I'm sorry he's gone."

Trey said nothing, but the ache in his heart intensified.

After the tour, Hans and Trey joined Aariah in the kitchen.

"Oh, Hans," Trey said, "I didn't notice a car. Did you rent one?
There's still room in the garage."

"No, I came in a taxi. I might rent a car tomorrow though."

"There's no need for that. Father has a nice Mercedes in the garage.
It's yours to use for as long as you need it."

Aariah served the *snack* she had prepared. It was the biggest snack
Trey had ever seen, but it didn't last long. Hans Olander could consume
more calories in a single sitting than Trey could eat in two days.

Following the meal, all three of them cleaned up, and then Aariah
said, "I think I'll go to bed. I guess you two will want to catch up on
the events of the day."

Hans cocked an eye. "Has something happened?"

"You could say that," Trey told him. He gave Aariah a chaste good-
night kiss, and she left the room with a reminder that there would be a
big breakfast in the morning.

"She's a sweetheart, Trey. God does work in mysterious ways, does
he not? I'll never believe He didn't orchestrate things so that you and
Aariah and Bonnie and I would find each other."

"I do feel blessed. I just hope she doesn't change her mind about me after all this mess has been cleared up," Trey said.

"Oh, my boy, my boy. Don't you fret about such a silly thing. That girl loves you. I can see it in her eyes and on her whole face. Don't you ever let her get away. Now, tell me what you've been up to, Detective Shotwell."

For the next hour, Trey brought Hans up to date on the investigation. "Do you mean to tell me you think Martin Talley actually survived the dip in the ocean? I would never have imagined such a thing to be possible."

"I can't help but wonder, Hans. I know it seems impossible, but he is a diver, and his partner in crime, Andrew Remington, AKA Mark Silmer, was on a rented boat at that time with deep-sea diving equipment."

"Do you think the package was the stolen paintings?" Hans asked.

"The size of the package Joe saw fits what I would expect. And I suppose if they'd been properly wrapped with plenty of protective padding, they might have survived being dropped in the ocean. It would have to be leak proof, but that could have been done. Now I'm thinking that the theft and the man overboard was all part of a well-planned plot to steal the paintings."

"So now we not only have to worry about the folks that jumped ship in New Zealand, but we also have to worry about the worm with the missing tooth. Actually, I'd love to get my hands on that guy again. He was a very unlikable character."

"So is my uncle." Trey rolled his eyes. "Let's get some sleep. I'm hoping that tomorrow will be another productive day."

It was late in London but early in Sydney when Inspector Hawk called Trey. Aariah had made a huge breakfast and the group was gathered around the table when Trey got the call. The two men talked for a moment, and then the private investigator said, "I found a connection between Victor Krause and your family, Trey."

"I knew there had to be one," Trey responded. "What did you learn?"

"The connection's actually with Lukas Nichols, your mother's little brother. It seems that clear back before your mother's murder, your uncle and Victor made a deal having to do with property that belonged to your grandparents," Hawk said.

"Property that he was cut out of when they died," Trey said. "I suppose you know all about the fact that my grandparents felt like Lukas had taken more than his share of the estate, and so they left everything to my mother."

"I don't know all the details, but I did know that he didn't get what he thought he would. That's where Krause comes in. He fronted Lukas some money with the agreement that it would be paid back once he got the inheritance," the investigator explained.

"Was that before or after my grandparents' death?" Trey asked suspiciously.

"I think I know what you're wondering," Inspector Hawk said. "It seems unlikely that Victor would be fronting any money to Lukas before they died, and that's a reasonable thought. But the fact is, it was before they died—a week before. This makes me wonder, as I am sure it does you, if Victor might have had something to do with their deaths."

"Exactly," Trey said. "Their deaths were totally unexpected. It was a traffic accident on a mountainous road in France. I know nothing more than that."

"It probably wasn't an accident. You see, the sum of money that Krause fronted to Lukas was about a million British pounds. Lukas was actually buying a piece of real estate your grandparents owned in Germany," Hawk explained.

"It seems to me that a deal between Krause and my uncle would have created trouble between the two of them. I don't see how it would have caused homicidal anger in Krause against my parents," Trey reasoned.

"You make a good point, Trey," Inspector Hawk admitted. "I had the same question, and I asked a couple of my operatives to look into it. So far, they've only confirmed that the two of them, Victor and Lukas, appeared in court together a couple of times when Lukas was trying to get his parents' will overturned. And they were said to have been quite chummy. My investigators were able to access a court transcript of a hearing in which your mother testified. She was able to establish times and amounts that Lukas bilked his parents for—large amounts. Lukas also testified, and the transcript made it clear that he expected the court to award him half of the remaining estate. I think both Victor and Lukas were shocked when your mother's strong stance won the day."

"So are you suggesting that Victor's anger was directed toward my mother rather than at Lukas?" Trey asked.

"That's my guess," the investigator said.

"So there's a chance the paintings were stolen and my mother was murdered because the two of them felt that she had cheated them?"

"It was a chance to get back some of what they felt they'd lost and a further chance to get revenge against your mother in a personal way. Which of them killed your mother is something we still need to figure out, but I think there's a strong possibility it was one of them. We'll have to somehow prove they were at the scene," Inspector Hawk said.

"I may have that information already," Trey said. "There's a couple on the cruise ship who bought my painting, the one that was stolen."

"You would be talking about Gil and Daphne Slader?"

"Yes, so you know about them."

"Detective, I make it my business to know everything that is related in any way to a case I'm working on. Of course, in this case, Damian Latimer told me about them. So what were you going to tell me?"

"Detective Denning told me yesterday that they admitted that the forged painting was one they consigned to the ship for sale. I am of course referring to the piece my father identified as one my mother painted and was stolen when she was killed."

"Yes, Willie told me about that," Hawk said. "They said they bought it from Krause, who had bought it from Lukas. We need to find Victor and Lukas, but of course they seem to be missing. It'll be up to you, if you find them in Sydney, to see if you can learn the truth from them."

"We're looking for them. But there's another twist," Trey said. He then related the story he'd learned from Joe Gibbons the day before.

"That casts a serious shadow over the Sladers. It makes me wonder if they're telling the whole truth, Detective. We have more suspects than we need," Hawk said. "But we're making progress. If what the Sladers say is true, that helps us build a case against your uncle. What's the weather like in Sydney, Detective?"

That question threw him. "It's quite nice really," he stammered. "What's it like in Europe?"

"About like you'd expect this time of year. It's cold and miserable. Maybe I'll join you down there, Trey. I haven't been to Australia for a while. I'll call Damian and see if he'll authorize it, and then I'll get back with you."

Trey's houseguests had only heard half of the conversation, so when he hung up they all looked at him expectantly. "I take it you want to know what that was all about," he said. And he explained it to them.

"This just gets more complicated all the time," Aariah said. "How will you ever know for sure who did what?"

"Do you doubt my skills at investigating?" he asked soberly.

She went red. "Of course not; it's just—"

"Hey, I'm just teasing," he broke in with a grin. He laid a hand tenderly on hers. "But in all seriousness, I am not as experienced as either Detective Denning or Inspector Hawk. I'm optimistic, not because I think *I* can get all the answers, but because I have the best help in the world. I just hope Damian is willing to authorize the inspector to come here. He's a brilliant man."

"I'm sorry; I didn't mean it like it sounded," Aariah said.

"I know," he replied, looking tenderly at her.

She smiled and then said, "I'm so worried about you, Trey." She looked up at the big Swede. "You'll take care of him for me, won't you?"

"I won't let anybody hurt this guy, you have my word, little lady," he said in all seriousness.

* * *

Trey called his office on the way there to explain that he was going to be accompanied by a friend. He'd told Hans earlier that it would be a good idea if he let them know before the two of them walked into the station.

"Trey, is that you?" Detective Inspector Rhett Smith sounded surprised.

"Of course it's me," he said. "Why wouldn't it be?"

"But you were killed this morning," Smith said.

"I don't think so," Trey said, totally bewildered. "Hans, do I look dead to you?"

Hans shook his head, equally bewildered.

"Inspector, I'm with a friend of mine who's going to help me for a few days. His name is Hans Olander," Trey said. "Now, why do you think I'm dead?"

"Well, somebody is," Inspector Smith said. "And we thought it was you."

Trey felt a much too familiar chill descend over him. "What's going on? I can assure you I'm very much alive."

"There was an explosion at your apartment. There's a body there. It's badly burned, and we can't make out the features. We assumed it was you, Trey," he explained. "Meet me there. I'm headed out right now."

Trey made an illegal turn and raced toward his apartment. "My colleagues thought I was dead," he explained to Hans as he negotiated the heavy traffic. "Apparently there was an explosion at my apartment. Someone else died, but I would guess it was meant to be me."

The Swede growled menacingly and shook his giant head, but he said nothing.

When he was still more than a mile away, Trey could see smoke rising into the air. When he turned onto his street, there was a snarl of police cars, fire trucks, an ambulance, and news vans blocking his way. He slid to a stop behind one of the news vans. "We'll go on foot from here."

Trey's heart was in his throat. As he got closer, he could see that the entire front of the apartment was gone. Smoke curled lazily up through where the roof had been. The entire apartment complex was single story. If it hadn't been, more destruction would have occurred. As it was, the apartments on either side had sustained damage, but it was unlikely that any of his neighbors had been injured.

The inspector had made it there ahead of Trey. He was standing on the sidewalk near the front of the building, a figure covered with a blanket on the concrete beside him. "Detective, I'm sorry," Inspector Smith said.

"It could have been worse. That could have been me."

"Thank goodness it isn't. We were sure it was until you called. Who did you say your friend is?" The inspector was looking up at the big man. Hans smiled down at him.

"This is Hans Olander. We met on the cruise. He's been assisting me."

"I was asked by Captain Johnsen on the ship to act as bodyguard for Detective Shotwell. We thought he was in danger. It looks like we were right," said the big Swede, in his deep, rumbling voice.

"You said there's no way to tell who this is, that he's too badly burned," Trey said.

The inspector nodded and signaled for the constable who was standing guard over the body to remove the blanket. As he reached down, a news photographer shouldered his way past Trey and pointed his camera at the covered body on the ground. "No pictures, mate," the inspector said.

The photographer paid no attention, and his camera began whirring as the blanket was pulled off. The inspector, his face mottled with rage, said, "Give me that camera."

The photographer, a man who stood well over six feet just snarled at the inspector and raised his camera and began to retreat.

"Hans, get the camera," Trey said.

A giant fist darted like greased lightning and plucked the camera away. The photographer grabbed for it, but Hans held it so high that the smaller big man could not reach it. Like a fool, he stamped his shoe on Han's foot. Hans dropped the large camera, shattering it, and lifted the man into the air until his feet dangled. "You shouldn't have done that," Hans said.

Hans was holding the front of the man's shirt so tightly that he couldn't say a word. The inspector signaled for a couple of uniformed constables to relieve Hans of his captive. Hans handed him over and looked down at the badly burned body on the ground. "Thank you, Mr. Olander," Inspector Smith said. "Some people have no respect for the dead."

"Glad I could help," Hans said. "Trey, look at his shoes." Hans pointed to the one part of the dead man's body that wasn't charred. Then the two men's eyes met. They each nodded in recognition.

"Do you know who this is?" Inspector Smith asked.

"From his shoes, I think we do," Trey said.

The shoes were blue and had sharp, pointed toes and slightly raised heels. Trey remembered seeing those shoes on Victor Krause after he and his French friend, Claudia Gaudet, had been knocked down as Martin and Danny had retreated in their attempt to get away from Hans.

Hans said, "I guess Victor's been found."

"Yes, it looks like it," Trey agreed.

The inspector said, "Victor Krause? Isn't that the name of one of the people whose pictures you have had us distribute?"

"One and the same," Trey said. "He hated my father. I didn't know why until last night; now I do."

"He clearly wanted to get rid of you, Detective, but it looks like his attempt to kill you with a bomb backfired," Inspector Smith said. "I'm just glad you weren't home, Detective."

"I'm temporarily staying at my father's house," Trey explained. "Actually, I guess it's my house now, and maybe it won't be so temporary after all."

"I'm glad you have a place to stay. Did you have a lot of valuable things in there?"

"The most valuable things I already moved. There are things I would have liked to save, but, well, I guess it's too late now," Trey said morosely.

"Why don't you go back to what you were doing? I'll keep you apprised of the progress of our investigation. When it's safe, I'll have you come back so you can take a look at what's left of your apartment."

Trey nodded. The enormity of what might have happened, what someone had planned to have happen to him, suddenly weighed heavily on him. "Would you like me to call the captain of the cruise ship and see if I can get you more information on the victim?"

"Yes, that would be helpful. And as you know, we'll need to have an autopsy and DNA testing to confirm the victim's identification," Inspector Smith said.

"Of course. Let's go, Hans."

As they walked away, Trey looked back just as an officer escorted a frantic woman to the Inspector. He couldn't tell what was being said, but he supposed Inspector Smith would tell him later if it was important. He mentioned it to Hans. The two men hadn't been back in the car for more than five minutes when Trey got a call. He looked at the screen. "It's the inspector. I'm guessing that the woman had something important to say. I better see what it is."

EIGHTEEN

"DETECTIVE, THE DEAD MAN AT your apartment did not set the bomb," Inspector Smith said.

"A witness saw someone dressed in black set a package by your door about a half hour before the explosion. She said he fiddled with it for a moment and then left.

"The witness was out for an early morning walk. She said that when she returned, a second man, one she said was wearing eccentric blue shoes, went to the door. She turned and watched as he lifted his hand to knock. That's when it blew," the inspector explained. "She's the one who called it in."

"It was a man who set the package there?" Trey asked.

"Actually, we don't know. It wasn't fully light yet, and the person had a black hoodie on. But the witness *thinks* it was a man," Inspector Smith said.

"Okay, thanks, Inspector. There are others who might have set the bomb," Trey said.

"That's why I called. The bomber's still out there somewhere. I'm not sure you shouldn't just go to your father's place and sit tight for a while."

"Thanks, Inspector, but I need to keep working. Hans and I will be cautious."

After the call, Hans said, "I think we should at least go back to your father's house and let Aariah and her grandmother know that you are okay. They might see the news and think you're dead."

"You're right, and then I'll call Detective Denning on the ship and then Inspector Hawk, if it isn't too late in London." He looked at his watch. "It should be okay. Maybe I'll call Hawk right now."

It only took a couple minutes to bring the private investigator up to date. "So Mr. Krause is now out of the picture. He still could have murdered your mother and father, and just because he's dead doesn't mean the danger to you isn't still very, very real."

"I'm afraid you're right," Trey agreed.

"I am at Heathrow International Airport as we speak, Trey. I was going to call you shortly to let you know I'm coming, but you saved me the trouble." Hawk chuckled. "I'll be there sometime tomorrow afternoon."

"I'll be glad for your help, Inspector," Trey said.

"I don't suppose you have any idea where Victor's sidekick, Claudia Gaudet is, do you?" the inspector asked.

"No, but I think I'll check here and in Auckland to see if she shows up on any airline passenger lists," Trey said.

"You do that, and I'll have one of my operatives do some checking here in London. Who knows, maybe she's here."

"Or in Paris," Trey suggested.

"Yes, that's possible. I'll have my investigators follow up on that end too. I'll call you the moment I arrive in Sydney," he promised.

Aariah, fortunately, hadn't heard the news on TV, so she hadn't yet had the chance to fall to pieces. Hans and Trey laid it out for her as gently as they could. She was understandably upset, but to her credit she didn't come apart. She did, however, hug Trey longer than she ever had before.

He placed a call to Willie on the cruise ship and told him of the death of Victor Krause. "I've already talked to Inspector Hawk. He's having some of his people check the airports in England and France to see if, by any chance, Claudia Gaudet has returned there. And I'm going to do the same thing here."

Aariah shed some tears when he and Hans prepared to leave again. He promised, as he seemed to be doing quite frequently of late, to be careful.

"I know you will," she said, "but I worry about you."

"I know you do, and I worry about you." As Trey spoke, a new concern struck him right between the eyes.

Whoever tried to kill him had thought that he was living in his apartment. If—no, *when* they learned where he was living, what was to stop them from doing the same thing to this house? That thought stopped him in his tracks.

"What is it, Trey?" Aariah asked, her face masked with worry.

Hans spoke up. "You just had the same thought I did, didn't you, Trey? You're afraid the bomber will find this place."

Trey nodded. He sat down, pulled out his phone, and dialed the number of Inspector Smith's cell phone. "Inspector, have you released anything about the victim of the bombing at my apartment?"

"Not yet. First we have to confirm that it is Mr. Krause, and then we need to notify his next of kin," the inspector said. "You know the drill, Trey. Is there something worrying you, like your father's house?"

"Exactly," Trey said. "There's a great security system in place here, but it's not foolproof."

"I've already ordered around-the-clock protection for your house," Inspector Smith told him. "The bombing this morning puts a whole new light on what you have been dealing with. I can now commit whatever resources are needed, and I intend to. There's already an officer on his way to your new home."

"Thanks, Inspector," Trey said.

"Oh, and if you don't mind, I'd like you to come back now and poke around a little."

"I'll do that," Trey said, hoping there were still some of his belongings that were salvageable.

When he got back, he donned some tall rubber boots a firefighter provided. Hans waited while Trey began to sort through the burned rubble that had been his home. Trey took his time and found a few personal items that were still okay. His bedroom was the farthest room from where the explosion had occurred, so it had sustained the least damage. Even though the smoke damage was severe, his clothes and shoes were in good shape. Everything would have to be laundered or dry cleaned, but it wasn't all ruined.

The room next to his bedroom was the one he had used as an art studio. It was in shambles. Had he not moved his paintings, they would have been destroyed. The art supplies that he hadn't moved to his father's house were useless now.

His kitchen and living room were damaged the worst. That was to be expected, as they were in a direct line of the blast.

He felt physically ill; it was all so overwhelming. But as he looked around, he thanked the Lord his life had been spared. He finally went back outside and said to Inspector Smith, "My clothes, shoes, and most everything else in my bedroom are salvageable. I'll need to air things out and launder most of my clothes, but other than that they're okay."

"I'd suggest you get your clothes out of there as soon as possible," the inspector said.

"I'll help you," Hans said.

"Thanks, Hans." He addressed Inspector Smith again. "Did you find out how Victor got here?"

"He had a rental car. It was parked about a block away. I had it impounded, and it's being thoroughly searched."

"I'm wondering where Claudia Gaudet, the woman Victor was hanging out with on the ship, is. If they find any evidence that indicates she has been in the car Victor was driving, I'd like to know it. If she's in Sydney and anyone locates her, I'd like to interview her," Trey said.

It was midafternoon by the time Trey and Hans had salvaged what they could and moved it to his father's house. Aariah and Charlotte insisted on laundering everything they could in the large utility room. Next Trey and Hans drove to the police station, where Trey made some phone calls to the airport in an attempt to determine if Claudia Gaudet had flown in. They'd only been there for about thirty minutes—with negative results—when Trey was alerted to a possible sighting of the gray Ford pickup that Andrew Remington had rented under his alias.

The pair sped across the city to the parking lot of a large shopping mall, where a pair of uniformed constables was keeping an eye on the truck. Trey and Hans watched it themselves for a little while, but when no one showed up, Trey approached the truck. He circled around it while Hans watched the neighboring vehicles. After the bombing at his apartment, Trey was particularly worried about another bomb. He didn't see anything to alarm him, but he'd made so many promises to be careful that he took his time. There was a large cardboard box in the bed of the truck but nothing else. Peering through the windows, he didn't see anything in the cab, not a single package or piece of paper or suitcase—nothing.

Trey stepped away from the truck without touching it and called for a bomb squad. He was curious about the big box in the truck bed, but he wasn't about to attempt to retrieve it. The squad, when they arrived, checked the truck carefully, first with a bomb sniffing dog and then with some sophisticated equipment.

"It looks like I've worried over nothing," Trey commented to Hans. "But I still don't want to touch that box. Sometimes dogs don't indicate there is something when there really is. They're not infallible."

"Don't they have a way to safely check the box out?" Hans asked. "You know, a robot or something?"

That's exactly what the bomb squad had. They put a robot in the back of the truck and cleared the area. Once all the neighboring vehicles had been moved by their owners, the crowd that had gathered was substantial; they were kept well out of the danger zone with the members of the bomb squad and the other officers. When all was secure, the robot's operator began to remotely control it, sending it to the edge of the box. Trey and Hans were among those who watched a large screen that showed everything the robot's camera was seeing.

Contact with the box did not result in an explosion. The robot slowly lifted one edge of the box. There was still no explosion. On one of the robot's arms was a retractable knife, a very sharp one. The knife was extended, and the robot stabbed it through the cardboard. When nothing blew up, the robot spent the next five minutes slicing the box open.

When it lifted the top up, the camera revealed the box's contents. Trey gasped. In the bottom of the box was the painting Trey had sold on the ship. Something was written across the painting, seriously defacing it. The painting was ruined. It was ten minutes before the canvas was extracted from the truck and Trey was able to read what was printed in bright white paint in small letters. It read, *This is what I think about your painting, Trey. Actually, it's improved now. Sorry, Daphne, but you shouldn't have bought such a worthless piece.*

Trey stared at the painting. It wasn't the same quality of his father's work, but it wasn't bad, either.

"Sorry, my friend," Hans said as he laid a giant hand on Trey's shoulder.

Trey only grieved over his painting for a moment, and then he stood up and said to Inspector Smith, who had just arrived, "I can get you some handwriting samples of my uncle, Lukas Nichols, as well as some of both Martin Talley and Simon Remington."

"Do I understand that you painted that?" Inspector Smith said.

"Yes. It's the one I sold on the ship and was then stolen."

"I'm sorry, Trey."

"I can paint more. And this gives me hope that the one my father painted that was stolen from the ship is now here in Sydney. I can't tell you how badly I want to find that one," Trey said with determination.

"I'll make whatever resources you need available to you," Smith promised. "And yes, we'll see if we can get a match on the writing. Get the samples as soon as you can."

"I'll do that. This is a big city, and I don't know where to start from here, but I'm thinking that we need to begin in this area. Would it be possible to have a few officers check hotels in the area and see if any of the suspects have been there?" Trey asked.

"We will do that, Detective."

"Then I'll go to work on obtaining the handwriting samples," Trey said.

As Trey and Hans drove across the city to retrieve a sample of Lukas's handwriting from Simon's house, Trey called Detective Willie Denning. As soon as Willie answered, Trey said, "We have my painting back. It's ruined, but we have it."

"What about the other one, your father's?" Willie asked.

"Not yet, but we're working on that. My superiors have freed up all the officers they can," Trey said.

"Is there something I can do to help?"

"Yes, I need handwriting samples from Martin Talley and Andrew Remington. There should be something there with Martin's handwriting, and I was hoping you could call your office in London and see if someone can round up something with Remington's handwriting," Trey said.

"I'll get right on it," Willie promised.

"I have been unable to find evidence that Claudia Gaudet flew into Sydney. But I need to check further. I was working on that when Remington's rental was located," Trey said. "Do you know if anything has turned up on her in England or France?"

"Not so far. Nor can we find any evidence that she has flown out of New Zealand. She may still be here somewhere," Willie responded.

"Here?" Trey asked. "Does that mean you're docked in New Zealand?"

"We are. I wonder now if maybe Victor did something to Claudia. Maybe her body will turn up somewhere in New Zealand."

"But it wasn't him that tried to kill me," Trey reminded Willie.

"Trey, you need to look beyond what you know," Willie said. "Just because he didn't set the bomb doesn't mean he didn't intend you harm. And there's more. Daphne Slader claims she heard Victor Krause make a threat against your father the day before he was killed."

"She's just now telling you that?"

"She says it slipped her mind. She says this whole affair has been very upsetting and she simply forgot."

"Why do you think she remembered now?"

"That's easy," Willie said. "Damian Latimer has offered another reward; this one is for any information that leads to your father's murderer. He's really angry. Damian liked your father, liked and respected him."

"Maybe a reward will help," Trey said. "When and where was the threat made?"

"Victor was in a lounge, and Daphne says he was talking to Claudia Gaudet," Willie said. "She claims he'd been drinking quite a bit and talking kind of loudly. She doesn't think he even noticed her and Gil. Anyway, Krause said something to the effect that he was going to kill Simon. She says he specifically said he'd stick a knife in his skinny chest."

"If Victor did it, he won't be confessing now, that's for sure," Trey said. "Daphne might be right, although, honestly, my uncle is still first on my list of suspects."

"Mine too. Now, what do you want me to do with the handwriting samples?"

Trey gave Willie a fax number and then said, "That's for the crime lab. They'll need originals at some point, but I think they can work off a fax for now."

"That sounds good. I'll send them. Do you want me to update Captain Johnsen on Daphne Slader's painting, the one you found?"

"Let me try to call him." Trey finished his conversation with Willie and made the call to Captain Johnsen a minute later. "Captain, one of the stolen paintings has been found, the one that belongs to Daphne Slader—it's worthless now." He explained why. "I guess you might as well make sure she's reimbursed."

"I already paid her," the captain said. "She's been hounding me, and I gave in. I guess I did the right thing."

When Hans and Trey got to Simon's house, they collected a couple samples of Lukas's handwriting.

"Will you be back soon?" Aariah asked hopefully as the men prepared to leave again.

"No. We may be out all night," Trey told her. "You're safe though. The house is under surveillance."

Aariah's eyes misted. "I hope you catch them tonight."

"So do I."

"She didn't tell you to be careful," Hans said as they got back in the car. "So I'm telling you for her."

NINETEEN

AFTER INSPECTOR HAWK ENTERED THE country, Hans asked Trey, "Would you mind if I went back to the ship now that your friend from London is here to work with you?"

"Missing a certain security officer are you?" Trey teased.

"I am, and since you're in good hands now, I thought I could use the remaining time on the cruise to work out and get myself in shape for the bouts I have coming up."

"You go, Hans," Trey said. "I'll be fine, but I'll look forward to seeing you when you return for your fights."

The two men shook hands, and then Hans headed for the airport in a cab.

* * *

Two days had passed since Hawk joined Trey, and despite a lot of officers talking to a lot of people, there were still no leads on Martin Talley or Andrew Remington. They hadn't registered in any hotels or rented any apartments in the area. The rental company picked up the truck when the police were through with it, reporting they had lost contact with Andrew, aka Mark Silmer, despite numerous attempts to contact him after he failed to return the truck. The effort to locate the two men had been expanded to areas farther from the parking lot where the pickup had been abandoned.

The only progress that had been made on the case was about the handwriting on the face of the painting. It hadn't been written by Lukas Nichols, Andrew Remington, or Martin Talley. Trey requested a sample of Victor's handwriting from the ship, even though he had died before the painting had been found. It also failed to match. Inspector Hawk had insisted that they also test a sample of Claudia Gaudet, which also was negative.

They did find that Victor had entered Sydney the day before he was killed, but despite a thorough check of the airports in Sydney and the surrounding areas, no record of Claudia coming into the country could be found. Inspector Hawk's agents in London, France, and Germany were also unable to find evidence of Claudia entering any of those countries. And finally, there was no record of her flying out of New Zealand. Hawk and Willie both wondered if she had, in fact, met her death in New Zealand before Victor Krause left. But then, three days after the disfigured painting and the gray Ford pickup had been found, Trey got a call from Willie on the ship.

"We found Claudia Gaudet," Willie said.

"Where?" Trey asked. "Is she alive or dead?"

"A little of both," Willie said grimly. "Mostly alive, though. She got beat up. She says it was Victor, that he beat her up and then left her for dead on a trail way up in the mountains somewhere. She had to hike back and was in so much pain and so hungry that it took her quite a while. She got patched up at a hospital and hired a taxi to drive her all the way to Picton, where we're currently in port. She hobbled onto the ship a couple hours ago."

"Wow!" Trey exclaimed. "Did she say why she left the ship in the first place?"

"She says Victor arranged for a rental car, that he wanted to show her some of the scenery the tour busses would never show her. She liked the idea, and she was so distraught over your father's death that she thought a little break from the ship might do her some good."

"That's interesting," Trey said. "Did she say anything else?"

"Quite a bit, actually," Willie said. "She and Victor met up on the ship and were renewing an old friendship. They were apparently having a really good time on their scenic trip in the country until they got into an argument. He suddenly became violent and hit her. This was on a hiking trail quite a ways into the mountains, at least eight or ten kilometers. She said she fought back, but he was way too strong for her. Anyway, at some point, she lost consciousness. When she came to, she says it was dark and that she was in some thick bushes several meters off the trail. She thinks he must have carried her there, dumped her, and then left, thinking she was either dead or would die there."

"I suppose she's angry."

"That's an understatement. She's irate. One of the first things she asked was if he was back on the ship. She wanted him arrested and jailed in Picton. She said she'd testify or do whatever else she needed to do to see to it that he was punished," Willie said.

"When I told her that he wasn't on board, she wanted to go back into Picton and make a complaint to the police there about him. But she was afraid to go alone in case he'd figured out she was alive."

"Did she go into Picton?"

"No. Instead, the New Zealand police came onto the ship and interviewed her here," Willie told him. "They promised a warrant would be issued for his arrest."

"Did you tell her or the local officers that Victor is dead?" Trey asked.

"We haven't told her because she's so distraught, but I called one of the officers and told him," Willie said. "Obviously, they won't be issuing any warrants for the *dead guy*, but they promised to follow up with an investigation into the assault of Claudia."

"That's an amazing story," Trey said. "Does she look like she's hurt badly?"

"She does. The ship's doctor examined her, and he said that she should have been kept at least overnight in the hospital that treated her," Willie explained. "I asked her why she didn't stay there, and she said it was because she was afraid he might go back, find her body wasn't where he'd left her, and go looking for her to, as she said, *finish the job*."

"I suppose the cops will follow up on all that in New Zealand?"

"They plan to," he said, "but they aren't going to make it a high priority since Victor is dead. And I can understand how they feel. She's sedated now, and the ship's medical team is keeping a close eye on her."

"When do you plan to tell her that Victor is dead?" Trey asked.

"Not until after we are out to sea again," Willie told him. "I have more questions for her, but she was getting tired and the doctor told me to leave her alone for a while and let her get her strength back."

"Will you ask her, when you can, if she remembers the threat Daphne Slader overheard?" Trey asked.

"You got it. I'll also ask her if Victor made any other threats or boasted—or even hinted—about killing your father," Willie promised.

Trey thanked him and hung up.

After Trey relayed the information to Inspector Hawk, Ruben said, "That is most interesting."

It was just a couple hours later that a report came in that a witness had finally been located who claimed to have seen someone matching Andrew Remington's description a couple miles from where the defaced painting had been found. The two men headed to the police station where the witness waited.

Lane Steiner was a man of medium height and weight. He was seated at a small table in an interview room, his head in his hands and his collar-length brown hair mussed and hanging forward. He looked up and brushed the hair out of his eyes when Trey and Hawk were introduced. Trey spent a few minutes giving the young man a little background on why it was important that they find Andrew Remington. Then he began his questioning. "First, Lane, tell me a little about yourself."

"Like what?" Lane asked.

"For starters, how old are you?" Trey prompted.

"I'm twenty-two."

"What kind of work do you do?"

"I'm an electrician."

"Do you live close to here?"

"No, but my girlfriend does . . . at least she did," Lane said as, once again, his elbows hit the table and his head fell into his hands.

Trey and Inspector Hawk looked at each other. The inspector shook his head. Trey looked back at Lane and asked, "What do mean by your girlfriend used to live around here?"

"I can't find her," he mumbled.

"What's your girlfriend's name?" Trey asked, his pen poised over a small notebook.

"Kori Acton."

"Can you describe her to us?" he asked.

"She's really pretty," he said.

"That's nice," Trey said, casting a glance at Hawk, who gave him a quick smile. "Besides pretty, what can you tell me about her?"

"She's shorter than me," Lane said.

"Okay, what about her hair?"

"Pink."

"Did you say pink?"

"Yeah, it was blue, but she dyed it pink a few days ago."

Again Trey and Hawk exchanged quizzical glances. "How long is her hair?" Trey asked.

"It's short and spiky," Lane said.

"What color are her eyes?" he asked.

"Blue."

"Okay, so now you say you can't find Kori, is that right?" Trey asked.

"Yeah," was the response.

"Lane, have you told the police that she's missing?"

"Yes."

"When?"

"Two days ago. I thought she was mad at me and was hiding from me."

"Why would she be mad at you?"

The young man finally looked up again, rubbed his eyes, and said, "Because I told her not to help that guy, that short guy you are looking for."

Trey showed him a picture of Andrew Remington. "This guy?"

"I think so," Lane said as he blinked a couple of times and then leaned closer to the photo. "He's older now, but it looks like him."

"What didn't you want her to help him with?" Trey asked.

"He said he'd pay her to write something on an oil painting. I told her I thought that was stupid. I told her maybe the painting was valuable."

"How did she respond to that?"

"She said she needed the money," Lane said.

"Did she do it anyway?" Trey asked.

"I think so. She said she was going to."

"I take it she hadn't done it yet the last time you talked to her," Trey suggested.

"She said she was going to do it that day," Lane said. "I asked her to wait, but she said the guy needed it done right away. I told her I'd go with her if she'd wait until I got off work, but she wouldn't. She said I was being silly. Now I can't find her, and I'm afraid something's happened to her."

Now that he had Lane talking, Trey wanted to keep him at it. "Lane, when did you see this man?"

"Kori showed me where he was staying. I drove past there the night before, and he was standing in front of the house talking to some other guy. She didn't want him to see her, so she ducked down, but I got a good look at him."

"He was staying in a house?" Trey asked.

"Yeah. I can show you the house if you want."

"Definitely, but first, did you see any cars by the house?"

"Yes, there was an old white car, a Honda, I think, and a gray pickup. It was nice. I'm pretty sure it was a Ford F150," he said. "It was beside the house. The guys were standing beside it when I drove past."

"Would you recognize the other man if you saw him?" Trey asked.

"The cops already showed me pictures of three other men, but the bloke had his back to me, so I didn't really see much of him."

Trey produced a picture of Martin Talley. "Did they show you this picture?"

"Yes, but I don't know if it's him or not."

"Does the hair look about right?" Trey asked.

"He had a hat on. I'm not sure."

"What about his height? The man in this picture, his name is Martin Talley, would be eight inches taller than Mr. Remington."

Lane nodded. "Yeah, it could be him, I guess. He was probably only a little taller than me but a lot taller than the little guy."

"Show him the other pictures, Detective," Inspector Hawk suggested.

Trey pulled out the pictures of both his uncle and the now-deceased Victor Krause. "Both of these men are also about the same height as I am," he said. He laid the pictures on the table beside the ones of Martin and Andrew.

"The cops showed me those too. If it was one of the three, it would be him," he said, plunking his finger down on the picture of Victor Krause.

"Lane, did you happen to notice the man's shoes?" Trey asked suddenly.

Lane looked at him in surprise. "Yeah, they were blue," he said. "I thought it was weird."

Trey couldn't help but think that blue and pink hair was also a bit weird, but he kept that thought to himself. He asked a few more questions, but he learned nothing more. Lane hadn't heard any names and didn't think that Kori had either. If she had, she hadn't told him. Trey also learned nothing more about where Kori might have gone. But he did now have another connection between Victor and Martin, even though it was only through Andrew Remington. Daphne Slader claimed she had purchased the altered painting from Victor, and now there was a chance, a very real likelihood, that Victor and Martin had a connection. Daphne was probably telling the truth.

Detective Shotwell, Inspector Hawk, and Lane Steiner drove to the residence where Lane had seen Andrew Remington and Victor Krause. The location was well outside the city in a sparsely populated area. They were met there by two other officers.

"You stay right here in this car," Trey instructed Lane.

The four men approached the house from the front and the rear. Trey didn't have a lot of hope, for there were no cars present. No one answered their knocks, nor was there any sound coming from inside. Trey felt strongly that they needed to have a look inside but knew they needed a warrant to do so. Hawk stayed at the house with the two cops who had helped them, and Trey drove back into the city and dropped Lane off at the station. With the help of another officer, Trey prepared a search warrant. The men located a judge who agreed to sign it, and then they returned to the house outside of the city.

The process, including driving time, took close to two hours. Inspector Smith sent more officers to help execute the search warrant. Trey was the first one to go in, his gun drawn and all his senses on high alert. The front door hadn't been locked, making entry very simple.

The moment they stepped inside, a powerful stench almost overpowered the officers. It was a smell that was all too familiar, and Trey's heart sank. Inspector Hawk, who was right behind Trey, said what Trey had already concluded. "There's something dead in here."

Indeed there was. They found the rotting body of a yellow dog in the far back room. It was clear that the dog had been clubbed to death, apparently in that very room. The odor was horrible. Trey stumbled back outside and gulped in the warm, clear air in an attempt to clear his lungs and nose of the horrible odor.

"I'll be ready to go back inside in a moment," Trey said when Inspector Hawk joined him. "I thought for sure we'd find the body of the missing girl, Kori Acton."

"I thought so too," Hawk agreed. "If she is dead, we might find her as well, just not in the house. I saw blood on the floor in the living room and the kitchen."

"Could it have been the dog's blood?" Trey asked.

"I don't think so. The dog was clubbed and didn't bleed much. And I think it was killed in that backroom by a baseball bat that was lying beside the bed," the inspector told him.

"Maybe it bit someone and ran to the bedroom, where it was beat to death. That could explain the blood," Trey reasoned.

"Yes, it could. Let's get back in there and see what, if any, evidence we can find."

For the next hour, Trey and the inspector worked with several other officers, carefully searching the house. The dog's body had been moved outside and placed in a sealed plastic sack. All the windows had been opened to try to at least temper the smell. One officer found a small can of white paint—which Trey suspected was used to apply the note to his painting—along with a small brush in a trash can outside the back door. There was also a small amount of dry paint on the kitchen table, likely where Kori did the work. An officer rushed samples to the lab to be compared with the paint on Trey's painting.

Behind the house was a dense thicket of trees and shrubs. Trey, Reuben, and two officers began a search of the area while other officers began a canvas of the neighborhood, interviewing anyone at home. The houses were scattered far apart with large lots that included small fields and wooded areas that ran back to the thick vegetation to the south at the base of a steep hill. There were no homes on that back side, just Australian wilderness.

The officers began to work their way into the thick vegetation, using sticks to probe for the dangerous, poisonous snakes that infested the country.

TWENTY

ONE OF THE OTHER OFFICERS beckoned to Trey and pointed at a mound of dirt a couple meters away. It looked fresh, even though some leaves, broken branches, and grass had been scattered across it, as if that would make it invisible. In the center of the mound was a large black snake. It was coiled, and its large head moved menacingly from side to side as its forked tongue flicked rapidly in and out of its mouth. The men stood back far enough that the snake could not reach them if it were to strike.

Trey shooed at it with his hands, but it didn't give an inch. It was as if it was protecting a deadly secret beneath the disturbed earth it occupied. One of the officers found a long, dead branch hanging low in a nearby tree and snapped it off. He poked at the snake with it. The deadly serpent drew its head back and struck at the branch, uncoiling to its full length. The officer poked again, and the long black creature finally slithered into the underbrush.

Trey looked at the mound more closely. Had they not been conducting such a thorough search, the mound may well have been missed. Shovels were brought in and slow, methodical digging commenced, the officers ever alert for the black snake.

The body of a young female with pink hair was uncovered about two feet beneath the surface. Kori Acton's body showed evidence of a knife wound to the chest. Dried blood had soaked her blouse. She still had ropes tightly tied around her wrists and ankles. Whoever killed her had used a knife, just like whoever had murdered Simon Shotwell had done.

The loose soil was carefully brushed away and photographs taken. Trey leaned over the hole and examined her bound hands more closely.

The fingers of her right hand had traces of white paint on them. He straightened up as he thought about the paint that had been used to deface his painting.

"She was just trying to make a little spending money," Trey said sadly as he approached Reuben a few feet from the grave.

"She found a dangerous way to make it," Inspector Hawk responded. "I wish she'd listened to her boyfriend. And I suspect that when he learns of her death, he'll wish he'd insisted she stay away from those men."

The inside of the house was given an even more thorough search after the body had been taken away. Forensic evidence was carefully removed. The process was far from complete, and it was getting late in the evening when Trey's cell phone began to ring.

He stepped outside the house where he had been observing the work of the forensic team.

"Detective Shotwell?" a familiar voice asked.

"This is Detective Shotwell," he replied.

"This is Joe Gibbons, down at the boatyard. You told me to call if I saw that guy again."

"Did you see him?" Trey asked as his heart sped up.

"No, but my hired hand did. I thought you'd want to know what happened here."

"I do. Tell me about it," Trey said.

"That guy, the short one, he came back while I was gone to the doctor this afternoon."

"Is he still there now?" Trey asked.

"No, he rented a boat again, loaded some diving equipment and a package about like the one he brought the other day, and headed out to sea," Joe reported. "When I got back I noticed that a boat was gone. I asked my hired man who he'd rented it to. He told me it was some really little guy, only about five feet tall and really ornery. I wouldn't have thought much of it if my man hadn't mentioned the bloke's size and that he had taken diving equipment and a package that was wrapped like it was meant to be waterproof on the boat with him."

"Was he alone?" Trey asked.

"He was, and he's been gone about four hours now."

"Did he tell your hired man where he was going?"

"Nope, just that he needed the boat for about four or five hours. He used the same name as he did the other day, Mark Silmer," Joe said.

"I'll be there as soon as I can," Trey said as he signaled to Inspector Hawk.

Within a couple of minutes, he and Reuben were driving frantically toward Joe Gibbons's private boatyard. It was a long drive; it took them almost an hour to get there. As Trey slid to a stop in front of Gibbons's dilapidated office, the old man came running out. "He's right over there," he shouted, pointing to where a small man was getting into an old white sedan. "He just finished loading his diving gear, but he doesn't have the package anymore."

Trey and the inspector had barely gotten out of the car when the Honda sped toward them, fishtailing and spraying gravel. It headed straight for Trey, who jumped back, falling to the ground as the Honda barely missed hitting him.

"It's Remington," Inspector Hawk said urgently as he helped Trey to his feet. "He meant to kill you."

"So I noticed. Thanks, Joe," Trey called out as he and Reuben jumped back into Trey's car, turned around, and pursued the fleeing Honda.

Trey called for assistance, but the Honda was leading them farther away from the city, and there were no police units available in the direction they were headed. The pavement ran out after a few miles, and they were forced to eat Andrew's dust. Trey was right behind him, but he had to back off when Andrew reached out a window and fired a couple of shots back at them.

"I could fire at him," Inspector Hawk said as the police car bounced on the increasingly rough and twisty road, "but it would be futile. The dust is too thick, and the ride is too rough."

"That's okay," Trey said. "Maybe he'll lead us to Martin or . . . someone. Maybe my uncle."

"Then I'll just hang on for the ride." Ruben chuckled. "But if we don't get him soon, it'll be dark, and he could get away from us on foot if he attempts to."

The day was pretty well spent. Trey had lost track of time while they'd worked the scene of the girl's murder. He pressed the gas pedal a little more, worried about the lateness of the hour. The road they were on was getting narrower, more twisty, and rougher. It led deep into a wooded area, through several miles of burned forest, then back into heavy woods again. They had been in pursuit for close to an hour, and the sun had set when the voice of Inspector Smith came through Trey's police radio.

"You take it," Trey said to Ruben. "I don't dare take a hand off the steering wheel."

"This is Ruben Hawk," he said into the mike. "Detective Shotwell is driving."

"What's your location?" Smith asked.

Ruben looked at Trey, who shook his head. "I don't know," he said. "I guess just tell him that I can't tell exactly, but I can tell the general area," Trey said. "Tell him whatever area the GPS shows."

Ruben relayed the information to Smith and then turned back to Trey, who gave a general description of the route Andrew had led them on. He was able to offer a reasonably good idea of the direction they had traveled and the area they were going through. Hawk relayed the information to Smith.

"Okay, I'm in the air in a helicopter headed your way," Inspector Smith told them. "But there's not a lot of daylight left."

"Just look for a large burned area. We're back into thick forest again, but we're kicking up quite a cloud of dust. We have our lights on now, but the suspect does not," Hawk told Smith. "If you get close enough, you should be able to see us. The suspect is armed. He fired a couple of shots at us."

"Unless he turns his lights on, he's going to crash," Trey said to Hawk after the inspector had put the mike up. Trey concentrated on the narrow road ahead, gripping the wheel tightly. The road had so many tight turns that he had been forced to slow way down. The Honda would be in sight one moment and then out of sight the next, but with the dust and the lack of lights on the Honda, it was getting harder to spot. Five minutes of frantic, dangerous driving later, Trey rounded a curve in the road.

"There he is," Hawk shouted.

Trey spotted the Honda at the same time Ruben did. Remington had run it off the road and slid sideways into a thicket of small trees.

They saw the suspect jump from the car and run through a clearing, limping slightly but still moving pretty rapidly. Trey gunned the engine until he was even with the spot where Andrew had left the road on foot.

"I'm going after him," Trey shouted as he leaped from the car. He hesitated only long enough to grab his flashlight. "I only have one of these. Stay with the car and see if you can direct Smith. They can land the chopper in the clearing."

"Watch for an ambush," Hawk warned him. "He might have his gun with him."

Trey crossed the clearing and entered the forest again. He kept the flashlight off most of the time, following Andrew by the sound of the man's steps and of slapping limbs as he forced his way through the thick vegetation. Another clearing opened up ahead. Trey spotted Remington, a dark form, nothing more, as he neared the far side. Then Trey stopped as he saw several shadowy forms just beyond the fleeing fugitive.

Had Remington been expecting to meet Martin and several others up here on the mountain? Trey wondered. Had he known where he was going? It didn't seem likely, and yet, someone was up there. He peered closer through the gathering darkness. Or *something*.

Trey moved forward again but slower, careful not to trip. The shadowy figure of the man he was pursuing wasn't being as careful. Andrew stumbled, went to the ground, then got right back up and charged headlong into one of the other figures. The sound of Remington's shout carried clearly through the air. It was not a shout of recognition but of fear. Trey pressed forward. Then he slowed and watched as a battle between two shadowy forms commenced.

Trey flipped on his light, holding it at arm's length to his side in case the light drew gunfire. His strong beam, however, identified a small herd of kangaroos. One of them, probably the biggest of the bunch, was pounding Andrew unmercifully. He could hear the thud of kicks as they landed. Andrew was attempting to duke it out with the kangaroo, kicking and attempting to throw punches, but the creature was far more skilled in the use of his feet than Andrew was with both his fists and legs. Andrew fell on his back, turned over, and tried to crawl away, but the kangaroo pursued him. The rest of them had gathered around like a crowd of spectators.

Trey drew to a stop. Andrew, curled up on the ground, was in defensive mode now. He was covering his head with his hands and screaming loudly. Trey pulled his gun. He had to stop this now or the infuriated kangaroo might kill the man. He aimed a few feet in front of the herd of kangaroos and fired a shot. The kangaroo that was doing the beating stopped and looked toward Trey. He fired again, over their heads this time, hoping they wouldn't charge him. But luckily the entire herd started to hop away from Trey's position.

Remington uncurled himself and got slowly to his feet. The large kangaroo took one giant hop back toward him, knocked him down again with those powerful back feet, and then turned and hopped away, each hop covering three or four meters. Trey surged forward, his gun in one hand and his light in the other. He still held his light to the side in case the man decided to shoot. "Stop! Police!" Trey commanded even as he heard the distant thump of an approaching helicopter.

Andrew dragged himself to his feet and shouted hoarsely, but he was so out of breath Trey couldn't understand his words. He shut the light off and stepped quickly to one side in case Andrew was going to shoot. But no shots came. Trey zigzagged toward Andrew. The fugitive made it to his feet and made for the nearby trees. He fell just as he reached them and then crawled out of sight.

Trey listened as the helicopter came closer. Then he moved to within about three meters of where Remington had disappeared. A couple minutes passed. Still not sure about whether his adversary was armed, he dropped to the ground, making himself a smaller target. He could hear twigs breaking and branches slapping as Andrew forced his way deeper into the thicket. Trey had no idea how long it would be before help arrived—although he could see lights from the helicopter behind him—but he wasn't about to charge into the thicket as dark as it was now. He looked back. The chopper was slowly lowering to the ground about where Trey thought he'd left Inspector Hawk and the car.

The noise of the chopper drowned out the sound of the retreating man, but suddenly a desperate scream came from the bushes, easily heard over the helicopter. Then it came again, louder and even more desperate. Trey stayed where he was, little bumps forming on his arms. He was conscious of the kangaroos as they entered the tree line to his right, but they didn't appear threatening, just curious, although the big one was in front of the rest of them.

Suddenly, Andrew charged out of the bushes, screaming and shouting for help. Trey turned his light on the suspect and felt a chill descend even as he rapidly backpedaled. Two snakes were fastened to Andrew. A very large one was coiled around his chest. The other was around his right leg. Andrew fell to the ground, beating at the snakes with his fists. Then his screaming stopped, and he lay still. The snakes uncoiled themselves and slithered back into the bushes. Only when they were out of sight did Trey move toward the fugitive.

"Help me," Andrew moaned, his breath labored, his arms and legs beginning to thrash helplessly.

Trey shined the light on him. Andrew's face was a mass of red welts, cuts, and bruises. One eye was completely shut. His lips were bleeding. His nose sat at an odd angle, blood trickling from it. On one arm there was a purple spot that was swelling rapidly. He was also bleeding from a couple of nasty scalp wounds and several of the cuts on his face. And his pants and shirt were nearly ripped to shreds. It was hard to differentiate what injuries had resulted from the car wreck, the angry kangaroo, the heavy trees and shrubs, and the deadly snakes. But all combined, the man looked near death.

Trey dropped to his knees. Andrew's mouth opened and closed. His one good eye stared at Trey. His breathing was labored. The kangaroos appeared to be moving closer; Trey could see them in his peripheral vision. But they weren't acting aggressively, so he didn't consider them a threat—yet. He shined his light directly on the rapidly swelling lump on Andrew's arm. There were two small holes there.

Snakebite.

Andrew's breathing became shallow. Trey holstered his gun, wondering if there was anything he could do to help the man, to save his life. He shuddered at the thought of giving mouth-to-mouth, but just then Andrew's breathing picked up a little. His lips moved. In a very weak voice, Andrew said, "They bit me. I'm going to die, aren't I?" He was thrashing his arms and legs weakly and rolling his head back and forth. What Trey could see of his face showed fear, the naked fear of a man who was about to die.

"Help's coming," Trey said helplessly, for he was pretty sure it would be too late for the injured man. "We found the girl with pink hair. Did you kill her?" he asked.

"I had to," Andrew said, struggling to get the words out and stopping the tossing of his head. "She . . . was . . . going . . . to . . . tell . . . the . . . cops . . . what . . . we'd . . . done." It took those words a long time to come out, and Trey was straining to make sure of what Andrew was saying. When the man's lips stopped moving, Trey knew he'd just heard a confession and recited it in his mind.

Trey was conscious of movement a few meters behind him. He turned his head, expecting to see the kangaroos closing in, but the faces of Inspector Hawk, Inspector Smith, and an officer he'd never met before were approaching. They had flashlights, and it was the reflection off the grass from their own lights that lit their faces enough for Trey to recognize them.

He turned his attention back to Andrew. He had another question. "Did Martin help you kill her?"

"Yes. We . . . had . . . to . . . kill . . . her," the ever-fading voice said.

"Did you throw my father's painting into the sea?" Trey asked.

Andrew attempted to answer, but whatever he was trying to say was smothered with a cough, and then his body relaxed as the life oozed out of him.

"I think he's dead, Trey," Inspector Smith said as he knelt. "But not before you got him to implicate Martin Tally in the murder. Good job, Detective. We'll get a warrant out. He'll be found; I'm sure of that."

Trey nodded an acknowledgment and then reached down and placed his fingers over Andrew's carotid artery. There was no pulse. Trey drew his hand back. "You're right; he's dead."

"Was it a snake that did this?" Smith asked.

"Two of them, after a large kangaroo had beaten him," Trey said, rising to his feet. "I don't know what he was thinking. He just ran right into that big kangaroo. Or maybe he was disoriented and thought it was me. Whatever made him do it, it was stupid."

Trey shined his light to the right again. The kangaroos were still congregated near the edge of the trees, grazing quietly as if nothing had happened. The largest one stood to his full height when Trey's light lit him. "Thanks, you big bloke," Trey said, and the other men chuckled.

TWENTY-ONE

A FEW MINUTES LATER, AS the men were attempting to load the body onto the helicopter, Inspector Hawk received a call on his satellite cell phone. He stepped away from the others and spent several minutes talking. By the time his call was ended and he had rejoined Trey beside the chopper, the body was loaded.

Inspector Smith was preparing to step up into the helicopter when he hesitated and looked back. He pointed to the other officer and said, "He'll stay with the wrecked car until we can get it moved. If you two need to get back to the city, go ahead."

Inspector Hawk said nothing about the phone call as the three men carefully made their way back to the road. The chance of encountering deadly snakes kept them all watching every step with care. When they were finally back in the car and headed down the mountain, Inspector Hawk said, "Now I can tell you about that phone call, Detective. It was from one of my operatives in London. He's been working on identifying the person who signs the stolen paintings using the name Ainslee Cline. My client, Damian Latimer, has been very generous, and I've been able to put a lot of recourses into the case.

"He authorized me to hire a couple of art experts to examine her work and the work of other artists, starting with the most obvious, Daphne Slader." He paused.

"And . . . ," Trey coaxed.

"Daphne Slader is Ainslee Cline," he said firmly. "We don't need to look any further."

Trey was stunned. "But she claims she bought mother's painting from Victor Krause."

"I'm not saying she didn't, but I am saying that when she bought it, it didn't have Ainslee Cline's signature on it," Hawk said. "Daphne did at least some of the paint over. The experts will testify in court to that."

"I guess I should call Willie and tell him," Trey said.

"I have a better idea," the inspector suggested. "I think you and I should join the ship tomorrow. I think you should be there to take the lead in questioning the Sladers. I don't want them to know we're even suspicious until we have them sitting in front of us. What do you say?"

"How do we get there?"

"The same way you got *from* the ship, my young friend. Actually, we can fly on a fixed-wing aircraft to whatever airport in New Zealand is closest to where the ship is, which we can figure out when we get back to the city. Then we'll hop in a chopper and fly out to the ship."

"That'll be expensive," Trey protested. He wanted to go back but was unsure of who would pay the bill.

"My client, as I said a minute ago, is very generous. He has instructed me to spare no expense. And that," Hawk said, "is exactly what I intend to do. The only people we'll tell that we're coming are Detective Denning and Captain Johnsen. And we won't tell them why, just that we are."

They arrived at the Shotwell house well after midnight. Security was still in place, and other than one light in the living room, the house was dark. Hawk was staying with Trey because the house was so large and comfortable and the food was great. Charlotte Bray might be along in years, but she was a great cook, and Aariah wasn't so bad herself.

The men parked in the garage, and then Trey entered the code to disarm the alarm while they went into the house.

"Trey, you're home." Aariah leaped from one of the plush sofas, dropping the book she'd been reading, and flew into his arms.

"What are you doing still up?" Trey asked after a long hug and tender kiss.

"I couldn't sleep, and I hoped you'd come along eventually. I figured you'd be hungry when you got here, and someone needed to heat the food up. There's lots of it. I hope you guys are hungry."

"As a matter of fact," Inspector Hawk said, "we haven't had a bite since early this morning."

"Have you been busy?" she asked as a cloud crossed over her face.

"You could say that," Trey told her with a shrug. "We'll tell you all about it over some dinner."

As they ate, the men explained to Aariah what had happened.

"So Daphne lied?" Aariah asked.

"Let's put it this way; she didn't tell the whole truth," Trey said.

"Does that mean she could be a suspect?"

"It does, and for that reason and others, Ruben and I are going to fly to New Zealand and then take a helicopter back to the cruise ship."

"And leave me here?" she asked as fear crossed her face.

Trey looked at Inspector Hawk, who shrugged and said, "She and her grandmother are booked on the ship. Why don't they come with us? I'm sure the captain will be fine with it. And that way, you and Willie and I can protect them."

Aariah's face lit up.

"Sounds great to me," Trey agreed.

* * *

Willie, Hans, Bonnie, Captain Johnsen, the corporate investigators, and three stewards met the helicopter early the next afternoon. They were all assigned staterooms, and their luggage was quickly moved there. At Hans's insistence, Trey was his roommate, and Aariah and Charlotte were in their former stateroom next door.

Charlotte was nervous, but Bonnie assured her they would be kept safe. Trey and Inspector Hawk were anxious to find and interview the Sladers as quickly as possible.

"I don't think we want them to know we're back on board until we bring them in and sit them down in front of us," Reuben said.

"As you know," Captain Hawk said, "we're not going to dock anywhere until morning, so it's just a matter of finding them on the ship. Why don't you wait in my office while I have my security team find and escort the couple to meet you."

Trey said, "That would be great, but I have one question first. What's the status of your camera surveillance system?"

"It's working. New equipment was installed, and it's working perfectly again," Captain Johnsen responded.

"Do you have any idea yet how it was hacked or who hacked it?" Trey asked.

Willie spoke up. "It could have been Victor Krause."

"Why do you say that?" Trey asked.

"One of the investigators back home learned he was a computer expert in Germany. He works with computers and was reported to be very knowledgeable. So far, he's the only one we've been able to identify who might have the expertise to do what was done," Willie said.

"Well, that's good to know," Trey said thoughtfully. "Did he by any chance leave a laptop in his room?"

"No, we've been through his room thoroughly."

"Okay, then let's get back to work," Trey said.

In less than half an hour, Gil and Daphne Slader were seated in the captain's office, facing Detective Trey Shotwell, Detective Willie Denning, and Inspector Ruben Hawk. The captain sat across the room.

"What's this all about?" Gil demanded haughtily. "We already know the painting we bought was ruined."

Trey took the lead. "I'll explain in a moment. I know you've met Detective Denning. But you haven't met Ruben Hawk. He's the head of the Hawk Investigations Agency in London. He's a retired inspector, having worked for thirty years with New Scotland Yard."

"What's a private investigator doing here?" Gil asked, with less haughtiness.

"He and his firm were hired to investigate the missing paintings and other matters," Trey answered. "He's working closely with me and officers in London, Sydney, and other locations."

"Who hired him?" Gil demanded.

"I'm afraid that's confidential," Inspector Hawk said. "If my client wants to disclose it, that would be fine, but I can't."

"But your client isn't here to do that, is he?" Gil said.

"No. I can reach him if I have to, but for now, it will remain confidential."

"It's probably that rich Frenchman, Damian Latimer," Daphne said, speaking for the first time.

Hawk neither confirmed nor denied it. "It doesn't matter who it is. You just need to know that I and my operatives have been working hard on this case." He looked at Trey, who nodded, indicating that he should proceed. So he went on. "We're here today to discuss something a couple of my men have learned. The information they gave me last night is rock solid. They've learned who Ainslee Cline is."

The inspector stopped and stared unblinking into Daphne's eyes. The color drained from her face.

"Who . . . who is it?" she asked, her voice trembling.

"You know who it is, Mrs. Slader," Hawk said coldly, his eyes still holding hers. "It's you. And any attempt to deny it will do no good. We have the proof. So the best thing you can do now is explain yourself. We have a handful of murders to investigate, so at this point I think it would be wise for both of you to cooperate."

As the Sladers looked at each other, Trey said, "This information implicates you in the death of my mother. If you did it or had anything to do with it, we will find out. I agree with Inspector Hawk that it would be in your best interest to cooperate."

Gil said, "My wife and I would like to confer privately for a moment."

Trey shook his head. "You've had plenty of time to discuss this matter between yourselves. We know that you, Daphne, painted over parts of my mother's painting. That clearly implicates you in the theft of that painting." The color continued to drain from her face. Her husband simply clenched his jaws and watched with angry eyes.

"Inspector Hawk personally located two other pieces you painted over. One of them is hanging in a private home in Germany. It is also one that was stolen at the time my mother was murdered. Would you like to explain, or do we simply need to arrest you, take you to New Zealand, and have you held while New Scotland Yard begins proceedings to extradite you back to London?"

Again Daphne and Gil looked at each other.

This time Detective Denning spoke up. "Detective Shotwell swore at his mother's grave that he would not rest until her killers were brought to justice. And that's exactly what he, with our help, is going to do."

"Tell them, Daphne," Gil said. "We didn't kill anybody, and we didn't steal anything. Tell them."

Daphne hesitated, but finally her eyes looked at Willie's face. "I told you I bought the painting from Victor Krause."

"Yes, you did, but you lied when you told me it was already painted over," the detective said darkly.

Her hands were shaking. Her husband was watching her, a touch of anger in his eyes. "Tell them, Daphne."

"Okay, yes, I lied. But I didn't know anything about the painting. There was no signature on it."

"Was the same true of the one that is now in Germany?" Trey pressed.

"Yes, but honestly, I didn't know they were stolen," she said.

"I'm assuming Victor also sold you other paintings that had no signature," he said.

"Yes."

"And you didn't know they were stolen?" Trey asked dubiously.

"I guess I suspected it," she said softly as her eyes filled with tears. "But I swear, I didn't know anyone had been killed."

"Where did Victor say he obtained them?" Trey asked.

"He said he bought them, but he didn't tell me who he bought them from. Why don't you ask him?"

"Do you know where he is?" Inspector Hawk asked.

"I know he didn't come back on the ship, but you can find him," she insisted. "And I'm sure you can make him tell you where he got them."

"Do you know where his friend, Claudia Gaudet, is?" the inspector asked.

She shook her head.

Willie said, "She's on the ship again. She claims Victor tried to kill her, that he left her for dead."

"That's horrible," Daphne said. "But maybe he told her where he got the paintings."

"Maybe, but we don't know that," Trey said.

"Then you need to ask her," Gil spoke up.

"I honestly doubt she can tell us," Trey responded.

"Then find Victor and make him tell you. Surely the police are looking for him if he tried to kill Claudia."

"They were but not anymore," Trey said.

"Why not? You've got to find him. He might have stolen them. He might have killed your mother," she said, her voice rising.

"We already found him. He's dead. Someone blew him up," he said.

The shock on the faces of both of the Sladers seemed genuine. Trey let it sink in for a minute. Then he said. "He was blown up, but the bomb was meant for me."

For a full minute, it was silent in the captain's office. Finally, Daphne asked, "Do you know who did it?"

"It was probably either my uncle, Lukas Nichols, or your friend Martin Talley," Trey said. "This means, of course, that you have more explaining to do. I—we, all of us, think you two are involved in Martin leaving the ship. It wasn't something he did on his own. At least two people helped him."

Daphne's shoulders slumped. "Danny," she whispered.

"If it was Danny," Gil said, his face turning dark with anger, "then he had help. I knew Martin was a bad influence on him." He looked across at Trey. "We know nothing about that. But I have a feeling Daphne's brother does. Get him in here, and he'll tell you. I'll make sure he tells you."

The captain got to his feet. "Would you like me to have security find him?" he asked.

"Absolutely," Trey said.

The captain made the necessary call, and then he said, "They'll have him here shortly."

Trey nodded and then said, "We'll wait and continue this when your brother gets here. But you need to realize that if he and Martin and someone else stole the paintings, then they are very likely responsible for my father's death and probably my mother's. And, maybe they'll implicate you."

"We didn't steal anything or kill anyone," Daphne said. "I swear to it." Trey said nothing, and after a moment she went on. "I know Martin and the paintings were found in Sydney, but can you tell us how they got there? Honestly, I can't imagine."

"Martin was seen in Sydney, and the paintings did both come to shore, but we don't yet have him in custody. I'm hoping you can help us locate him."

"In Sydney?" Gil asked. "We'd be no help there."

"We'll see," Trey said.

"He had help, didn't he?" Daphne asked.

"Yes, he did."

"Do you know who helped him?"

"Let's ask your brother about that," Trey said, neatly sidestepping Daphne's question.

Daphne seemed sad, but Gil was clearly enraged.

"When they bring Danny in, don't say a word until we tell you to," the wise and experienced Inspector Hawk said. "I can see you're angry, but we need for you to keep your cool. If you don't, we may not get a thing out of Danny."

"If you really want to get him to say anything, you just need to give me about ten minutes alone with him," Gil said, barely able to contain his anger.

"That won't help, Gil," Daphne said, pleading with both her voice and her eyes. "If either of us should spend some time alone with him, it should be me."

"You're too gentle," Gil said. "I can make him talk."

"Let's let the cops try first," she said as she wiped tears from her eyes. She looked over at Trey. "You said you didn't find Martin yet, but what about your father's painting?"

"No, but I have an idea where it might have gone," he said just as the door opened and two officers ushered Danny into the room.

One look at Gil and Daphne, and Danny wilted.

TWENTY-TWO

AFTER DANNY HAD BEEN SEATED—ABOUT three meters from the Sladers—Trey introduced Inspector Hawk, and then he said, "I understand you've already met Detective Denning."

He nodded, and Daphne said, "Please, Detective Shotwell, can I just say one thing to my brother?"

Trey looked at Willie and Hawk. They both nodded, but the inspector said, "Make it short, and no questions at this point. Is that understood?"

She agreed, and Trey said, "Go ahead then."

"Okay." She faced her brother. "Danny, I'm terribly disappointed in you. If you know what's good for you, you'll answer every question these men ask you, just like Gil and I have done. Don't lie, and don't hide anything."

"What's this all about?" Danny asked, trying to appear nonchalant but failing miserably at it.

"It's about you and Martin," Trey said.

"Martin's gone. He fell overboard," Danny said. "He's dead."

Daphne turned to Trey. "He doesn't know," she said.

"Apparently there are some things you don't know about," Trey said. "I know what happened. Martin is very much alive. He turned up in Sydney with the stolen paintings. So don't act like you think he's dead. Now, who helped you get Martin and the paintings overboard?"

Danny's mouth opened and closed without a sound coming out.

Daphne caught his eye. "They have it figured out, Danny. So talk."

"How do you know?" Danny asked, slumping in his chair.

"Your friends weren't as smart as they thought they were. They brought the paintings into a boatyard near Sydney on a rented boat.

They're in a lot of trouble, but so are you. You can make it easier on yourself if you simply tell us what your involvement was and who the other person was."

"*Now*, Danny," Gil said, ice in his voice.

The look that Danny received from Gil was all it took to open his mouth. "It was all Martin's and Victor's idea," he said. "I just helped them. That's all. They promised nobody would know I helped. They promised."

"Have you never heard the old saying that there's no honor among thieves?" Trey asked.

"What do you mean?" he asked.

"People who steal often tell on each other. I've learned already that you and Martin stole the paintings and that Andrew Remington picked Martin and the paintings up and took them to Australia. Now, I'm going to give you a chance to tell me more. Start with who helped you boost Martin over the railing."

"I don't think I should."

"Why not?"

"He'll kill me," Danny said.

"Victor?" Trey asked.

"You said you didn't know who helped us." Danny's chin quivered.

"I didn't say any such thing, Danny. But since we both agree that it was you and Victor Krause who helped Martin get away, why don't you tell me how you stole the paintings."

"Detective Shotwell, you don't understand. Victor's a dangerous man. If he thinks I told you, he'll kill me. I know he will."

"And I know he won't touch you."

"Is he in jail?" Danny asked.

"No, Victor's dead," Trey said. "He died in Sydney."

"Are you sure? Did you see him?"

"I saw what was left of him. He was blown up. Now, let's start at the beginning, and you can tell us all about it."

Danny turned to his sister. "Do I have to?" he asked with a whine.

"Yes, you have to," Gil answered for his wife, his eyes filled with rage. "Believe me, you will either tell them or you will tell me, and I think it would be safer for you to tell them."

Danny hung his head. "Okay, but it wasn't my idea, it was Victor and Martin that thought it all up."

"Thought what up?" Trey pressed.

"The theft from your mother," Danny said.

"Were you there?" Trey asked.

"Yes."

"Did you kill my mother?"

"No, you gotta believe me. All I did was help take the paintings. I carried two of them out to the van, and when I went back in, Mrs. Shotwell was lying dead on the floor," Danny said. "Martin handed me another painting and told me to take it to the van. He grabbed another painting, and we jumped in the car and took off. I asked him why he killed her, said that Victor told us not to hurt anybody. He said he had to, and he drove away really fast."

"Was the van black?" Trey asked.

"Yes."

"Where was Victor during all this?"

"I don't know," Danny said.

"What did you do with the paintings?" Trey asked, glancing at Daphne. She was sitting with her head in her hands, sobbing. Gil was glaring at Danny, his fists bunched.

"Martin told me he gave them to Victor."

"And Victor sold them to your sister?"

"Yeah, I guess so," Danny said.

"So the whole scheme was Victor's, is that right?" Trey asked.

"I guess so. Martin told me it was."

"Wait a minute. Are you saying you never heard Victor give the order to steal my parents' paintings?"

"No, but Martin said he did," Danny insisted.

"Danny, do you understand that even if you didn't kill my mother, you can be tried for murder just by being there committing a crime when she was killed?" Trey asked.

"But I didn't do it. I didn't know Martin was going to. You've gotta help me. Please," he begged. "I'll tell you anything you need me to."

"Okay, let's talk about the thefts here on the ship," Trey suggested. "Whose idea was that?"

"Martin said it was Victor's idea."

"Is that why Martin and Victor came on this cruise?" Trey asked.

"Yes."

Gil couldn't restrain himself. "You brought that fool Martin on our trip *knowing* he was going to steal paintings?"

"We didn't know Daphne was going to buy that one. We didn't even know it was going to be on the ship. We only planned to take the other one. But then Martin said Victor wanted us to take the one you painted too."

"Was that before or after we bought it?" Gil demanded.

"It was before," Danny said.

"Who broke into the room where the paintings were stored?" Trey asked, cutting off Gil before he asked anything else.

"Martin did," Danny answered. "He used some lock-picking tools he brought with him."

"Have you seen him use them before?" Trey asked.

"He uses them a lot," Danny acknowledged.

Gil looked like he was about to explode. Trey wasn't sure how long the man could contain himself. He glanced at Willie, who stepped closer to Gil. Daphne looked totally defeated. Danny was sweating profusely.

Over the next few minutes, Danny rehearsed how they'd covered the paintings in some plastic Martin brought on the ship. "Then we took them up to our room and wrapped them even better," he said. "They had to be water tight. We padded them with towels and newspapers, and then we wrapped them together and covered them with lots of plastic and taped them up really good. Then, we took them down to the walkway."

"Danny, where was Victor? Was he with you when you stole them?'"

"No, he met us on the promenade deck."

"You were being watched, Danny. The witness said it looked like you were fighting or struggling with Martin," Trey told him.

"We were just acting, in case anyone saw us. We didn't want anyone to know Martin was planning to go in the water. It had to look like he was thrown in. Everybody was supposed to think he was dead."

"They did," Gil growled. "He should have been."

"How did anybody figure it out?" Danny asked. "I mean, who thought Martin didn't really drown?"

For the first time, Inspector Hawk spoke. "That would be Detective Shotwell."

"How did you know?" Danny asked Trey.

"I learned he was an experienced diver. When we found out that he and his friend Andrew Remington had been arrested for diving to a wreck and stealing treasure, it made sense that the two of them could have arranged all of this," Trey said.

"Where are Martin and Andrew? Are they in jail in Australia?" Danny asked.

"Andrew isn't. He's with Victor," Trey said.

"But Victor is . . ." He stopped and looked at Trey with wide eyes. "Is he dead too?"

"Yes, he is."

Danny slumped. "How did he die?"

"That's another story. You don't need to know that right now," Trey said, and then he abruptly shifted the focus of the questioning. "Was it you and Victor who kidnapped Aariah and threatened her?"

Danny, to Trey's surprise, got a blank look on his face. "I don't know what you're talking about," he said.

Trey pursued the line of questioning for a few more minutes but finally concluded Danny hadn't had anything to do with that. Once more Trey shifted the focus. "Danny, why did you kill my father?"

Danny threw himself back in his chair. "I didn't have anything to do with that," he shouted. "You gotta believe me. I've never killed anyone."

"So are you saying Victor killed him?" Trey asked

"I guess. I don't know. It wasn't me. That's all I know."

"Surely Victor said something to you about it," Trey pressed.

"No, I swear. I don't know anything about it."

They talked for another hour or so. Gil and Daphne were eventually allowed to ask their own questions, and Detective Denning and Inspector Hawk asked some as well. They learned that Andrew had planned to swim underwater to the area near the ship, towing more diving equipment for Martin. Danny also told them that Martin and Andrew had planned to use submersible GPS units and radios to find each other. The boat that Andrew was going to use, as per their plan, was left far enough from the ship's route that it wouldn't be noticed. And Danny said they also enclosed a GPS unit with the paintings that sent a signal to the thieves' radios. According to Danny, the preparations were all supposed to make it relatively simple for Andrew to locate both Martin and the paintings.

Finally, the paintings were to be hidden in Australia for a few months before being taken back to London to be "fixed," as Danny told it, and then eventually sold.

"You didn't really think I'd do it for you, did you?" Daphne asked. The sadness she'd displayed had turned to fury.

"No, he was taking them to someone else," Danny had responded.

They learned a few more details, and then Danny was turned over to the cruise investigators, who put him in the ship's brig. Daphne and Gil were allowed to go back to their suite.

It was Trey who said, "We're still missing something. Danny knows something he hasn't disclosed."

"I think the Sladers know more than they've admitted," Willie said. "Maybe they should be arrested too."

"Maybe so, and yet, I don't know . . ." Inspector Hawk said and trailed off. He thoughtfully rubbed his chin for a moment and then spoke again. "Trey's right. We *are* missing something, but it doesn't have anything to do with Danny."

"Uncle Lukas," Trey said suddenly. "He's probably the missing piece."

"So what we need to do is go back to Sydney and find Lukas—if he's there," Hawk said.

"I agree. And I'd like to find Martin Talley. He's a bad guy, that's for sure, but I can't help but wonder if he might be a scapegoat for the Sladers and Danny," Trey mused. "Maybe he killed my mother, and maybe he didn't. All we have right now is Danny's word."

"When we catch up with Lukas and Martin, we'll learn more, Trey."

"I think we need to get back there, Inspector. How long will it take for us to make arrangements to return?"

"I'll make some calls while you check with your department and see how the manhunt is going," Hawk said.

Trey called Inspector Smith, who said, "I'm glad you called, Detective. I just learned that Martin Talley has been apprehended."

Trey pumped one fist as he held his phone in the other hand. "That's great news, Inspector. Where was he caught?"

"He was at the airport, attempting to leave the country. An off-duty officer who was checking bags recognized him from the pictures we distributed. Talley was carrying a single bag past the check-in area," Inspector Smith said. "With the aid of several officers from airport security, he was able to arrest Martin."

"I can't wait to talk to him," Trey said. "Inspector Hawk is trying to arrange transportation back to Australia for us right now. And just so you know, we have a coconspirator here on the ship who claims Martin Talley is the person who murdered my mother."

"That's good to know; we are charging him with the murder of Kori Acton, as well. You may rest assured that Talley won't be going anywhere, so you'll be able to interrogate him whenever you get back."

"I don't suppose anyone has seen Lukas Nichols or Vanie Velman," Trey said.

"No, but the search is on. What else did you learn from your suspects on the ship?" Inspector Smith asked.

Trey briefly summarized the information gained from the Sladers and Danny Bidwell, and then agreed to let the inspector know when they would be arriving back in Sydney. As Trey finished his call in the hallway outside the captain's office, Inspector Hawk joined him from where he'd been on his phone a few meters down the hallway.

"You must have good news," Hawk said. "I saw you pump your fist."

"They caught Martin Talley."

"Great," Hawk said. "But it's going to be tomorrow before we can get back to Sydney. We might as well just relax this evening and be ready to meet the helicopter first thing in the morning."

"I'll let Aariah and her grandmother know," Trey responded. "Maybe we could all have dinner."

Also joining them for dinner an hour later were Willy Denning, Hans Olander, Bonnie Springer, and the generous Frenchman with the fat checkbook, Damian Latimer. They discussed Martin's capture, Danny's confession, the violent death of Victor Krause, and the close scrape with death Claudia Gaudet had experienced at the hands of Victor. They also talked about the death of Andrew Remington and his partial confession that the painting Damian had purchased had been buried at sea. The ongoing search for Lukas and Vanie was also mentioned.

Damian said, "Maybe Martin will tell you where my painting was left and if it was secured in such a manner that it wouldn't drift with the ocean currents so it could be retrieved."

"That's my hope," Trey said. "But who knows with Martin."

"If you had coordinates on it, I'd be willing to pay a diver to attempt to retrieve it," Damian said.

"I know a good diver," Hans said, his eyes looking at Bonnie.

"I'd give it a try," she said. "I've had quite a bit of experience."

"We have to pinpoint it first, and that won't be easy," Hawk interjected. "Trey and I and the ladies here," he said, indicating Aariah and her grandmother, "will be returning to Sydney tomorrow. We'll just have to see what we can do."

Aariah cleared her throat. Trey glanced at her and saw that she was fidgeting nervously. "What is it, Aariah?" he asked.

"Well . . . ah . . . Grandmother and I have been talking about it. We'd kind of like to finish the cruise, if that's okay with you. Grandmother would like to at least see a little bit of New Zealand. Then when we return to Sydney, your case should be finished and maybe we can get our lives back to normal."

"That would be fine. You should be safe on the cruise now," Trey said even as he felt an aching in his heart. He would miss her, but it would only be a few days. Of course, when the cruise was over, she and her grandmother would probably be going back to Melbourne. He said nothing about any of that. After all, he had work to do in Sydney, and with his uncle still unaccounted for, despite Martin's arrest, Trey could still be in danger—and that could put the women in danger as well. Maybe they would be better off on the ship than in Sydney.

"I'll make sure they're okay here and see that they have a good time for the rest of the cruise," Bonnie said. "You go back and find your uncle and be assured that Aariah and Mrs. Bray will be safe."

"We'll come back to Sydney before we return to Melbourne," Aariah said.

Trey took her hand. "I'll miss you, but I understand."

"And I hope all of you will be there to see me thrash a few opponents," Hans said with a huge grin.

"We wouldn't miss it," Aariah said. "What about you, Bonnie?"

"I'll be there. I'm going to take a few weeks off after we land in Auckland," she said. "I want to get to know this big bruiser a little better." She blushed lightly as she said it, and Hans grinned again. Then she added, "And if Martin cooperates and tells you where the painting is, I'd be glad to try to recover it."

"Then we'll see what Martin has to say," Trey concluded.

* * *

Later that evening, Hawk got a call from one of his agents in London. He relayed the information to Trey. "It seems that an acquaintance of Lukas's is under the impression that your uncle and his girlfriend intend to buy some property in Australia and establish a second home there."

"He must be making some money then," Trey said.

"Maybe, but remember, Miss Velman is wealthy. They could be using her money. But it could also mean that he and Vanie may not be trying to make a quick getaway. And it gives us a way to find them," Hawk said. "When we get back to Sydney, I think we should begin to contact real-estate companies. Who knows, maybe we'll get lucky."

"I hope so," Trey said.

TWENTY-THREE

MARTIN TALLEY HAD AN ATTITUDE. But he was also trapped in a situation of his own making. He had mysteriously disappeared from the ship between Australia and New Zealand at the same time as the paintings, and yet he stubbornly insisted he'd had nothing to do with the paintings being stolen.

"Yes," he said after several minutes of interrogation by Trey and Inspector Hawk, "I did jump off the ship. I'm an expert diver, and I knew that my friend Andrew Remington was in the area to meet me and help me get to Australia. And we did, and that is our business."

"You left Australia on the cruise. It seems like it would have been a lot simpler to just stay there in the first place," Trey reasoned.

Martin shook his head. "You don't understand. Daphne and Gil Slader were making my life miserable. I hadn't expected that. So I contacted Andrew, we made the plan, and as you can see, it worked. You have no reason to hold me. I have done nothing wrong. I didn't steal anything."

"We have sufficient evidence to send you back to London to face murder charges," Trey said coldly.

Trey thought he saw a slight tic in Martin's eyes, but the man recovered quickly. "Who am I accused of killing? I'm not a killer."

"My mother, Rita Shotwell."

"That's insane," Martin said hotly.

"We have a witness," Trey said as he leaned toward Martin. "You'll be going to England and facing trial there. And you'll also be tried for stealing five very valuable paintings on the day you murdered her."

Martin's face went red. "Who told you all this? Whoever said it is a liar."

Trey leaned back again. "You'll find out who it is in good time, but we'll get back to that. Have you talked to Andrew lately?" Trey, of course, knew that he hadn't. He also knew that nothing had been released to the press about Andrew's death. He wanted to see what Martin would say about Andrew.

"No, I haven't seen him since he brought me here from the ship. I think he already left for London. He told me he had some diving contracts there," Martin said.

"That's interesting," Trey said, poking a finger toward him. "He told me you had him take my father's painting that you stole from the ship and then had him hide it under the sea, secured so it would stay down. He says it's safely wrapped and will be fine when you go after it later."

There was a definite tic in one of Martin's eyes. He looked down at his hands for a moment, as if giving himself time to think, and then he looked up. "It's not true. There's no way he would have told you that because it didn't happen."

"He also told me you helped him kill a girl with pink hair who you used to deface the piece I painted, the one Daphne bought and you stole," Trey pressed.

"That's a lie! Why would I even bother to steal that piece of junk you painted?" he asked with a sneer.

Trey again ignored his response. "He also says you tried to kill me by setting a bomb at my apartment."

"That's ridiculous. If I had done that, you'd be dead." Martin forced a chuckle and added, "Why would I try to kill you? I'm not a killer. I told you that before."

"You're right about one thing, Martin. I didn't get killed, but Victor Krause did. You should have warned him about what you had done," Trey said.

Finally, it seemed like Trey had struck a weak spot in Martin, for he could see fear in the man's eyes now. Martin began to squirm nervously on his chair but still said nothing.

Inspector Hawk said, "I think you can gather from the questions Detective Shotwell has been asking that before you go to London to face charges there, you'll have to answer to ones here—Victor's murder and the murder of Kori Acton, the girl you hired to paint a note on Detective Shotwell's painting. You do plan to charge him with those, don't you, Detective?"

"Inspector Smith has already seen to that," Trey answered. Hawk already knew that, but he wanted Martin to hear it. Then Trey again addressed Martin. "I'm afraid we happen to believe Andrew, not you, Martin."

"Where is he?" Martin asked with much less bravado than he had previously displayed.

Trey looked Martin in the eye. "I thought you just told us he went back to London. Well, I'm here to tell you he didn't. I caught up with him the day he took my father's painting back out to sea. Why don't you think about things for a while, and we'll talk to you again."

They left Martin, and when they did, both men could see he was rattled. "I think he'll tell us more," Hawk said. "But first, I think we need to take a look at his belongings."

They did, but it was no help. "Let's look through Remington's wallet and the car he was driving. I know that's already been done, but I think we should do it with an eye out for GPS coordinates," Inspector Hawk suggested. "With all the money my client is spending, I'd sure like to get his painting back."

Once again, they got no results. "Unless we can get Martin to tell us, that painting might be lost," Hawk moaned. "One thing looks pretty certain. Martin's going to be spending the rest of his life in prison."

The next morning, Trey was notified that Martin wanted to talk to him. He and Inspector Hawk drove directly to the jail. Martin, when he came in, appeared quite arrogant again. After they were seated, and the recorder was running, Trey said, "You asked to speak to us," he said.

"Yes, I did," Martin replied. "I've been thinking about these trumped up charges ever since you talked to me yesterday. I'm not going to take the fall for anyone. I've decided that I need to look out for myself instead of protecting other people, who, it appears, are ready to throw me to the wolves."

"What other people would that be?" Trey asked.

"There are several. First, you need to know that Gil and Daphne Slader are the ones who ordered the theft of your parents' paintings.

And it wasn't me that they sent in to do it; it was that German, the one you say is dead."

"Victor," Trey said softly.

"That's right. Victor stole the paintings for Daphne and Gil, and he's the one who murdered your mother, Detective Shotwell," Martin said.

"And how do you know that?"

"He told me," Martin said.

"When?"

"It was about a year ago. He and I had become acquainted through the Sladers. We were talking one night in a pub in London. He'd had too much to drink, and when that happens, he talks too much," Martin said, grinning and exposing his yellow teeth. Trey watched his face, conscious of the large gap where Hans had knocked one of those teeth out. Martin shifted in his hard wooden chair and then went on. "We were talking about Daphne and Gil. I told him I thought they were nice people and that Daphne was a good artist.

"Victor laughed at me. He said, 'You think they're nice? Let me tell you about them.' And that was when he told me that they'd hired him to steal a bunch of paintings. After he told me he'd given them to Daphne and got paid, I told him I knew all about how Rita Shotwell had been murdered. He laughed again and said, 'I did it.'"

"Just like that?" Trey asked.

"That's right," Martin said.

"Did he tell you what he hauled the paintings away in?" Trey asked.

"He said it was a black van, one of those without windows in the back," Martin answered without any hesitation.

Trey and Hawk asked him more questions about what Victor had told him, and then Martin said, "Daphne paints over the pictures Victor steals for her. Victor told me that too. She uses the name Ainslee Cline. She even does a few original paintings using that name. There, you have it. I'm not protecting them anymore."

Trey drummed his fingers on the table for a moment, watching Martin intently. Martin's eyes were continually shifting. Trey assumed it was because he was nervous over one of two things—either Martin was lying or he was worried that squealing on the Sladers would come back to bite him, that they would somehow make him pay. Trey let him stew for a minute more, and when Martin didn't say anything else, Trey quit drumming his fingers and asked, "You stole the paintings off the ship, isn't that right?"

Martin got a tic in his eye again. "I did that for Daphne and Gil. They promised to pay me."

"So you lied about that yesterday? You said you didn't steal any paintings."

"I didn't. Gil, Daphne, and Danny did that."

"So it's just coincidence they threw the paintings into the ocean at the same time you jumped in?"

"It must be; I don't know what happened to those paintings. I didn't know they'd even been stolen."

Trey thought for a moment. Martin was changing his story so fast it was making Trey's head spin. First he'd admitted stealing them, and then he'd denied knowing anything about it. Both versions could not be true. Trey stared at the man for a minute, thinking about what to say next. "Martin, I might be able to believe you about the Sladers having Victor steal the paintings from my parents and even of him killing my mother, but I know about the paintings from the ship. We have one of them. And there's no way it could have gotten back to Australia all by itself."

Martin ducked his head. Trey waited. Finally, Martin said, "Okay, I admit I knew about them. But the Sladers made me do it. They put a little transmitter in the packaging and gave me a receiver. They threatened me. You've gotta understand, Detective, they're dangerous people. When Gil told me I had to help them, he said if I didn't, they'd kill me. And they would have," Martin said.

"So it was already planned with Andrew Remington, is that right?"

"Yes," Martin finally admitted with downcast eyes. "I called him from Daphne's satellite phone and told him I was going to get off the ship and how I planned to do it. If he's telling you something different, it isn't true."

"So he found you in the water and gave you some diving gear, and then together you found the paintings with the help of the little homing device?" Hawk asked, leaning in.

"Yes."

"Where are they now?" Trey asked.

"I don't know. I think Andrew double-crossed me. He must have talked to Daphne after talking to me."

"Martin, we have one of the paintings, the one Daphne bought. It's defaced, a note written on it in acrylic paint by a girl named Kori Acton," Trey emphasized. "She's dead now, murdered. We found her buried in a shallow grave behind the house you and Andrew were staying in." Trey paused and watched Martin's face. What he saw was a man who appeared to be on the edge of admitting defeat.

Trey forged ahead, hoping to push him over that edge. "Andrew told me that the two of you killed and buried her because you thought she was going to go to the police. That's true, isn't it?"

Martin, his head bowed, said, "I didn't do it. Andrew did."

"But you were there, weren't you?" Trey asked.

All the response that question got was a small nod of the head.

"Martin, where's the other painting you stole?"

"I didn't steal it. Daphne did. I told you that already. All I did was agree to get it to Australia. And I did that with Andrew's help. I don't know where it is now," he said. "I guess Andrew put it back in the ocean if you say he did, but I didn't know he was doing it. Maybe you need to ask *him* if he is so willing to tell you stuff."

Inspector Hawk got up. "I need to make a couple of phone calls, Detective Shotwell. I'll be right back."

Trey watched him leave, wondering what in the world he was doing. To leave in the middle of an interview like this one was highly unusual, but since the interview was being recorded, he decided to continue to question Martin. "Why would Andrew double-cross you? I thought you were good friends."

"He would do anything for money," Martin responded.

"Even double-cross his friend?"

"Probably. He must have. I'd like to talk to him. Where are you holding him? Is he in this same jail?"

"No, Martin, he is not in this jail," Trey said.

"He lied to you," Martin said. "If you'd let me talk to him, he'd tell the truth."

"Martin, Andrew's dead," Trey said.

Martin rocked back in his chair, a look of shock on his face. "He lied!" Martin said weakly, visibly shaken by the news. He said nothing for a moment, and then he went on. "If he's dead, how could he have told you the stuff you say he did?"

"He was dying when he told me."

"Then nobody will believe it," Martin said, but he didn't say it with much conviction.

"Actually, Martin, the law calls that a deathbed confession. They're almost always true, and judges and juries believe them."

"Did you shoot him?" Martin asked.

"No, I didn't shoot him."

"Did somebody else, then?"

"No, he wasn't shot."

"Then what happened to him?"

"He lost a boxing match with a very large and angry kangaroo, and then, trying to get away from the kangaroo, he crawled into the bushes and met a couple snakes."

"He died from a snake bite?" Martin asked with horror on his face.

"Two snake bites, actually," Trey informed him. "He died a very painful death. But he told me the truth as he was dying. Now, I have another question for you. Did you place the bomb at my apartment that killed Victor?"

Martin, though the day before seemed to have been hesitant about that very question, did not hesitate this time. He said, "No. I had nothing to do with that."

"But you knew about it? Is that right?"

"No, that's not right. I didn't know about it. Why would you think I wanted to kill you? I've told you over and over that I'm not a killer. Yes, I've done some bad things. Yes, I'm a thief. I admit that, but I didn't try to kill you."

Trey sat back. For some strange reason, he thought Martin was telling the truth this time, but he decided to put a little more pressure on him. "I know you don't like me, Martin. And you know I don't care much for you. I didn't appreciate the way you treated my friend Aariah on the ship, and I think you knew I'd come after you for stealing the paintings. That's why I think you wanted to kill me."

"But I didn't know you'd come after me. I thought everyone would think I had drowned," he said with a bit of a whine in his voice. "Daphne said she would make sure everyone thought so."

"She tried," Trey said. "But I wasn't convinced. So why did you set that bomb for me?"

"I swear I didn't do that," Martin said.

"Then who did?"

He shrugged his shoulders. "I have no idea. Maybe it was Victor. Maybe he was careless and blew himself up."

"No, it wasn't Victor."

"Then I don't have any idea," he said. "But I didn't do it. I swear."

Even though there were reasons to believe Martin was that killer, Trey had doubts. Officers were checking with real-estate agencies all over New South Wales and beyond in an attempt to find where Lukas might have purchased property. He had to find his uncle, and when he did, he was pretty sure he would have found the killer of his father as well as Victor. And perhaps even his mother.

He threw one more question at Martin. "Did you kill my mother, Rita Shotwell?"

"No!" Martin practically shouted. "I told you already. Victor did that."

"Are you sure it might not have been my uncle, Lukas Nichols?" Trey asked, throwing the question out there just to see what kind of reaction it might get.

"Lukas Nichols? I don't know Lukas Nichols. I already told you. Victor told me he did it."

Inspector Hawk reentered the room then. "How is it coming?"

"I think we're through here," Trey said. Then he turned again to Martin. "If you think of anything else you should tell me, ask for me, and I'll come again."

"I think I've told you everything," the dejected man said.

"Well, just in case, I'll be available."

Trey and Ruben walked outside into the blinding sunlight. "I'm thinking about staying here until summer comes in England," Ruben said with a grin.

"Seems like a good idea," Trey responded. "You could work here when it's summer and then go back to England when it's summer there." The two men chuckled as they climbed into Trey's police car, and Trey pulled out to the street.

"Tell me about the rest of the interview with Martin," the inspector said, "and then I'll tell you about the calls I made."

After giving him a short summary, Trey said, "Maybe you disagree, Inspector, but let me tell you what I have concluded. I think that Martin is, for the most part, telling the truth this time."

Trey looked across the car at Ruben as he answered, "I agree with you. Now, let me tell you who I called and why."

TWENTY-FOUR

DAPHNE AND GIL SLADER WERE in their cabin on the cruise ship when there was a knock on the door. "Not you guys again," Daphne said when she opened the door. The presence of Detective Willie Denning, Officer Bonnie Springer, and the two cruise line investigators obviously irritated her. "What do you need now?"

Gil was on his feet, and he joined Daphne at the door. "Why don't you step out here, both of you?" Willie said.

They did as asked, albeit reluctantly. "You're both under arrest," Willie announced, and the officers pulled out handcuffs. Bonnie handled Daphne, who was cursing and kicking. She spun the woman against the wall, pulled her hands behind her back and expertly put the cuffs on.

Gil went ballistic, but he was no match for the three men and was soon in handcuffs as well. "What is this?" Gil demanded angrily as the two captives were led down the hallway. Doors opened and then shut rapidly as they passed by. "I'll own this entire cruise line before I'm through with you. You have nothing to arrest us for."

"Actually, Mr. Slader, we do," Willie said, "and you both know it."

Daphne kicked at Willie but missed. Bonnie wrapped her arms around the smaller woman and lifted her from the floor. "Gil's right, you know," she said as she continued to struggle. "We've done nothing wrong. We'll sue you all personally—and the entire cruise line. This is false arrest."

The charges were recited to the couple as they were led down to the brig, where they were searched and placed inside. Danny was then led out by the two cruise line investigators. Gil and Daphne were cursing and making threats. "Danny, you'll regret helping them, you little skunk," Gil snarled.

"I didn't," he protested, but the investigators hustled him away before he could say anything more.

Bonnie shut and locked the iron door to the small cell. She and Willie ignored the angry couple and walked briskly away. From there they went directly up to the captain's cabin. "They're in custody, Captain," Willie said.

"Did they give you any trouble?" Captain Johnsen asked.

"Nothing we couldn't handle," Bonnie said with a chuckle.

The captain snorted. "To think I gave them back the money for the painting they bought and then stole . . ." he said, his voice trailing off. He shook his head and then started speaking again. "If I understand you right, you can prove that they stole the paintings, but so far, you don't have evidence that they murdered Mr. Shotwell."

"Your investigators are questioning Danny as we speak," Willie said. "Hopefully, they can get him to tell them exactly what the Sladers are responsible for. But we do have solid evidence on the theft of the paintings. And my colleagues in London are building a case for the theft of the Shotwells' paintings ten years ago and the murder of Mrs. Shotwell. We do not believe they killed Rita Shotwell themselves, but they did order the theft of the paintings, and her murder occurred as a result thereof."

"But you don't have solid evidence on that yet?" he asked.

"Not yet."

"Okay, you've done good work. Keep me advised of any further developments. And Bonnie," he said, turning to his tall security officer, "I'd like you to let Miss Stanton and Mrs. Bray know that the Sladers are in custody. This has been a terrible experience for them. I'd like them to be able to enjoy what's left of the cruise, even though I fully intend to see to it that they receive a full refund. While you do that, I'll invite Damien Latimer to the cabin and bring him up to date on the arrest of the Sladers."

"I'll call Detective Shotwell and inform him," Willie volunteered.

* * *

Trey's cell phone rang as he and Inspector Hawk were walking into the realty office where Inspector Smith and a constable were waiting for them. Trey waved a hand at Smith and then stepped back outside again when he saw who the call was from. "Willie, is Aariah okay? Did you get the Sladers?"

"Aariah's fine. Bonnie just went to inform her and Mrs. Bray that we've arrested the Sladers," Willie said. "They're cursing up a storm, but they're right where we want them."

"What a relief. I've been kicking myself for letting Aariah and her grandmother stay on the ship. I really didn't realize that Daphne and Gil were the thieves and possibly my father's killers," Trey said. "They seemed so cooperative. How did they act when you arrested them?"

"They went nuts. But you should have seen the way Bonnie single-handedly put Daphne in handcuffs." Willie chuckled. "Are you making any headway in Sydney?"

"I'm standing outside a realty office as we speak. All I know so far is that Lukas and Vanie Velman came in looking for some property to buy. I'll know more shortly."

"Let me know what you find out," Willie instructed him.

"I will. By the way, how is Claudia Gaudet doing after her close call with death?" Trey asked.

"She's resting. I don't know if she's even left her room since the doctor finished patching her up," Willie informed him.

"Okay. I'll talk to you when I know more. I'm going inside now," Trey said.

"Detective," Inspector Smith greeted him, "you'll need to go to Tasmania. It seems that your uncle is buying a piece of property a few miles from Hobart. The Realtor says it isn't terribly far from Port Arthur on the Tasmania Peninsula."

Trey nodded. "I've been there before, to see the famous prison where convicts from Great Britain were sent to perform hard labor back in the eighteenth and nineteenth centuries. Do you have an exact location of the property they're buying?"

"We do," he said. "Inspector Hawk is writing it down right now. He'll go with you; I've also arranged for someone from the police force there to give you backup."

They were flown to Tasmania by a New South Wales police pilot and arrived in Hobart in the early afternoon. From Hobart, they took a helicopter to Port Arthur, where they were met by a pair of uniformed constables who had already arrived at the property. It was a small but very nice house with a magnificent view of the surrounding area. A light-green Ford Territory, a small Australian-built car, with a sticker from a Hobart rental company was parked in front of the house.

The officers positioned themselves strategically, and then Trey went to the front door and knocked. Lukas himself answered. "What in the world are you doing here, Trey?" Lukas asked in surprise.

"We need to talk," Trey said.

"Come on in." Lukas was acting friendly, not like the angry threatening man he'd been on the promenade deck when Danny and Martin had inadvertently knocked him down. "Vanie, we have company," he shouted over his shoulder as Inspector Hawk joined Trey near the door.

"Uncle Lukas, this is Inspector Ruben Hawk, formerly of New Scotland Yard and currently the owner of a private investigation firm in London. He may also have a few questions for you," Trey said.

Lukas's face darkened, and his eyes narrowed. "I don't know what's going on, but whatever it is, I hope it doesn't take too long. Vanie and I are trying to make our new vacation home presentable." By the time they had entered a moderately large living room with only a few chairs scattered around it, Vanie had appeared.

"Sorry about the chairs," Lukas began. "We haven't had a chance to get any furniture yet. We're just using what came with the house. Pick a seat, if you'd like."

They all sat down in a semicircle, and then Lukas said, "So what is this visit about? I hope it's to tell me that you've arrested the person who killed your father, Trey."

"We're making headway, but we haven't made any arrests yet. We were hoping you could help us," Trey said. "You left the ship so suddenly that we couldn't get back with you. We barely figured out where you had gone."

"I don't know how I can possibly help you, Trey. As you know, your father and I didn't exactly have an amicable relationship," Lukas said. "I think he always believed I had something to do with my sister's death."

"Did you?" Trey asked quickly.

"Of course not," Lukas said. "I had no reason to harm her—or your father either, for that matter, since I think, from the look on your face, that you think I killed him."

"That's what we're here to talk about," Trey confirmed. "And as far as any reason you might have had to harm my father, we know about the promissory notes you signed each time my mother lent you money and that you failed to pay as much as ten pence on."

Lukas's face paled. "How did you know that?"

"My father kept them all. I found the notes a few days ago," Trey said coldly.

"Okay, so maybe I did sign a few notes, but Rita told me I didn't have to repay them. I'm sure your father knew that."

"I would have thought he would have told me that," Trey said. "But he didn't."

"So are you here to collect on them?" Lukas asked. "Is that what you brought this man for, to have him find out what assets I have so you can take them?"

"No, that's not why he's with me," Trey said.

"I'm working for a client who has paid me to find the paintings stolen from the ship and to assist in finding whoever killed Trey's father," Inspector Hawk broke in.

"I don't know who stole the paintings. It wasn't me or Vanie, and we didn't kill your father," Lukas said.

"I hope that's true," Trey said in all honestly. "If you didn't do it, maybe you can point us in the right direction."

Vanie and Lukas exchanged glances. Then Lukas stared at the floor for a moment before saying, "I have an idea. I have a picture at home in London that you need to see, Trey."

"That's not a lot of help here," Trey said.

"It can be," Inspector Hawk said. "Is there anyone there who can access it for you, Lukas?"

"Yes, there is. I have a neighbor who's watching my flat while I'm gone. But I would have to call him," Lukas said.

Hawk pulled out his satellite phone. "Give me the number." The inspector entered the number Lukas recited and handed over the phone. The inspector said, "Have him find the picture. I'll have an agent meet him at your house." Ten minutes later, one of the inspector's agents was headed for Lukas's London address. "My man will photograph your picture and e-mail it to me. We can look at it on my phone."

While they waited, Trey said, "Why don't you tell me what we're going to see and how you think it will help us solve my father's murder?"

"I'd rather show you the picture first. It'll speak for itself, I promise," Lukas said. "While we wait, let us show you this little place of ours. Actually, it's mostly Vanie's. It's her money that is paying for it, but she's kind enough to share with me."

Vanie stood, moved over behind Lukas, and laid a hand gently on his shoulder. "Lukas, this is *our* vacation house, not *mine*."

He smiled up at her. She smiled back, very tenderly, Trey thought.

"Come, see what we have here," Vanie invited.

Thirty minutes later, the e-mail appeared on Hawk's phone. He opened the attachment, which took a minute, and then handed his phone to Lukas. "Is this the picture?"

"That's it. Here, Trey, look at this."

Trey took the phone and peered closely. He used his fingers to enlarge the picture and centered it on the faces there. Then he realized what he was seeing: his father and a beautiful woman, holding hands and smiling broadly. A chill descended all the way from the top of his head to the tips of his toes.

The chill did not fade as Lukas explained the picture and what it meant.

"I'm glad you showed me this," Trey said.

"It may not mean anything, but it could," Lukas said.

"We've got to go." That picture had Trey thinking. Everything was beginning to come into focus, but he still wasn't entirely sure that what he was thinking was correct. He had to know.

"If you think I owe you the money, I'll—" Lukas began.

Trey cut him off. "I don't need the money. What's past is past. You don't owe me anything."

Lukas's eyes grew big. "Are you sure?"

"Yes, I'm sure. The inspector is my witness and so is Vanie. Let's go, Inspector," Trey said. "I think we're finished here."

"Trey, we'd like you to come visit sometime when you have a couple of days—and, of course, bring your special someone," Lukas said kindly.

"Thank you, I just might," he answered.

As the two men headed for the helicopter, they shouted a thanks to the Tasmania constables and assured them that everything was under control. It was too noisy onboard the helicopter to make any phone calls, but as quick as they were back in the fixed-wing aircraft, both Trey and Inspector Hawk got on their phones.

* * *

Aariah and her grandmother had enjoyed some time in the sun and were headed back to their rooms when they heard running footsteps behind them. They turned just as Bonnie called out.

"Aariah, I was just looking for you."

"What's wrong?" she asked in alarm. Her grandmother's face went white. "Did the Sladers get out of the brig?"

"No, but we need to talk. Are you going to your room?" Bonnie asked.

"Yes, to rest a little before dinner," Aariah answered. "Why don't you come in and tell us what's happened. I assume something has happened."

"Well, yes, sort of," Bonnie said.

Once they were back in the room, they all sat down, and Bonnie said, "Willie Denning just got a call from Trey." She spent the next few minutes telling them what Trey had called about, and Aariah felt a shock wave run through her.

"Is he sure?" she asked.

"No, but he's sure enough not to take any chances. I think it would be best if the two of you had dinner brought to your stateroom tonight," Bonnie said.

"Okay," Aariah agreed meekly.

"I'll arrange to come with the steward who brings it," she said. "If you don't mind the company, maybe I'll have them bring me something too, and we can eat together. I have to do a couple of other things first, but don't open your door to anyone unless it's the steward and me. Don't open for a steward if I'm not with him. Of course, if Willie or the captain happen to want to talk to you, you can let them in. But that's all."

Aariah nodded her head in agreement, and Bonnie left. Aariah turned the dead bolt and fastened the chain.

"I wish we'd gone back with Trey," Mrs. Bray said sadly. "This has been a horrible experience."

Aariah wanted to disagree, but she couldn't. "At least I met Trey. He's worth it."

Her grandmother did not reply.

TWENTY-FIVE

INSPECTOR SMITH MET TREY AND Ruben as they stepped off the airplane in Sydney. "Come back to my office," he said. "There's something I need to show you."

"We'll follow you," Trey said.

The inspector set a blistering pace through the city. When they arrived at the police station, the three of them jogged inside. A short five minutes later, as they viewed security footage from a hotel on the western edge of the city, the rest of the pieces fell into place.

"That does it," Inspector Hawk said. "We need to get back to the ship. I'll make arrangements while you call Detective Denning. You know what to have him do."

Trey did know, and with hands he was having a hard time keeping steady, he made the call. "What do you mean the camera system is down again?" he said. "Victor's dead."

"I'm just telling you. It just went down a minute ago."

"Are you headed to their room yet?" Trey demanded.

"I'm on my way. I'll have Bonnie check the other stateroom and then meet me," Willie said. "I'll get back with you."

* * *

"There's no one in the stateroom," Bonnie reported to Willie. "No one answered the door. I tried my master key, but it didn't work, so I kicked the door open. It's empty."

Willie was running. "Hurry, Bonnie. Meet me up there."

Willie ran past Hans, who asked, "Hey, where you going? I was looking for Bonnie."

"Follow me," Willie shouted over his shoulder. The huge Swede didn't need to be asked twice, nor did he ask for an explanation. He just began to run.

* * *

Aariah and her grandmother sat huddled together on the sofa, where they'd been for most of the past hour. "I guess I should order up a meal," Aariah finally said.

"I don't know if I can eat anything," Charlotte moaned.

"We have to try."

"Okay, I guess you're right."

"What would you like me to have them bring for you?"

"Just some salad and soup," the old lady said, standing when Aariah did. Charlotte went around the corner toward the restroom, and Aariah stepped over to the ship's phone. She picked it up and dialed room service. Before anyone picked up the other line, she heard a soft moan. She dropped the handset as she saw her grandmother being shoved around the corner, a gleaming knife at her throat.

* * *

Willie held up his hand as the three of them approached the stateroom, and everyone stopped running. He whispered to Bonnie, "Knock on the door. Hans and I will stay out of sight of the peephole."

Bonnie knocked, but there was no response. She tried once more, but she turned away, her face grave. "Something's wrong."

"I have a plan, but the timing must be perfect," Hans said. "Listen carefully." He explained, then they all looked at their watches, and Hans slipped silently down the hallway.

* * *

Claudia Gaudet held a knife to Charlotte's throat, but in her other hand, she was carrying a laptop computer and a roll of silver duct tape. "You and I are going for a trip, Aariah," Claudia said. "Take my computer and set it on the bed until I tell you we're ready to leave."

Aariah did as she was told even though she was shaking so badly she could hardly hold the laptop. She almost dropped it before she reached the bed with it. But she did manage to put it down without damaging it. Then Claudia, her eyes gleaming with a deranged light, held out the duct tape. "Take this and bind the old woman so tight she can't move. And tape her mouth too."

"Why are you doing this?" Aariah asked with a sob as she took the tape. The knife was never far from her grandmother's throat as she worked. She wondered if she could knock the weapon away. She watched for her chance.

Claudia, it seemed, knew what she was thinking. "Don't try anything, Aariah, or I will carve your grandmother up, and you and I will get out of here anyway."

Aariah was afraid Claudia would follow through on the threat, so she simply did what she was told, hoping she would have a chance when they were farther away from her grandmother. "Where are you taking me?" Aariah asked as she taped.

"We're going to leave the ship."

"But we aren't even at a port."

"You will make sure we can. That boyfriend of yours, my Simon's son, he came on a helicopter. You will convince the captain to have one come for us," the woman said, her eyes blazing with a wild look.

"Why? How are you involved? They already caught the people who stole the paintings. They're in the brig," Aariah said.

"Yes, they stole the paintings. It was a pretty shrewd plan too. Victor told me all about it when we were in Sydney."

"But . . . but . . . you said that Victor left you for—"

"Dead," Claudia said with an evil chuckle. "I lied. I got the injuries in a little car wreck after I got back to New Zealand. No, no, girl. *He* didn't try to kill *me*; I killed him. I put a bomb beside your lover boy's door, but it wasn't meant for Trey, although he also deserves to die. No, I meant it for Victor. He was always so gullible, and he was so in love with me he'd do anything I asked. I despised him. I placed the bomb at Trey's apartment. Then, a little later, I had Victor go up and knock on the door. I hid and watched. When he was where I wanted him, I detonated the bomb. Boom! End of Victor. I didn't need him anymore."

Aariah was just about finished with the taping when she felt her grandmother go limp. "Grandmother!" she cried out.

"She's not dead, you foolish girl. She just passed out from fright. I think that's enough tape to keep her from causing a scene. Now it's time for me and you to go."

"But they'll see us on the cameras," Aariah said, hoping to somehow change the crazy woman's mind.

But Claudia cackled. "They don't work again. Victor, he was useful for some things. He could hack into any computer system. I'm a quick learner. He taught me how, and then, the poor fool, I didn't need him anymore. You see, all I needed was that little laptop right there." She cackled again. "Face the door. If you don't do exactly what I say, you will feel the wrath of this sharp knife I stole from one of the kitchens. I do get around, don't I?"

"You killed Simon Shotwell," Aariah said as she watched the French woman point the knife in her direction.

"Of course I did," Claudia said.

"Why? You said you loved his paintings." Aariah caught sight of a shadow of movement on her balcony through the drawn drapes and felt a surge of hope. She had to keep the woman talking.

"I loved his painting, yes. But I also loved him. We were to be married. Then that pretty little artist, Rita, caught his roving eye. He told me he was going to marry her instead. I begged him not to, but he dumped me and married her anyway."

"That was a long time ago," Aariah said as the shadow moved again behind the drapes.

"Yes, I wasted sixteen years trying to win him back, but he wouldn't leave Rita. So I had Rita leave him." She cackled again.

"I thought Victor killed Rita," Aariah said.

"No, all he did was steal the paintings for that Slader woman. I killed Rita, but poor Victor was so in love with me that he told me he'd never let anyone arrest me for it. He promised to say that he did it if anyone ever suspected me." Once more she cackled. "He's gone now. Yes, Victor's gone, and it's time for us to go."

Just then, there was a loud knock on the door. "The pests, they're back again. Well, there's nothing they can do. Victor also taught me how to interfere with anything that had to do with electronics or computers, so their key card is useless." There was a second loud knock.

"Answer it," Claudia commanded. "Then when you get it opened, tell them to stand out of the way. If you don't, I will kill you. And you've got to know I mean it."

"I know you're in there, Aariah. Open the door right now." It was Bonnie's voice, loud and commanding.

There was less than a second after she shouted before the door suddenly began to shudder. "That woman is going to bust the door down. Well, let her, and then we'll go out. They're not going to—"

Claudia didn't get to finish that last sentence. A giant hand grabbed her arm and slammed it so hard against the wall that she dropped the knife. Then a second giant hand grabbed the other arm. Claudia could only kick and scream.

"All's clear in here," the deep rumbling voice of Hans Olander boomed, echoing off the walls of the small stateroom. Then softer, he said, "You can open the door now, Aariah."

* * *

The cruise ship docked early the next morning. The first person on board when the door was opened was Detective Trey Shotwell, and waiting for him just inside was Aariah. She flew into his arms. He hugged and kissed her and held her tightly. "I don't want to ever let you get away," he whispered.

"I don't want you to ever let me go, not ever," she whispered back.

"Okay, you two, that's enough," the deep rumble of the Swede came from behind them. "You're embarrassing Miss Springer and me." Then a deep chuckle followed.

In the captain's cabin, after the prisoners had been turned over to the New Zealand Police, Trey listened to Aariah's story.

When she finished, Detective Willie Denning said, "Claudia confessed fully to me. She told me what she told Aariah."

"Why did she tell me she'd killed Trey's parents?" Aariah asked. "That was a confession, wasn't it? Didn't she know I'd never keep a secret like that?"

Willie got very serious. "Of course she knew. You don't think she would have ever let you tell anyone, do you?"

Aariah's pretty face went white. "I guess not."

Inspector Ruben Hawk spoke up then. "I've never seen a case with so many suspects—and all but one were guilty of one part of the scheme or another."

"Yes, all but one," Trey said meekly. "My uncle is a plotter and a lazy man. I thought surely he was behind it all, and yet he was the only innocent one of them all. I feel badly about suspecting him."

"You shouldn't feel too badly, Detective," Hawk said. "After all, you forgave him of a huge debt, which, by law, you could have collected. That was very generous, and I'm sure he knows it."

The captain spoke up. "Okay, please give me a recap. I would like to know who did what. I still don't have the whole story."

"Trey, go ahead," Inspector Hawk said.

"You couldn't make something like this up," Trey began. "To start off, Claudia Gaudet was in love with my father, and I guess my father had also fallen for her. But then he met my mother, and Claudia was no match for her. Anyway, Claudia was determined to win him back. He was equally determined that it would never happen.

"Daphne and Gil Slader paid Victor to steal the Shotwell paintings so Daphne could alter them and sell them under the signature of her alter ego, Ainslee Cline. They claim they didn't know Victor had a connection to Claudia. They also didn't order anyone to be killed. But Claudia knew what Victor was doing, and she slipped into the house while Victor and Danny were loading some of the paintings. She stabbed my mother and then slipped quietly away. Later, Claudia told Victor what she had done, and he promised to keep her secret even if he had to confess to it. He was as in love with her in his sick way as Claudia was in love with my father in her own twisted way," Trey said. He paused for a moment, making sure everyone still followed the narrative.

Then he went on. "Now we come to the cruise ten years later. Daphne consigned one of the paintings to be sold on the ship, the one my mother called *The Scottish Farmer*. That was where things began to unravel. My father and I recognized it. Daphne and Gil already had a plan in place that involved her brother, Danny; Danny's friend Martin; Martin's friend Andrew; and of course, their old friend Victor. They stole the paintings and threw them overboard, carefully wrapped and with a small homing device enclosed."

The captain interrupted. "Didn't someone tell me that Claudia and Victor were bidding against each other at the art auction?"

Trey smiled. "I think I told you. Believe it or not, neither of them knew the other was at the auction. When they realized what they were doing, they quit bidding against each other and teamed up."

"I think I'm beginning to see," he said. "Claudia came to purchase a Simon Shotwell painting and, I assume, to make a last effort to try to win back the heart of her old flame."

"I think so," Trey confirmed.

"And Victor came to steal one of your father's paintings for the Sladers."

"Exactly." Trey nodded. "So, as we know, they stole the paintings. They took the one of mine that Daphne bought to make it look like the Sladers were victims and keep us from suspecting them. The Sladers never did know that Victor had recruited Claudia into their little scheme. Victor and Claudia were in on it together at that point. Victor was so infatuated with Claudia that he told her he'd get the painting away from Martin when they got to Australia and give it to her. It was Victor who hacked the cameras, by the way, following the plan ordered by the Sladers. Claudia watched him do it and probably later had him instruct her further, acting, I'm sure, like she was admiring him for his skills," Trey said. "Remember, she had spent a lot of time with Victor over the years and probably learned a lot from him."

Trey looked over the captain's head for a moment. Then he took a deep breath and said, "Claudia hacked it herself the last time, just before she went after Aariah. Anyway, it was Victor and Danny who helped Martin throw the paintings over and then helped him over. The ship passed, and Martin and Andrew met. Martin put on diving equipment, and, I learned later, they had some small propeller packs of some kind that they both used. Anyway, they located the paintings, and then swam to the rented boat and headed for Australia."

"Who kidnapped Aariah and sent the threatening note?" the captain asked.

"It was Danny and Victor, but the note was Claudia's. She went totally off after killing my father when he made it clear that he would never take her back."

"I'm confused about one thing," Captain Johnsen said. "Aariah was assaulted in the hallway when Simon was murdered. Who did that? It was someone larger than Claudia. Was it Victor?"

"It was. He helped Claudia, and she promised him that once Simon was dead, she would marry him. He left the stateroom first, saw Aariah coming up the hall, and knocked her out. Claudia and he then snuck back to their own rooms. Claudia left the ship with Victor and took him to Australia to get married—or so she told him. Instead, she got rid of him and came back, looking as innocent as a little lamb."

"Where's the missing painting?" Captain Johnsen asked. "Damian still wants it back."

"And he will have it, if Bonnie is willing to do a little diving," Inspector Hawk responded.

"Do you know where it is, Inspector?" she asked.

"I do now. Andrew mailed the GPS coordinates to his address in London before he actually took the painting out there. One of my agents intercepted it. The note indicated he was going to secure the package to the ocean floor at that exact location."

"Let's go get it then," Bonnie said with a grin. "I'm ready, and I know I can do it. That nice Frenchman deserves to get his painting back."

EPILOGUE

BONNIE SUCCESSFULLY RECOVERED THE PAINTING from the ocean floor a few miles from shore. The piece was still perfect despite all it had been through.

Hans fought his matches in Sydney, won both of them, and then announced to his fiancée, Bonnie Springer, that he was retiring from wrestling and going to do what he'd gone to college for. He was going to be a civil engineer in his native Sweden and hoped she would accompany him, which she readily agreed to do.

After they were married, Aariah and Trey settled down in his father's huge house and even provided a room there for Aariah's grandmother. They went to church together every Sunday, even Charlotte Bray.

All surviving suspects went to prison. The only ones that had no chance of ever getting out were triple-murderer Claudia Gaudet, the worst of the lot, and Martin Talley, convicted of killing Kori Acton, the girl with pink hair.

Trey finished the painting his father had worked on while on the cruise and presented it to Damian Latimer as Simon had promised before his death. Trey didn't give up his job as a cop, but he also worked hard at his hobby and became a well-known painter in his own right.

Two years later, the Shotwells took their infant daughter, who they named Rita, and Charlotte Bray on another cruise, and this time they all got to see New Zealand. That same year they also visited Lukas and Vanie—who had finally married—in their modest house in Tasmania. It was on that visit that Trey learned something he'd never known before.

Lukas and Simon had actually visited for a few minutes on the cruise ship, and in that visit, Simon had admitted that even though he had been upset with Trey's choices regarding becoming a cop and a Mormon, the real reason he left London was to get away from Claudia Gaudet. It had worked for ten years. And then she found him.

ABOUT THE AUTHOR

CLAIR M. POULSON WAS BORN and raised in Duchesne, Utah. His father was a rancher and farmer, his mother, a librarian. Clair has always been an avid reader, having found his love for books as a very young boy.

He has served for more than forty years in the criminal justice system. He spent twenty years in law enforcement, ending his police career with eight years as the Duchesne County Sheriff. For the past twenty-plus years, Clair has worked as a justice court judge for Duchesne County. He is also a veteran of the US Army, where he was a military policeman. In law enforcement, he has been personally involved in the investigation of murders and other violent crimes. Clair has also served on various boards and councils during his professional career, including the Justice Court Board of Judges, the Utah Commission on Criminal and Juvenile Justice, the Utah Judicial Council, the Utah Peace Officer Standards and Training Council, an FBI advisory board, and others.

In addition to his criminal justice works, Clair has farmed and ranched all his life. He has raised many kinds of animals, but his greatest interests are horses and cattle. He's also involved in the grocery store business with his oldest son and other family members.

Clair has served in many capacities in the LDS Church, including full-time missionary (California Mission), bishop, counselor to two bishops, young men president, high councilor, stake mission president, Scoutmaster, and high priest group leader. He currently serves as a Gospel Doctrine teacher.

Clair is married to Ruth, and they have five children, all of whom are married: Alan (Vicena) Poulson, Kelly Ann (Wade) Hatch, Amanda (Ben) Semadeni, Wade (Brooke) Poulson, and Mary (Tyler) Hicken. They also have twenty-four wonderful grandchildren. Clair and Ruth met while both were students at Snow College and were married in the Manti temple.

Clair has always loved telling his children, and later his grandchildren, made-up stories. His vast experience in life and his love of literature have contributed to both his telling stories to his children and his writing of adventure and suspense novels.

Clair has published more than two dozen novels. He would love to hear from his fans, who can contact him by going to his website, *clairmpoulson.com*.